N. 3-4-16

Praise for
angel fire

"Gruesome, gory, baffling, shocking, awesome—and incredibly
suspenseful describe this mystery."
—*The Oklahoman*

"A captivating tale."
—*Tampa Tribune*

"Remarkable and emotional debut . . . The touching love story that plays
out in the background is refreshing in its sincerity and emotional depth."
—*New Mystery Reader Magazine*

"Worthy of widespread acclaim. She has the ability to write with great
beauty in describing the landscape of this character-rich debut . . . well
recommended."
—*Deadly Pleasures Magazine*

"An excellent debut novel . . . A smart, well-developed mystery
that will leave you hanging on every page as you devour this
book. . . . There's a new author on the scene, Lisa Miscione.
You don't want to forget this name!"
—*Book Review Cafe*

"Taut prose, insidious suspense, psychological motivation, police
procedural sidebars, and a would-be lover make this debut from a former
member of the publishing world a real winner. Don't miss it!"
—*Library Journal* (starred review)

"Miscione hits the ground running, quite literally . . . in her debut
novel featuring crime writer Lydia Strong. . . . There's a surreal and
nightmarish quality to the story. . . . It remains gripping and terrifying
right through the carnage of its final scene."
—*Publishers Weekly*

lisa unger

writing as
Lisa Miscione

angel
fire

a novel

broadway paperbacks
new york

BROADWAY

The setting of this book was inspired by the beauty and mood of the Santa Fe and the Angel Fire, New Mexico, areas. Readers intimate with these very real places will realize that I have taken significant geographical, topographical, and architectural liberties as per the demands of the narrative, my vision, and my imagination. *Angel Fire,* as well as its characters and setting, is entirely a work of fiction.

Copyright © 2002 by Lisa Miscione
Preface copyright © 2011 by Lisa Unger
Excerpt from *The Darkness Gathers* copyright © 2003 by Lisa Miscione

Published in the United States by Broadway Paperbacks, an imprint of the Crown Publishing Group, a division of Random House, Inc., New York.

www.crownpublishing.com

Broadway Paperbacks and its logo, a letter B bisected on the diagonal, are trademarks of Random House, Inc.

Originally published in hardcover in slightly different form in the United States by St. Martin's Press, New York, in 2002 and subsequently published in paperback in the United States by St. Martin's Press, New York, in 2003.

Library of Congress Cataloging-in-Publication Data
Miscione, Lisa.
Angel fire / Lisa Miscione.—1st ed.
p. cm.
1. Murder victims' families—Fiction. 2. Women journalists—Fiction.
3. Mothers—Death—Fiction. 4. Santa Fe (N.M.)—Fiction.
5. Missing persons—Fiction. 6. Crime writing—Fiction. I. Title.
PS3613.I83 A54 2002
813'.6—dc212001048665

ISBN 978-0-307-95309-4
eISBN 978-0-307-95310-0

Printed in the United States of America

Cover design by Mumtaz Mustafa

Cover photography by Dave Curtis/Trevillion Images

10 9 8 7 6 5 4 3 2 1

First Broadway Paperbacks Edition

To my parents, Joseph & Virginia Miscione
Who gave me the tools to build the craft on which I travel . . .

To my husband, Jeffrey
The North Star,
The red sky at night,
The wind inside my sails . . .

Preface
by Lisa Unger

I was nineteen years old when I first met Lydia Strong. I was living in the East Village, dating a New York City police officer, and attending Eugene Lang College, the undergraduate school of the New School for Social Research. I was sitting in a car, under the elevated section of the "1" line in the Bronx, waiting—for what I can't remember. But in my mind that day, I kept seeing this woman running past a church. She was in New Mexico. And all I knew about her was that she was a damaged person, someone in great pain. Running, for her, was salve, religion, and drug. That was Lydia.

I pulled a napkin and a pen from the glove compartment and started writing the book that would become *Angel Fire*. It took me ten years to write that novel, mostly because the years between age nineteen and twenty-nine were, for me, years of hard work and tumultuous change. But also because during that time, I let my dreams of becoming a writer languish a bit. Lydia was faithful; she waited.

In spite of a first-rate education, a career in publishing, and a strong desire to write fiction, I didn't know much of anything when I was writing my first novel. I don't think you *can* really know anything about writing a novel until you've actually written one. (And then you go to school again when you sit down to write your second, and your third, and so on.) All I knew during that time was that I was truly fascinated by this woman occupying a place in my imagination, and I was deeply intrigued by her very dark appetites. I was enthralled by her past, by the mysteries in her present, and why she wouldn't let herself love the man who loved her. There were lots of questions about Lydia Strong, and I was never happier over those ten years than when I was trying to answer them.

I was fortunate that the first novel I ever wrote was accepted by my (wonderful, brilliant) agent Elaine Markson, and that she fairly quickly brokered a deal for *Angel Fire* and my second, then unwritten, novel *The Darkness Gathers*. I spent the next few years with Lydia Strong and the very colorful cast of characters who populated her life. And I enjoyed every dark, harrowing, and complicated moment with them as I went on to write *Twice,* and then *Smoke*.

I followed Lydia from New Mexico, to New York City, to Albania, to Miami, and back. We trekked through the abandoned subway tunnels under Manhattan, to a compound in the backwoods of Florida, to a mysterious church in the Bronx, to a fictional town called Haunted. It was a total thrill ride, and I wrote like my fingers were on fire.

I am delighted that these early novels, which I published under my maiden name, Lisa Miscione, have found a new life on the shelves and a new home with the stellar team at Broadway Paperbacks. And, of course, I am thrilled that they've found their way into your hands. I know a lot of authors wish their early books would just disappear, because they've come so far as writers since they first began their careers. And I understand that, because we would all go back and rewrite everything if we could.

But I have a special place in my heart for these flawed,

sometimes funny, complicated characters and their wild, action-packed stories. I still think about them, and I feel tremendous tenderness for even the most twisted and deranged among them. The writing of each book was pure pleasure. I hope that you enjoy your time with them as much as I have. And, thanks, as always, for reading.

angel fire

chapter one

Lydia Strong ran. She ran until her muscles cramped, until her lungs were on fire. She ran until she couldn't run any farther. And then she kept running. She ran like she had something to prove, and would die trying to prove it, if necessary. Down the dirt drive from her home, nestled in the foothills of the Sangre de Cristo Mountains north of Santa Fe, off onto the rocky path that led past the church in Angel Fire.

When she ran, she was lost and she was found. She left behind the chaos of her thoughts and fears, left behind her life, her work. In running she found an animalistic kind of peace. She was a living organism motivated only by her physical self, the desire to rest and the drive to go on, go farther, and farther still. She was only her lungs and her legs. It was painful but it was quiet. This ritual served as Lydia's only religion these days.

She did not deny the possibility of a god or a godlike force, but organized religion . . . out of the question. Still, this August morning, like most mornings, she felt a tug at her heart as she ran past the small white church. The Church of the Holy Name sat proud and undeniable by the side of the dirt road. White and immovable like the moon, it rose from the dust and the weeds. It was just as it was one hundred years ago, solid and righteous as if it had grown from the earth like a mountain. It was so sure of itself, its walls painted orange, pink, purple by the rising sun.

As a child, she had attended church with her mother every Sunday. It was always an event, because her mother was a devout woman. The joy Marion Strong took in the church service was contagious, for Lydia loved her mother fiercely and had wanted, then, to be just like her in every way. She was excited to wear one of her most precious dresses. She would walk with her mother proudly, imagining that people who saw them would think she was an adult, since her shoes made noise just like her mother's as their heels clicked on the sidewalk.

Once inside the church her mother would give her four quarters, two for lighting a candle for each of her dead grandparents and two for the collection plate. They would sit in the center pew. Lydia waited with restless anticipation for the time to sing. When the organ sounded and the hymns began, with all the might of her few years Lydia would sing her heart out, for she knew all the words. Her mother would look down at her, smile and sing in her high, melodic voice. Lydia felt such a sense of belonging. Everybody, it seemed, was there for the same reason. Everybody sang together and everybody smiled and shook hands. "Peace be with you."

Of course she hadn't thought about it at the time, but she wondered now if her mother had missed her company when she turned into a rebellious teenager, shunning everything that smacked of institution and refusing to go to church with her "on principle." Her mother never forced her to go; she never lectured or manipulated her with guilt. Her mother just looked away and shook her head. Lydia remembered that small break in the ground beneath their feet as the first in the chasm that would grow between them in her early adolescence.

After her mother's death, Lydia had tried to return to the church. The loss of her mother had left a hollow place in her heart where the wind blew through. But the service seemed empty, contrived, rather than rich with meaning and faith. Not beautiful, as she remembered. And when it occurred to her that she had never been to mass without her mother, had never entered a church without holding her mother's hand, she felt deeply sad. Rather than filling the void where her mother's love had been, her visit made her feel the loss even more profoundly. Now when people asked her about her religious beliefs she answered, "I'm a runner."

Always, as she ran past the white adobe church by the side of the dirt road, she saw her mother's face and remembered the clicking of her shoes on the sidewalk. On this August morning, the desert air still cool, not yet fully heated by the blazing sun on the rise, she thought she heard her mother's voice, almost audible, on the wind. She stopped and turned around, running in place. The sound of her own labored breathing was so loud in her head she had to quiet herself to hear anything else. But there was only the silence of sand and wind in the trees. Then, in the distance, its sound almost lost in the breeze and the Sangre de Cristos, a crow screamed. The sound was mournful and, Lydia thought, had a tinge of panic to it.

chapter two

Every year in the weeks preceding the anniversary of her mother's death, an agitated restlessness overtook Lydia. It interrupted her sleep, her work. And instead of lessening over time, almost fifteen years now, it had worsened. This feeling often compelled her to wander in the night, or to drive aimlessly for miles, or to do other things that she would rather forget. A battalion of shrinks had never been able to cure her. She had long given up on psychiatrists and their cabinets filled with happy pills. It was the same feeling on a larger scale as when she'd misplaced her keys or wallet and couldn't rest until she laid her hands on them again. Except that she wasn't sure what she had lost and she had the desperate feeling that it would never be found. But that she would keep looking for the rest of her life. It was something about herself that she had stopped trying to explain, something she had grown to accept.

On this night her restlessness caused her to leave home, and for the second time, run the route past the Church of the Holy Name. The clock read 11:58 P.M. when she left her house. She had been rolling sleepless in her bed when the feeling took her. She tried to ignore it, to clear her head and force herself to fall asleep. But her muscles ached for a run. And something deeper inside her ached for it, too, for the exertion and for the exhaustion that followed when her body had been pushed to its limit.

It was as if an invisible string connected to her heart had pulled her from beneath the covers, and she'd rushed to pull on her running gear, knowing the sooner she was moving, the sooner she would be relieved of the restlessness. As soon as her battered Nikes hit the road and the rhythm of her breathing was the only sound in her head, she was free.

When she reached the church she stopped running. Everything was the same as it had been that morning except, of course, the night sky. But tonight her imagination conjured a nightmarish vision of what might be behind the wooden doors. A rich offering to a strange god; murdered animals with their throats cut spilling dark blood on pristine white fur; tropical fruit, overripe and opened not with knifes but with greedy fingers, spilling seeds and sick-sweet juice onto the altar. A vast array of flora, roses so red they seemed black; orange, white, fuscia gladiolas opened like mouths. Everything piled together, a plenty of hideous beauty wet with new death. There would be the buzzing of flies, and perhaps the echo of chanting voices somewhere from a distant room. Something she would not want to investigate—but would have to.

A noise brought her back to this moonlit night in front of the church. How many times a day did she drift away like that into her own fantasies? How many times were they so twisted? It seemed she had always been that way.

The noise came again. A soft shuffling from behind the church. She was immediately drawn toward it, her curiosity piqued. *Finish your run. Leave whatever it is alone. An animal, a priest, whatever—it's nothing.* But of course Lydia had to follow the noise—just to see what the darkness held.

When she walked behind the church, she came upon a garden. She had never seen it during any of her daily runs. It was surprisingly fecund, rich with exotic flowers unfamiliar to her.

Surrounded by a low white picket fence, the garden was bursting with itself. A path wound through it in the shape of a figure eight, illuminated by a lamp mounted above the back door to the church, which stood open. Orange like fire, purple like bruises, fuchsia, emerald, the exotic flowers stood tall and proud like well-shod socialites confident in their beauty. They swooned in the light breeze, bringing their perfume to her nose.

Through the open door she saw a man. Tall and thin, with curly hair the black of India ink, there was something odd about the way he moved, reaching his hand out in front of him before he committed his body to any action. He moved slowly, patting the air for a stool that stood before the altar. And as she moved closer to the door, Lydia could discern his blank stare—how he didn't use his eyes to see but rather his touch or his hearing. She realized he was blind.

It dawned on Lydia then that she had seen him before but had not noticed he was blind. The truth was that she had been drawn to the church even before she had purchased her house. Staying at the Eldorado Hotel in Santa Fe, she had driven up to Angel Fire looking for property. Lost on the winding back roads of the resort town on an early Sunday morning, she had come upon the church as it was filling for mass. On a whim she pulled over, parked her car, and entered. She told herself that she had attended the mass to see what kind of people lived in the town more than anything. But she could remember nothing about the parishioners, only the unassuming, simple wood-and-stone interior of the small building. And the man who played guitar at mass, how his music had moved her that day. She had stood in the back for a while, listening, then she left. A man standing outside the church with a broom handed her a booklet about Jesus' love; she thanked him.

A few hours later, the broker who was showing Lydia property brought her to the house she would close on soon after. It was to be her second home, her hideaway, as she spent most of her time in New York.

She had never returned to the church for mass even after she bought the house. In the year and a half she had owned it, she'd been there a total of three months, this last visit being the longest, almost five weeks now. As she stood in the night, watching the blind man, she wondered if he would sense her there but he seemed intent on what he was doing, polishing a guitar that sat on a wood table to the right of the stool. Soon he placed it on his lap, tuned it briefly, and began to play. It sounded lovely but suddenly she felt like an intruder. She turned and began running again, glad to be on her way. The sound of his guitar followed her longer than seemed possible, though the desert night is silent and sounds carry.

By the time she returned to the long and winding drive that led back up to her house, she felt better. She slowed to a walk and was not afraid as she made her way through the quiet, dark cover of the trees shading the road. In spite of the horrors she had witnessed in her life, Lydia was rarely afraid for her physical safety. It was almost as though, having seen the face of evil in her work as a true-crime writer and sometime consultant for the private investigation firm of Mark, Hanley and Striker, and even in her own childhood, it had lost its power over her. After all, wasn't that why people feared the dark: because they couldn't see what lurked there? Lydia knew what the darkness held, knew it well.

Her approach to the house triggered the motion sensors and the night flooded with amber light. Something scurried into the bushes as Lydia punched the keypad lock and stepped out of her muddied sneakers before stepping onto the bleached wood floor of the back foyer. She punched numbers into another keypad inside the door and reactivated the alarm. The lamp outside went out. She didn't bother turning on lights as she walked through the dark house; she ascended the spiral staircase to her bedroom, stripped her clothes, damp with sweat from her body, and lay upon her bed. She thought to get into the shower before sleeping but sleep came for her deep and fast.

Later that night she visited the church garden again, in her dreams. Usually her sleep, when it came, was a dark cocoon, an escape. None of the banalities and few of the horrors of her life had ever followed her there. It was the only place where her mind was ever blank.

In her dream, past the garden and through the door, she could see the blind man playing his guitar, but she could not hear the music. It was as if a sheet of soundproof glass separated them. She did not run away, as she had earlier, but easily manipulated the latch and pushed the gate open. She walked onto the path—the flowers had changed. There was a darkness, almost a maliciousness to the way they swayed in the light breeze. She knew they were talking about her—saying cruel and unfair things that would only seem more true if she tried to deny them. She let them gibber on about her. *Fuck the flowers,* she thought angrily.

She walked through the garden and the open door. The blind man turned his head. *He must have heard me,* she thought. But his eyes seemed to have lost their blindness—he saw her.

"She's here," he said simply, smiling kindly.

Lydia smiled back, relieved. "Oh, you can see. I'm so happy for you."

"The only important thing," he said, looking past her, "is what *you* see."

She followed his eyes and saw her mother. Not as Lydia chose to remember her from her childhood, but as Lydia had last seen her.

Her arms were tied over her head, her wrists bleeding and black and blue from her struggle. Though she smiled beautifully at Lydia in the way she always had, her eyes rolled back into her head and her face was ghastly white. Her throat was slit from ear to ear, and blood bubbled in and out as she breathed. Her ankles were tied in the same manner as her wrists, and her panties, covered in blood, were down, tangled around the ropes. Her white nightgown was ripped and filthy with dirt and blood and semen. She was forty-five years old.

Lydia tried to speak but was choked by her rage and her horror, just as she had been nearly fifteen years before.

"Mom," she managed, "let me help you."

"No, dear," she said, "let *me* help *you*."

Lydia began to scream as the blind man played his guitar.

chapter three

The light had long faded from above the New York City skyline before his thoughts returned to Lydia for the first time that day. Jeffrey Mark closed the file he was looking at, removed his glasses, and rubbed his tired eyes. The offices of Mark, Hanley and Striker were quiet now. He could hear only the hum of a vacuum cleaner down the hall and smell the burnt bottom of a coffeepot someone had forgotten to turn off.

He spun his chair around to look out at his view of the city. A million squares of light reached into a starless sky. *A million lies, a million heartbreaks, a million crimes to match,* he thought. He wondered again where in the hell she was and why she hadn't called. He supposed he should be used to this by now after fifteen years. But instead it seemed to be getting harder. He stared at his dark reflection in the plate-glass window. He looked older and more tired than he liked to imagine himself. He unconsciously rubbed his right shoulder.

He remembered the first time he saw Lydia Strong, fifteen years ago. He was twenty-five then. The death of her mother had been his first case with the FBI. Marion Strong was one of thirteen women murdered in their homes in the New York area in three years. One of the more memorable details of the serial killer's MO was that he would make sure to leave his victim where she would be found by her children returning home from school. All of the victims were single, working mothers with at least one teenage child.

Jeffrey was assigned to the case because no one else wanted to be the junior man under Roger Dooley, a twenty-five-year veteran with a miserable personality and a tendency toward obsession. Unwashed, mostly, and reeking of fast food and failed relationships, Dooley was the most unpleasant, bitter man Jeff had ever known—and that was when he was in a good mood. Every lead in the case had turned cold in Dooley's hands for three years. This investigation looked to be his last before retirement and he couldn't stand to end a superstar career on a losing streak. He was a real prick and Jeffrey hated him. But he was a genius investigator, and Jeff would learn everything he knew from the man.

They may never have found the killer if it hadn't been for fifteen-year-old Lydia. She had an eye for detail and an active imagination. Some days before her mother's murder, she had noticed a man in the parking lot of the local supermarket. She had noticed him because of his bright red hair, and the way he had stood staring at her and her mother beside a red-and-white car that reminded her of her favorite TV show, *Starsky and Hutch*.

"Look, Mom, that man is watching us," she remembered telling her mother.

"Lydia, don't stare. Get in the car," her mother had told her sternly, not in the mood for another of Lydia's fantasies. But Lydia was already playing a game in her mind, pretending the man was following them. She wrote down his license-plate number in blue eyeliner on the back of a note passed in class from one of her friends. She was pretending, but in the back of her mind, the man looked familiar to her. In fact, he had been watching them for months.

Going through the house with detectives, she had also noticed one of her mother's earrings was missing. Not from the pair Marion was wearing when she was murdered, but from a pair of garnet studs Lydia coveted and had borrowed the day before but carefully replaced in her mother's jewelry box.

"She's a natural detective," Dooley had said, with something like resentment in his voice.

In a matter of hours they had traced the plate to Jed McIntyre, a freelance engineering consultant living in Nyack, New York. When they raided his home, he was in his underwear, drinking a beer in front of the television. He smiled as he was led away in the cold night.

"You idiots," he kept repeating. "You idiots."

In the subsequent search of his home for evidence, they found thirteen photo albums filled with pictures of his victims and a large jewelry box with twenty tiny, velvet-lined drawers. Thirteen of them held one earring from each of his victims—minute, glittering trophies of his deeds.

Lydia coolly identified Jed McIntyre in a lineup a week later with a strange, trancelike composure. She looked dangerously close to floating away into her grief-stricken mind. Jeffrey was afraid for her and took her to his office so she could avoid the hordes of reporters that followed her everywhere.

"I need to be left alone," she had said to him, "just for a minute."

But as he closed the door and walked down the hallway, he had heard a scream that he carried with him still, that would, to him, forever be the very sound of grief. He ran back to his office to find Lydia sitting on the floor screaming and sobbing. He dropped to his knees and took her in his arms and rocked her until she stopped. She became limp with grief and fear, whimpering for her mother.

Sometimes he still saw her that way when he looked into her gray eyes over dinner or when they were working. He remembered her small, gaunt features taut with stress and terror on that first day. Her eyes heavy-lidded, blinking slowly—they would seem almost reptilian if they weren't so warm and intelligent. She'd had an odd strength and maturity for an adolescent. Her voice never quivered when they interviewed her, but she never made eye contact. She sat next to her grandfather, who sat with a protective arm around her as tears fell from his eyes.

Even now, though at thirty she was an award-winning journalist and an author, an investigative consultant with Jeffrey's firm, and a strong and accomplished woman, when they were alone he could see the demons in her still. He could see the little girl inside who had never really healed but had been locked away in the attic of her subconscious. He knew one day she would have to be let out. He only hoped he would be there when it happened.

He had been trying for weeks to reach her at her Upper West Side apartment in New York and on her cell phone. The number to the house just outside Santa Fe had been disconnected. That was not unusual, as she changed her numbers often. He could find her, he knew, if he really tried. But he always let her be, let her come to him.

Five years ago, he had left the Bureau and started his own private-investigation agency with two other former special agents. The firm Mark, Hanley and Striker Investigations, Inc. had started in a studio apartment in the East Village. With one phone line and one computer, a couple contacts at the Bureau, and a couple of informants on the street, he, Jacob Hanley, and Christian Striker had built the firm to what it was today: a suite of offices on the top floor of a high rise on West Fifty-seventh Street, employing over a hundred top people, grossing more money last year than Jeff would have thought possible. At first they took the cases no one else wanted, cases the police had dropped or deemed unsolvable, like desperate parents with no money looking for lost children, welfare fraud investigations. Hanley had a nose for finding the lost. Striker had a gift for surveillance. And Jeffrey, military and FBI to the core, had a hard-on for the facts, the evidence, the crime-scene details. As far as Jeff was concerned, the facts were the only element of any case that could be totally trusted. People lied, intuition failed, but facts, if followed carefully, would always lead to the truth. Working closely with government agencies they quickly earned an inside reputation as the guys the FBI and the police called when their hands were tied, when their leads had gone cold and they were about to give up.

But it was Lydia who had put them on the map as the firm that could solve the unsolvable. Her *New York Times* best-seller about the Cheerleader Murders, a case she had solved while consulting with them, had catapulted Mark, Hanley and Striker into the national spotlight.

Jeffrey, Jacob, and Christian had flown out to a suburb of New Orleans to investigate the disappearance of four high-school girls. Later dubbed "the Cheerleader Murders" by the local media, these girls, all blond with blue or green eyes, had been on the same pep squad. They were among the prettiest, most popular girls in school, by all accounts bright, with good grades and good manners, from happy homes. Looking at their faces in photos, Jeff could easily see what features were attractive to the killer, or so he thought. They were nearly identical in demeanor, with the same bobbed silky hair, wide smiles, unblemished skin. They could have been sisters.

After four weeks, the girls were presumed dead. Jeffrey and his partners, called in by the local police, were working under the

assumption that whoever was doing the abducting was a man connected with the school: a gym teacher, bus driver, janitor. They
had several suspects under surveillance. They were leaning pretty
heavily on a mentally retarded janitor who had a history of violent
behavior during periods in his life when he neglected to take his
medication.

But nothing felt right. The pieces weren't falling together. So, as
was often his move when he hit a dead end, he called Lydia in for a
fresh perspective. Her gift for intuiting elements of a case that eluded
him had been an aid to him many times before. Jeffrey, a confirmed
"just the facts" man, had learned respect for Lydia's intuitions and
their value in an investigation where the facts led nowhere.

Lydia was displeased when she arrived. "Well, 'You can take
the man out of the Bureau . . .' right, Jeff? This is a typical FBI
witch hunt," she complained. "I have a feeling you guys couldn't
be farther from the truth."

She was referring to their treatment of the suspects. During
the investigations, long-buried secrets had been surfacing like bodies dredged from a river. The gym teacher's wife had accused him,
during a vicious custody battle, of sexually molesting his daughter.
A bus driver had revealed that he was a recovering crack addict. A
female gym teacher, who was big and burly like a man, was discovered to have had a sex-change operation. They were shaking up
that quiet suburb and actually not getting anywhere.

Lydia began speaking to the girls' classmates. The picture they
painted was not the idyllic one presented by parents and teachers.
A tight clique, popular and beautiful enough to be the envy of
every other girl in the school, the girls were nonetheless secretly
feared and hated by most of their friends and classmates. Viciously
mean and brutal, they were predators, choosing the homeliest and
most unpopular students to taunt and humiliate.

Their most recent victim was a sixteen-year-old by the name of Wanda Jane Felix. A notably overweight, unusually tall, bespectacled girl with poor personal hygiene and a severe case of acne, Wanda had few friends and was painfully shy. By all accounts, she was a kind and exceptionally smart girl. But having moved to the area only at the beginning of the school year, she must have been lonely. In short, she was an easy mark. The four girls had befriended her for a week, treating her like royalty, giving her a makeover and taking her to the movies. Then on Friday afternoon, they invited her to the exclusive and much-anticipated Saturday night keg party. The unsuspecting Wanda accepted, thrilled with her new friends and social status but unaware that the girls were mocking her.

On Saturday night they proceeded to get her drunk on Orange Blossoms, a sickly-sweet combination of orange soda and cheap vodka. When she passed out, they stripped her of her clothes and left her on the lawn of her parents' home. Virtually every "popular" kid in school was witness to her humiliation. And for those who weren't, there were color photographs available. Wanda had not returned to school since the incident, two weeks prior to the disappearance of the first girl.

Lydia's heart ached for Wanda. "Imagine the rage, the shame," said Lydia sadly, showing Jeffrey the horrible photographs procured from a cooperative student.

"I don't know," Jeffrey had replied. "Sounds like a normal high-school Saturday night to me."

But all joking aside, he could see where she was going. Lydia felt that Wanda or somebody close to her was behind the disappearance of the girls.

"You really think a teenager could be capable of this?" asked Jeffrey.

"I do."

The motive was there, certainly. And in view of the total lack of evidence surfacing against the other suspects, Jeffrey and Lydia went to question the girl, accompanied by local police with a warrant to search the premises.

And in fact Lydia's theory proved to be right.

With the help of her mother, a diagnosed paranoid schizophrenic, Wanda Jane had abducted each of the girls in her mother's station wagon, tortured and then killed them. The bodies were found in freezers in the basement of the Felix home. The girls had been mutilated, golden hair shaved, pretty eyes gouged out, pearly teeth smashed with a hammer. Apparently, though, Wanda's mother, Kara, had done all the killing. Wanda, Kara later confessed, would have been satisfied with disfigurement. But Kara could not forgive the ugly deed done to her daughter, and finished each of them off with a .22 caliber bullet to the temple.

It was their first formal case together, though Jeffrey had consulted Lydia many times in the past, often breaching ethics to share facts with her and gain her opinion, her insight. She had taught him respect for things unseen, for intuition, for "the buzz," as they called it. It was a good match. He kept her grounded; she took him places he might never have gone without her.

The Cheerleader Murders was a typical Lydia Strong story, one she would have wanted to investigate and write about had she come across it in her endless scanning of the nation's newspapers. Lydia chose local cases with a peculiar twist, something that called to her, like a child abduction that wound up leading to a child-slavery ring or the unsolved murder of a local Florida woman that was shown to be tied to Santeria. She seemed always to be searching local papers and the Internet, looking for something that gave her "the buzz." Her only criterion was that the case be as dark and twisted as possible. The focus of her books was never the victims, though she believed they were often the key to the solving of crimes. In fact, critics had accused her of treating the victims as incidentals in her work, of treating them as evidence rather than as people. But what drove her was the mind of the killer, the details of the crime, and the process by which it was solved.

Jeff knew it was a search for answers, that she was trying always to understand why some people did the evil they do and what turned them into demons. As if by understanding them and exposing them to the light, she could make the monsters smaller and less frightening.

He looked at the phone a final time before rising, grabbing his black cashmere coat from the hook by the door, and leaving the office. He braced himself against the unseasonably cold fall air as he pushed through the glass doors and walked up West Fifty-seventh Street toward the subway.

chapter four

Groggy from a fitful night's sleep, Lydia walked unsteadily to her kitchen and brewed a pot of Hawaiian Kona coffee. Wrapped in a white terry-cloth cotton robe, she sat down in the window seat and stared out at the Technicolor Santa Fe morning sky, trying not to think about her nightmare and what it meant. When the rich scent of the coffee reached her, she turned her head and surveyed the kitchen. It was a large white room, immaculately clean. The appliances were brand-new, state-of-the-art machines that had barely been used. She was satisfied with how the room looked, everything in order, nothing out of place except for the unruly stack of papers on the kitchen table.

The creative mind by its nature, Lydia had long ago concluded, is restless and cluttered—constantly shifting in thought and action until it settles on something that can engage it for more than a few moments. She read newspapers that way, skipping from article to article, looking for something interesting, something different. She clipped items if she felt there might be something to look at more closely. They collected in piles around her house that she would sort through later to pick out things that struck a chord with her and then read more thoroughly.

She had done little but read since she arrived in Santa Fe over four weeks earlier. Mostly local papers, though. Her subscriptions to national newspapers piled up in her office, her e-mail went un-checked. She didn't feel ready for another story yet. Not yet. Her last article, for *New York* magazine, had been about a socialite with Munchausen's syndrome by proxy who was on trial for poi-soning three of her four children. It was a long time before anyone suspected her because she had killed one child in Paris, one in Switzerland, and one in New York City. Esmerelda von Buren, known to her friends as "Esmy," was a most narcissistic and ter-rifying sociopath. And after dealing with her, her heinous crimes, and the shallow, snobbish world in which she lived, Lydia figured she needed a good two months of doing nothing in Santa Fe be-fore she even thought about writing something new. But some subconscious memory of the articles she had clipped was giving her the buzz, that little edge of excitement she got when she knew something wasn't quite right, that there was a puzzle in need of solving. And ready or not, she couldn't resist.

Gathering the articles in her arms, she carried them into her living room. The room, filled with plants and small, potted trees, was flooded with sunlight. The southern wall was completely glass, below which was a precipitous drop into the valley of the mountains. She had an unobstructed view of the landscape, a sight she considered one of the most beautiful in all the world. She had told Jeffrey once that to wake up and see it in the morning gave her faith in the nature of the universe. No matter how wrong so many things were, no matter what tragedy, what chaos existed, this landscape still remained. He had laughed a little, telling her to stick to journalism and leave the poetry to someone else. But he knew what she meant. There was something peaceful about incorruptible beauty. But right now she barely noticed it. She was inside her head.

She placed the articles on her stone coffee table, then walked over the bleached wood floor back to the kitchen for a cup of coffee—very light, very sweet. She walked back into the living room, absentmindedly touching the white adobe wall, blemishing the pristine surface with a three-inch smudge of newsprint. She placed the cup on the table beside the clippings but not before spilling a few drops on the elaborately patterned dhurrie rug. She hunted for a cigarette, then a lighter. Finally, she settled on the plush cream chintz sofa and began sorting.

Like a sculptor searching for form hidden in a lump of clay she flipped through the pieces of newsprint. They must have whispered to her, otherwise she wouldn't have clipped them. She had found many stories this way, scanning papers and looking for connections other people had missed. She knew it was there, she could feel it.

As she sifted through the pile, she thought of Jeffrey. It was her dream last night that had brought him into her thoughts. He was so intimately connected in her mind to the murder of her mother. She realized it had been five weeks since they last spoke and she desperately wanted to hear his voice. She missed him like she missed the smell of the ocean, barely noticing until she caught the scent once again, and then it could bring tears to her eyes. She looked at the phone and knew he was thinking of her—waiting every day, in the back of his mind, for her to call, only really thinking of her when he was alone in his office late at night or in bed. But some kind of discipline kept her from calling, some need to see how long she could go without hearing his voice. She despised dependence in herself.

One of her shrinks had confronted her about her relationship with Jeffrey, commenting on how complicated it seemed to be and asking what he meant to her. It was an insightful question, but she was not about to share her personal feelings with some stupid doctor, in spite of the fact this was probably the point of therapy. It *was* complicated; she loved him, she needed him in her life. Maybe it was because she had met him when she was so young, or that he had played a rescuer/protector role for her initially, but for a long time she had almost hero-worshiped him. He was everything a man should be: strong, brave, honest, honorable, reliable—everything she aspired to be. She considered him to be an omnipresent, omnipotent force in her life, more than friend, more than brother, just everything. But when he had been shot, about a year earlier, something about the way she felt had shifted within her. The thought of him being gone from her life was unbearable and the fact that he had suddenly been proved as human, that he was fragile and mortal like she was, like her mother, had forced her to recognize that she was and probably always had been in love with him. So, of course, she was compelled to get as far away from him as possible without actually putting him out of her life. Love like that was not safe for anyone.

She turned her attention to the clippings. In the pile, she found an article about a trend of people abandoning cars in the desert. One old Cadillac was found with its lights still on, a dirty baby doll in the backseat with its head pulled off. The possibilities intrigued Lydia. Another article concerned itself with the high incidence of methamphetamine addiction among local teens. A housewife had died by hanging herself but the article stated that she'd been found wearing "leather accessories" and intimated that rather than suicide, her death may have been "accidental." *I guess "autoerotic asphyxia" and "suburban housewife" don't go well together in the same sentence,* thought Lydia. It was amazing what you could find going on in small towns if you knew what to look for. Lydia was sure there were no idyllic small American towns and probably never had been. Behind the quaint and charming facades of Everytown, U.S.A., there was some ugly rot, some un-imaginably twisted lives.

The articles that attracted Lydia today were notable not just for their strangeness, but by their potential connections to each other and the larger force that might be at work behind them.

(AUGUST 10)
BREAK-IN AT SURGICAL-SUPPLY WAREHOUSE:
Various Instruments in Small Quantities Are Missing

(AUGUST 15)
ABANDONED BARN BURNED, ARSON SUSPECTED

(AUGUST 16)
TEENAGER MISSING FROM THE CARE OF FOSTER FAMILY

(AUGUST 21)
DRUG-ADDICTED COUPLE DISAPPEAR:
A Long-suffering Victim of Domestic Abuse and Her Husband Missing

And there was one more story that made the back of her neck tingle.

Since she'd arrived in Santa Fe, she had been following a story about a little boy with leukemia, the son of a congresswoman, who had lost his German shepherd, Lucky. The dog had run away from the boy's father during an evening walk near their home in Angel Fire. As the kid lay dying in his hospital bed, he wanted nothing more than his dog back. Of course, this was the kind of tearjerker that the media jumps all over: DYING BOY LOSES HIS BEST FRIEND—WHERE, OH WHERE, HAS MY LITTLE DOG GONE? Tripe. Sadly, the boy died before his dog was found.

But according to today's paper, the dog's body had been found yesterday morning in a church garden, its belly opened from stem to stern. Lucky's organs had been removed with precision and skill, with a scalpel. When the blind man who lived at the Church of the Holy Name noticed the smell, he went out to the garden to investigate and fell over the dog's body. Lydia thought about her daily runs past the church, her imaginings last night about the garden, and about her nightmare. A dark chill climbed her spine and she felt a flutter of fear in her belly.

"Ready or not, here we go again," she said aloud, without really meaning to.

Her mother had always called her a dreamer and a storyteller because Lydia was forever concocting tall tales to entertain herself. She had always loved to read and found books much more interesting than the real world. After reading *Alice in Wonderland* at the age of ten, Lydia had spent hours at the creek in the woods behind her house waiting for a clothed forest animal to lead her to a magical world. After reading *The Lion, the Witch and the Wardrobe*, Lydia had completely disassembled her mother's armoire looking for the gateway to Narnia.

Rather than be disappointed by the failure of life to imitate art, she kept a journal, which she filled with her grand adventures. On the pages of her black-and-white-mottled composition book, she slew dragons with a enchanted emery board, stole magic from a warlock and kept it in a compact which she carried in her backpack (using it when necessary to defend the innocent or to clean her bedroom), led a band of orphans by ship to an island where a rich, lonely woman who could love and care for them had been exiled by an evil witch.

As she grew older, Lydia tired of fairy tales, but not of story-telling. She found she had the ability to perceive certain truths by observing the subtle nuances others failed to notice. She was thirteen when she first realized her ability.

One day when her mother brought her home early from school because Lydia had the flu, she noticed two cars parked in her neighbor's driveway. One she recognized as her neighbor's car but the other she had never seen there before. She felt instantly that something was very wrong.

She watched out the window of her bedroom. Her neighbors, Taylor and Claire Brown, a young couple who had lived there for over two years, both worked during the day. Claire had become friends with Lydia's mother.

"What do you think is going on over there, Mom?"

"It's none of our business. Now, I thought you were sick. Get into bed."

But soon as her mother left the room, Lydia was back at the window. She saw a petite well-dressed woman leave the house. The woman walked quickly, looking around and glancing at her watch. Five minutes after she drove away, she saw Taylor leave the house. He paused and looked at her mother's car and then glanced nervously over at Lydia's house.

Lydia moved behind the curtain to avoid being seen. Then he, too, got in his car and drove off. Lydia was certain he was having an affair.

Perhaps it was because when Taylor and Claire had them over for dinner at their house that Sunday, Lydia had noticed they didn't touch or smile at each other. Perhaps it was because when Claire came over for coffee the week before, Marion and Claire spoke in hushed tones so that Lydia couldn't hear. Maybe it was because both Taylor and the stranger had seemed anxious and self-conscious when they left. But Lydia was certain of her conclusion.

"You have to tell her," she said to her mother.

"Tell her what? Just because a young couple is having problems doesn't mean one of them is cheating, Lydia. They're thinking of selling that house; that easily could have been their real estate agent. These fantasies are going to get you into more trouble than you can handle someday."

Lydia insisted. "Then just tell her that you saw a strange woman in her house."

"No. I'm not going to cause trouble like that. Shame on you, Lydia. You're thirteen years old; you have no idea how complicated relationships are. In fact, though you think you're a genius, you can't imagine even a fraction of what goes on in the world. Claire and Taylor need to work out their problems on their own—without meddling neighbors."

Her mother led her back up to her bedroom and closed the shades. Lydia fumed as Marion tucked her in for the second time. But she was tired and sick and fell asleep.

When she woke up that evening, she heard the sound of a woman crying. She walked quietly down the carpeted stairs and heard Claire's voice from the kitchen. Claire had found another woman's earring in her bed, the last straw in over a year of verbal abuse and suspected infidelity. Claire had packed a bag and was leaving that night to go to her mother's home just a town away.

From her perch on the step, she saw her mother through the

banister slats, though Claire had her back to Lydia. Her mother raised her eyes from Claire, sensing Lydia's presence. Marion raised her eyebrows and shrugged sadly, as if to say, *You were right. Too bad.*

Lydia would remember this incident as the first of many that taught her a powerful lesson: an object out of place, a furtive gesture, something left unsaid could be indicators of a hidden truth. Most people, wrapped up in their own inner narratives, their own secrets, never noticed the subtleties of dishonesty. But very few things escaped Lydia's notice.

She never acknowledged her peculiar ability with any gravity until the death of her mother years later. Until then, it was always a game. Life was a series of little mysteries and Lydia was a detective putting the clues together.

"Mom, I'm telling you, I've seen this guy before. He's following us," she told her mother urgently. She was imagining herself in an *ABC Afterschool Special.*

"Oh, Lydia, for Christ's sake, he is *not* following us."

"He was standing in the parking lot watching us and when we drove away, he pulled out after us."

Her mother glanced uneasily in the rearview mirror. Lydia was making Marion nervous. She *had* seen the man and he looked very strange; Marion just thought he was some pervert leering at her daughter. And she *had* seen him pull out after them. She made a right turn suddenly without signaling. The red car went driving by without even slowing down.

"Wow, Mom. Good going, you lost him," Lydia said dramatically.

Marion looked over at her daughter and they both started laughing. Lydia put the cap back on her blue eyeliner.

"I got the license-plate number," she said.

"Good for you," said Marion said, playing along. It was a game for her now, too. The threat, real or imagined, was gone.

But Lydia couldn't drop it so easily. She was trying to remember where she had seen the man before. She knew she had. It was bothering her, making her feel uneasy.

She had the same feeling now, as she contemplated the clippings before her, the Santa Fe sun reaching into her window and heating the room like a greenhouse. It seemed like ever since the death of her mother she'd been hunting demons, trying to reveal their faces to the world so they couldn't walk around masquerading as normal people, surprising innocent women in the night or little children as they slept.

She turned her mind to the Church of the Holy Name and how she had been there the night before and again in her dreams. What would it mean if all the pieces fit together as she imagined? She felt a tingling of the senses, as if she'd heard a scream in the night that had awakened her from sleep. As if she were lying, paralyzed in the dark, hearing the scream echo in the silence, hoping that it would come again so she could spring into action—but praying that it wouldn't.

chapter five

Her study was the heart of the New Mexico house. It was a large room with a twelve-foot ceiling, decorated in warm browns and rusts, deep plum and evergreen, all the colors she found most soothing. The western wall was lined with shelves from floor to ceiling, wall to wall, each shelf filled with the books she had read and written in her life. She kept them all, could never bear to throw any of them away. The southern wall, like most of the southern walls of the house, was glass, exposing the view she cherished. On the floor, a rich brown wall-to-wall carpet felt like velvet beneath her feet. Beside the glass wall a large sofa and over-stuffed chair of sienna Italian leather faced each other. Over the couch she had draped a blanket given to her by a Tibetan monk. Velvet pillows of gold, green, and red picked up the colors of the blanket. Between the chair and table lay a huge wooden door she had purchased from an auction of an eighteenth-century Spanish castle and converted into a coffee table resting on a mahogany base. The wall behind the couch was a clutter of original black-and-white photographs from Alverez Bravo, Ansel Adams, Tara Popick, and a photo of herself taken by Herb Ritts for a profile written for *New York* magazine. A gothic iron candelabra sat on top of the table. On the floor over the carpet lay a large, elaborately embroidered Oriental rug.

Her desk, made of a rich, varnished mahogany, was nearly invisible beneath piles of notes, newspapers from around the country, videotapes, and her computer. Her chair was covered in the same Italian leather as the couch. The wall behind her desk was covered with awards she had won over the years, her Pulitzer the centerpiece among them.

The room, utterly silent, warm, and profoundly comfortable, was a womb. Here she found in turn solace, inspiration, seclusion. She had spent many hours sitting in her leather-bound chair, staring out the window, since she'd had the house built two years ago. She was untouchable here, completely relaxed. The only people who had ever been inside were Jeffrey and her grandparents when they came to visit. It was here she sat, surfing the Web, looking for more information on the items she had clipped from the paper.

The missing people Lydia had read about in the clippings clearly were not the concern of anyone important. Shawna Fox was a chronic runaway. It seemed like the investigation was half-assed, but the argument she had had with her foster parents led police to assume she had taken off just like she had from her three prior foster homes. The boyfriend, Greg Matthews, insisted vehemently that Shawna never would have left him, but no one seemed to give his opinion much weight. Christine and Harold Wallace were recovering addicts who had been in and out of rehab for most of their adult lives. Their disappearances probably wouldn't even have been notable if every single thing they owned, including their wallets and car, hadn't been left behind—and if they hadn't owed two months rent to their landlord. He was the one who had reported them missing to the police. There were no detailed profiles of any of the victims in any of the papers. The bigger *Albuquerque Journal* did not even carry a mention of the events, except a small item about the surgical-supply warehouse break-in.

There was of course a slew of articles on the congresswoman's son and his battle with leukemia, the missing dog, and the family's graceful forbearance in the face of tragedy. The usual human-interest stuff. But Lydia could find nothing more on the Internet to expound on the *Santa Fe New Mexican* article that reported the dog's body having been found mutilated at the Church of the Holy Name. *So what do we have here, Sherlock?* she asked herself in the sometimes mocking, sometime scolding tone that was her inner voice. It was partially her, partially her mother . . . Whoever it was, she could be a real bitch.

Not much, except the buzz. What she had was three of what the FBI Behavioral Sciences Unit termed "high-risk victims," people like prostitutes, drug addicts, or runaways whose lives or actions make them an easy mark for predators. She had arson and animal mutilation, two elements of the textbook "triad" of warning signs for a serial offender. Missing hospital supplies and a dog that had had his organs removed with "surgical precision" according to the local paper. And then there was the Church of the Holy Name and the blind man, whom she'd seen and dreamt about. The only thing connecting the church to the rest was that the dog had been found there. But still . . .

She typed the church name into the search engine, expecting a few listings for bingo games and charity events in the *New Mexican.* Instead she found 243 matches from newspapers and national magazines across the country.

Juno Alonzo, the blind man she'd seen playing his guitar the night before, was a bit of a celebrity. In fact, there were those who believed he was a healer and a psychic. Juno had lived at the church since he was a child. His uncle, Father Luis Claro, had raised Juno since his mother had died.

Most of his life had passed without incident until just two

years earlier, when a woman who had been blinded in a car accident claimed he had returned her sight. An autistic boy was
allegedly cured by Juno's touch. A man claimed that Juno had
contacted his dead wife and solved the mystery of her death. Of
course, upon these stories hitting the mainstream media, the sick,
dying, and curious of the world had descended upon Angel Fire
like locusts, accompanied by the obligatory media circus. Juno
Alonzo had refused interviews, claiming he had nothing to do
with any of the healings. He made only one statement to the
media: "If the people who have come to see me have been cured
of what ails them, then it is God's will and has nothing to do with
me." And when a young boy Juno visited in the hospital died after
a failed organ transplant, the melee died down. People went away
and Juno was forgotten again.

As Lydia read on, she vaguely remembered hearing about the
story. It was before she had bought her home in Santa Fe. She
chalked it up as a sensational type of story common to the supermarket tabloids. People were always looking for miracles in
the dark unknown of the world, forever looking for the face of
the Virgin Mary on the side of buildings, looking for Elvis in Las
Vegas, looking for order in the chaos of life. This type of searching
tended not to interest Lydia. There was enough in the real world
that needed figuring out. *I guess it never occurred to anyone that if
Juno was a healer, he probably could have cured his own blindness,*
she thought sarcastically. *But maybe that was God's will too.*

At the end of the list of articles about Juno were two items
from 1965. She couldn't believe the local paper was so on the ball
as to have digitized their archives back that far, but maybe they
had a lot of time on their hands. The first item was about a Serena
Alonzo, who had murdered her husband by setting their house
on fire while he was passed out drunk. She claimed to have killed

her husband because he beat her and she feared for the life of her unborn child. The item had come up in the search because her brother, Father Luis Claro, was a young priest at the Church of the Holy Name. Serena was tried, convicted, and sentenced to life in prison. Which turned out to be a pretty short sentence, according to the next item, because Serena had died while giving birth to her son in a prison hospital. The boy, Juno Alonzo, was born blind. Father Luis took custody of him and planned to raise him at the Church of the Holy Name where he resided.

It was an interesting backstory, but Lydia wondered if anyone at the police department had information on current events they wanted to discuss. Though she doubted anyone would be rushing to the phone to take her call, Lydia knew most people she called were rarely happy to hear from her, especially the police. Chief Simon Morrow of the Santa Fe Police Department was certainly no exception. When she made a call, she had questions; for whatever reason, they usually seemed to be questions people weren't eager to answer. She had been hung up on, sworn at, had her life threatened. She didn't take it personally. And she was very persistent. Lydia had asked some hard questions of Chief Morrow in the past, questions that would lead to her Pulitzer. He had given answers that ultimately had led to his resignation from the St. Louis Police Department. She had thought his career was over then, deservedly so. But he had turned up in Santa Fe like a bad penny, as Lydia's mother used to say.

Lydia was on hold, and she could almost see Simon Morrow rubbing his sweating middle-aged balding head unconsciously as he sat in front of his phone, trying to decide whether or not to take her call.

"Ms. Strong, how can I help you?"

"Chief Morrow, it's good to hear your voice," she said with mock cordiality. "Really."

"How long have you been in town?"

"Long enough to pick up on a few things."

"Such as?"

"I was wondering about Lucky."

"Lucky?"

"Yeah, the dog that was found mutilated at the Church of the Holy Name. You might remember, Lucky was missing a few vital organs when he turned up."

"Sad story. What about it?"

"Is there an ongoing investigation?"

Morrow paused for what she assumed was his attempt at dramatic effect. "Ms. Strong, you are aware that the mutilation and death of a dog, while tragic, does not warrant a murder investigation."

On the other end of the line, Lydia was practically salivating. She was tapping her pen rapidly against the pad on her desk. She could smell it. She could taste the blood in her mouth. "I am quite aware of that. I just thought, in connection with some of the other peculiar criminal activity in the area—for example, the surgical-supply warehouse or the missing-persons cases you have open—there might be some connections to be explored."

"I see. Thank you for your input, Ms. Strong, but I fail to see how this concerns you." He was, she knew, attempting to sound cold, intimidating, but there was an almost imperceptible quaver to his voice that told her he was hiding something.

"Just consider me an involved citizen."

"With an overactive imagination."

"That's what you said the last time we spoke, Chief. Do I have to remind you how wrong you were?"

"There's nothing here, Ms. Strong. Nothing at all."

"Are there photos of the location where the dog was found?" she pressed.

"No."

"Okay, we can play it this way if you want to," she said, her voice level and soft, "but we'll be talking again soon. Sooner than you'd like, I bet."

"I'll look forward to it. Really."

As Simon Morrow slammed down the phone he issued a string of expletives. Continuing to curse, he rose quickly, knocking over a cold, black cup of coffee.

He barely saved the photos of Lucky's mutilated body that lay spread across his desk.

chapter six.

Her run the night before had soothed Lydia's restlessness, but only temporarily. But morning had turned to afternoon and the afternoon to early evening as Lydia had sat at her computer, and her focus was beginning to drift.

She began to think she would call Jeffrey and ask what he thought about the articles and their possible implications. But then she began to think of other things. Memories of her mother began to sear her, and her restlessness began to feel physically uncomfortable. She shut down the computer and got up to stretch. The house was silent and lonely. She had to get out.

She walked to her bedroom and entered the walk-in closet, started flipping through the rows of designer clothes that she collected with zeal.

When she let the impulse take her, it took her to extremes. Sometimes it would come on her hours or days before she acted upon it. Her conscious mind would push it away until it could no longer be ignored. Even now, as she pulled the sleeveless black Armani dress over her lean, tightly muscled body and slipped her slender feet into high-heeled Gucci black leather pumps, she barely acknowledged what she was about to do. She wrapped her lustrous blue-black hair into a loose French twist and held it in place with two red lacquer chopsticks. She applied no makeup to her pale skin except a deep-red shade of MAC lipstick, to accentuate her stormy gray eyes. It wasn't that she didn't take responsibility for herself and her actions. It was only that she had about as much control as a junkie looking for a fix. All she was aware of as she headed out the door was a sense of relief that she wouldn't be spending the night alone.

In big cities like New York, the game was more dangerous, the quarry more unpredictable, more plentiful. In Santa Fe, she would usually find herself in the hotel bar of the Eldorado, maybe in a restaurant off the square, possibly a dive bar by the side of the highway. It didn't matter.

"May I help you, miss?" She was greeted by the smiling maître d', a young man who looked too young to be wearing a tuxedo.

"Just a drink. I'll sit at the bar."

The bar was more crowded than usual. Though the permanent residents of Santa Fe had opposed the construction of the Eldorado, the luxury hotel was packed with tourists year-round. Opera season, ski season, Indian Market, the art galleries on Canyon Road drew the country's idle rich. It had proved to be good hunting grounds the last time she had visited.

She spotted him at the end of the slick black bar. He was young, mid-twenties; his thick, dark hair was pulled into a ponytail at the base of his skull. He exuded wealth, his black cashmere sweater draping elegantly off taut pecs and strong shoulders. His Rolex glittered in the dim track-lighting above him. A martini, half-finished, sat before him. He traced the edge of the glass with a gentle fingertip. Melancholy, contemplative, definitely alone. She sat down across from him, a good distance, but directly in his line of vision.

"Ketel One, straight," she told the bartender, an elegantly dressed black man with a shaved head and a diamond stud in his right ear.

Her eyes swept the room. A couple nuzzled in a cozy booth with the intimacy of people who could see only each other. A group of well-dressed, bejeweled older women, obviously on vacation from their husbands, had had too much to drink and were laughing loudly. A young woman, trying to look more sophisticated than she was in a sequined dress and cheap satin shoes, sipped a white zinfandel and watched the door expectantly. A tall, muscular man walked in the door and stood awkwardly as the maître d' outfitted him with a jacket that was too small. Before he put it on, she noticed a tattoo on his arm. In the darkness of the room she could barely make it out, but it looked like a crucifix. The maître d' then escorted him to a small table in the back of the bar; Lydia imagined it was to keep him out of sight of the better-dressed clients.

When the man across the bar raised his eyes, he caught hers. She did not look away. Like always, she compared him to Jeffrey. Like always, there was no comparison. But he would do. He was quite handsome. She liked them dark and brooding. He smiled a practiced smile. She smiled back with equal skill and lowered her eyes, shyly. How she loved the game. She raised the glass to her lips, feeling the cool vodka burn her tongue and slide down her throat. She did not look at him again. If they did not come to her, she would walk away. But they usually came. And when she raised her eyes to glance at him again, he was on his way over to her. Chopin played mournfully in the background, as ice cubes in crystal glasses and the murmur of conversations were a music of their own.

She wondered what line he would use: *"In town on business or*

*pleasure?" "What kind of man would keep a woman like you wait-
ing?"* She'd heard them all. When he seated himself beside her, he
surprised her.

"I could drown in those eyes of yours," he said without looking at her. A slight Italian accent tinged his words. Of course.
Only European men were so smooth. American men were clumsy,
arrogant.

"Thank you," she answered.

"Can I buy you a drink?"

Within the hour they were in his suite, decorated in predictable Southwest decor; it straddled the line between opulence and
hotel tackiness uncomfortably. With three straight vodkas under
her belt, Lydia felt the welcome lightness that accompanied these
moments. He had turned the lights down low and they danced
slowly to a Mexican ballad on a stereo system piped into the room.
The smell of his cologne was intoxicating. His large hands on the
small of her back made her feel safe and wanted, though she didn't
know him at all. When she closed her eyes, he was the right build
so that she could imagine he was Jeffrey.

She hated herself a little in these moments, like a junkie going
back to the needle. This pursuit was empty, she knew. The effort to satisfy the desire never met the gaping need within her.
Here, she could have closeness without the risk of love, she could
take without giving, she could have something she wasn't afraid to
lose. She'd always had an intellectual perspective on her flaws and
it never made any difference when she tried to change.

He looked into her eyes as one hand traced the smooth skin
on her arm and the other delicately took down the zipper on the
back of her dress. "It is all right?" he asked softly.

"Yes."

She helped him slip off his sweater. He was beautiful. *Apollo,* she called him in her mind. Paolo was his name, she remembered vaguely. He kissed the straps of her dress away and the garment fell to the floor. As he gently cupped her breasts in his hands, kissing them, she undid his pants and reached inside, feeling him hard for her. He groaned at her touch and kissed her mouth with such passion it startled her. He pulled her leg up and she wrapped it around his, moving herself against him. Then he lifted her and carried her to the bed. She leaned on her elbows and watched him step out of pants and black silk boxers.

"Very nice," she said, smiling.

He pulled off her white lace panties with a boyish smile. "You are also 'very nice,' as you say. Beautiful, perfect."

She laughed, thinking the less he spoke, the better. He lay beside her and traced the center line of her body with a delicate touch. She quivered, ticklish, aroused. And then she was on top of him. She kissed him as she moved her hips in slow, luscious circles. He held her tightly at her hips, pulling himself deeper and deeper into her. She watched his face as he surrendered to his pleasure, moaning. She loved that moment of true yearning; she knew it so well in her own heart. To see it in another made her feel less alone.

It was close to midnight as she pulled her clothes back on. He slept soundly, snoring lightly, sweetly, like a child. She glanced back at him. He was lovely. As she closed the door and walked down the hall, she wrapped her arms around herself as if to protect her heart against the ache that was already setting in. The feeling she would go to the ends of the earth to avoid, the hole in her insides where the wind blew through, was creeping up on her, pulling at her with black ghost-fingers.

In her car in the parking lot, she wept, deep, true tears that welled from some secret place inside her. Tears she couldn't understand, and couldn't escape.

When Jeffrey's phone rang at four A.M., he knew it was her before he picked up.

"Where are you?" he answered.

"Santa Fe."

"Do you know I've been trying to reach you?"

"I know. I'm sorry."

"Right." He cleared his throat. She heard him struggling not to sound the combination of relieved and angry that he was. "Well, what are you doing?"

"I came to hide out for a while but I've run into something down here. Will you come?"

"You want me to drop everything and come to New Mexico?"

"Are you working on something big? Something no one else can handle?"

"Not really."

"We both know you don't have a life," she teased.

He laughed. He could use a vacation. And he did want to see her. "I'll call you with my flight information tomorrow. You can pick me up at the airport."

chapter seven

Jeffrey fought the urge to turn around and bolt from the gangway that led to United Airlines flight number 133 to Albuquerque. It was the same irrational feeling of impending doom that always assailed him when he boarded a plane. He tried without success to control his adrenalinized fear response, the dry mouth and sweating palms, the shallow breathing. Lydia thought it was the funniest thing in the world that someone who had faced down some of the most dangerous, desperate men in the country without a notable rise in his heart rate, experienced abject terror at getting on a plane. "It's safer than getting into a car," she'd said. And he knew this intellectually. But you had control over a car. If the engine failed on your car, you didn't plummet thirty-five thousand feet into the ocean. But he kept moving up the narrow aisle, stowed his carry-on in the overhead bin, and squeezed his big frame into the tiny window seat. He liked the window seat because he wanted to be able to see if there was a problem, like black smoke coming from the engine, or maybe an errant bolt of lightning in a cloudless sky. Then, of course, there was the possibility of in-air collisions because of the increasing number of planes in the sky, and pilots who spoke different native languages from the air traffic controllers. To say nothing of the potential for drug addiction and alcoholism among the pilots, airplane mechanics, and air traffic controllers. Really, anything could go wrong at any moment. "You know too much about this shit," Lydia had commented. "Ignorance is bliss. Besides, you walked away from a bullet fired into you at point-blank range. You're charmed."

The thought of the night he was shot about a year ago always filled him with yearning for Lydia.

He took a bullet, the only one of his career, in the shoulder during the apprehension of a child-killer he and his partners had been hunting for a year with the New York City Police Department. The chase led them to the rooftops of the projects in the South Bronx on a moonless rainy night. Younger and faster than most of the men working the case that night, Jeffrey found himself alone on the building-top, gun drawn, the rest of the team a good minute behind him, running up fifteen flights of stairs. The faces of the murdered and missing boys were burned into Jeffrey's mind, and he was more than determined to bring their tormentor to justice. The rooftop was a black field of shadows, doorways, and ventilation shafts, any one of them a place to hide. The street noise, even twenty floors up, made it impossible to hear the labored breathing or the shuffle of footsteps that might give Jeffrey the advantage of knowing where the perp hid. Jeffrey's mistake, of course, was that he wasn't afraid at all. Had he been, he would have been more cautious. Instead he rounded a corner too quickly and came face-to-face with the criminal, who fired a round at him. Luckily the bastard was a bad shot, and instead of getting Jeffrey in the head, the bullet passed through his right shoulder, just to the right of his protective Kevlar vest. The other men on the team took the killer down.

He didn't remember much else until he awoke hours later in a hospital bed, feeling heavily drugged and vaguely aware of a dull pain in his shoulder. It took him a second to remember what had happened and where he was. The room was dim and the heart monitor beeped steadily. Lydia must have been standing there in the doorway for a moment before he turned his head and saw her. He remembered thinking that he was dreaming. The lights behind her glowed like a halo around her head. She looked so beautiful and strong, her long black hair spilling over her shoulders, her white T-shirt clinging to her breasts. He smiled dreamily, wanting to take her into his arms.

Suddenly she seemed to lose her strength and leaned against the doorjamb, closing her eyes. When she opened them again, tears spilled down her pale skin. In all the years he had known her, he hadn't seen her cry since the death of her mother. Now she looked frightened and helpless, like the child he remembered. He struggled to sit upright.

"Lydia, I'm fine."

She walked into the room and sat in the chair by his bed. She took his good hand tightly and pulled it to her face. She held it there with her eyes squeezed shut, as if she were praying. They both knew she crossed the line that moment. He had realized as he lay there, his throat dry with emotion, that he had crossed it long ago.

He was moved to silence by her tears. He wanted to beg her to stop before his heart broke but, at the same time, her tears were answering a question he had never asked of her. He had always known that she cared for him deeply and, in a way, relied on him. He knew he was the only one she truly allowed into her life. But he was never sure where her feelings began or ended. She had always maintained a protective distance from him, appearing and then disappearing from his day-to-day life. As she sat by his bedside, bathing his hand with her tears, she closed that distance.

She had said to him once, "Never love anything so much that if fate snatches it away, your whole world turns black."

He knew it was too late for that now—for both of them.

"Lydia, I'm okay," he repeated softly. He lay very still, afraid to move his hand, afraid she'd let it go.

She searched his face to see if he was lying. Then she nodded and sat back in the chair, keeping her hold on his hand. He watched as she struggled to recover herself. Her skin was flushed, she stared away from him. Anyone else would have thought her face lacked emotion, her small features were taut and still. But her gray eyes told the tale to him alone.

"Don't you ever die on me, Jeffrey. Don't you ever," she whispered.

She seemed not to be able to stop the quiet, choking sobs that shook her shoulders. He would almost rather take another bullet than ever hear that sound again.

"Lydia," he began, the words he had wanted to say for years on the tip of his tongue.

She stopped him. "Don't, Jeffrey," she said gently.

He let it go, too afraid to go forward. They sat in silence, hand in hand, until he drifted off to sleep.

She stayed with him in his midtown apartment for almost a month. She cleaned, she cooked, she nursed him with a tenderness he wouldn't have believed of her. Not that she was a cold woman. But getting close to her was like trying to get a bird to eat out of your hand. You had to hold that bread crumb out consistently and for a good long time before you earned enough trust to approach without generating a flight response. She slept in his guest room, though she had her own apartment in New York City overlooking Central Park West. She stayed until he became restless to go back to work and she was satisfied that he was well.

Then Lydia left, went off to Europe to find out if Esmy von Buren was really killing her own children as her former mother-in-law suspected. Jeffrey didn't try to make her stay, just kissed her lightly on the mouth.

"I'll always be here, Lydia."

"So will I." And she flashed him a rare smile.

He strapped himself in now, and was glad to see that the door had closed but no one was sitting beside him, even though he probably would not at any point "take off his seat belt and move freely about the cabin" as the pilot would blithely suggest. Didn't people know about wind shears?

The plane began taxiing down the runway, picking up speed. He wondered, as he had wondered a thousand times, what would have happened if he had pushed her that night in the hospital. It might have taken only the slightest nudge. Perhaps she would have opened to him like a hothouse orchid. Or perhaps she would have shattered into a thousand pieces, like a carelessly handled porcelain doll.

But as it was, since their month of living together almost a year ago, she'd put more distance between them than ever. At the height of the FBI investigation of Esmy von Buren, which Lydia had been responsible for getting started, she called him almost every day, but they spoke only about the case. He'd seen her only a handful of times when she returned to New York for Esmy's trial. Then, two months ago, with Esmy tried and convicted of three counts of murder and Lydia's article turned in to *New York* magazine, Lydia took off. She left a message on his home machine, though she could have easily reached him on his cell phone.

"I need a rest after this case. Christ, I'm exhausted. I'll call you. Take care of that shoulder."

The plane was racing down the runway, doubling its speed

by the second and making his adrenaline pump. He let his head be pushed back by the force of takeoff and closed his eyes as he felt the wheels leave the ground. Why had she stopped him when they were so close? The last safe moment had passed between them—there was no real pretending to each other that their relationship ended with friendship. But he would rather see her preserved in the environment she created for herself than watch their relationship crumble if he came too close. So he endured the painful distances and the torturous closeness. He would continue, he knew, to come when she called.

chapter eight

The Church of the Holy Name was dimly lit by the fading sun as Lydia entered. Awed by the hush of the sacred room, at once she felt like a child and an intruder. She consciously pushed the vivid images of her dream from her mind. Still she felt a flutter of nerves in her stomach. She kept expecting to see her mother. *Why did you come here now?* she asked herself, as if something outside her had made the choice to stop suddenly on her way to the airport.

As she walked cautiously down the center aisle toward the altar, the old, immaculately polished wood floors groaned loudly beneath her lizard-skin boots.

"Is someone here?" Juno Alonzo materialized in a doorway that had been empty a moment ago. He was a tall man, almost six feet, and thin. His eyes seemed fixed on her—jet pools in a landscape of strong but gentle features. Full, red lips sloping into a square jaw, chiseled cheekbones leading to a high, deeply lined brow. But his face was more than the sum of these parts. There was something mesmerizing about it, like a portrait come to life. He was easily the most beautiful man—in an ethereal, almost angelic way—she had ever seen. She had the urge to confess all her sins to him and do penance in his arms.

He spoke again. "Hello?"

"Mr. Alonzo?"

"Yes?"

"I'm Lydia Strong."

"The writer?"

"Yes."

She wondered for a moment if he would treat her with suspicion and then turn her away as he had to other writers who came to interview him. But instead he smiled and approached her with his hand outstretched in greeting, as if he had been expecting her.

"A pleasure, Ms. Strong. My uncle has read your work to me from magazines and I've listened to you interviewed on National Public Radio. I had heard you had a home in the area."

When she took his hand in hers, he covered it with his other, gently pulling her closer to him. It was a warm and powerful grip, full of a strange energy that made Lydia flush and smile lightly in spite of herself. They stayed like that for a moment longer than would have seemed appropriate in another context. And as she stood captivated by his unseeing gaze, her small hand folded in his large one, she was tempted to believe what she had read about Juno. She wondered suddenly if he did have the power to enter people's dreams. It was a ridiculous thought but it stayed with her. She would give anything to have one last chance to talk to her mother, to say good-bye, to say she was sorry . . . for what, she didn't know. She would give anything to show her mother the accomplishments she had made in her career, to hear that her mother was proud of her. Would it cause her mother pain to know she wasn't married, that she never went to church? Would Marion be angry or disappointed? Lydia wanted to know these answers so badly sometimes.

She looked at Juno, searching his face for some hint of the supernatural. *Like what—some kind of glowing tattoo—a third eye?*

she thought. But even her own internal sarcasm couldn't dampen the irrational and inexplicable feeling of hope that welled in her. And the images from her dream haunted her, were a tune stuck in her head, repetitive and annoying.

"Please, sit down, Ms. Strong. Tell me what I can do for you." He led her to a pew with his hand on the small of her back. "I assume you are here to talk about Christopher Poveda."

"Who?"

"The boy who died recently of leukemia."

"Actually . . ."

"Sometimes God calls his children home, Ms. Strong. And there is nothing on earth any of us can do."

"I'm sure that's true, Mr. Alonzo. But I am here to ask you about Lucky, the boy's dog you found dead in your garden." She felt uncomfortable as she watched his face darken, aware and a bit ashamed that her interest must seem sordid to him.

"Yes?"

"Do you have any idea how the dog got there?"

"There are many people who believe that I have the power to heal. But there are many that disbelieve it—vehemently. These types of people have perpetrated acts of violence against me and this church in the past, may God forgive them."

She listened carefully to his words and his voice, listening for a note out of key that would signal to her that he had something to hide. One of the first things she had learned at the FBI academy, being one of the few authors ever allowed to attend, was that most liars gave themselves away without ever saying a word. She scrutinized him openly, looking for a tapping foot, a clenching fist, any revealing unconscious bodily movement. But he was solid, fixed. He concentrated on his words, choosing each carefully, speaking slowly. He seemed to speak as some people wrote, picking words specifically for their nuance and rhythm.

"So you imagined that to be an act of vandalism. Someone expressing anger that you were unable to heal Christopher?"

"I can't imagine why anyone else would have done such an awful thing."

"Forgive me, but it doesn't seem to make a whole lot of sense. Why would you kill one creature to express rage that another could not be saved?"

"It's a good question and one I have been asking myself since I fell upon the dog's body."

Usually, skepticism of others was part of Lydia's natural state of existence. The words people spoke, the faces they wore in public, were rarely the path to the truth about them. The inconsistent phrase, the shifting gaze, the unconscious movement were much more certain, though more subtle, indicators of the real story behind the face. She was looking for any of those things now. Hoping for one, in fact. Because as much as the possibility that this man was a psychic and a healer had appealed to her just moments earlier, now she inexplicably wanted him to reveal himself as a fraud.

"May I see where you found him?" she asked, though she wasn't sure what she could possibly find there.

He led her through the church, again with his hand on the small of her back. It was an odd gesture, at once intimate and authoritative. His large hand made her feel small and, as a result, vulnerable and a bit shepherded. She wondered if this was a consciously manipulative action on his part.

He held the back door open for her and she walked into the lush garden. She hadn't noticed it before, but in the center, nestled in a bed of leafy green fernlike plants was a small statue of the

Virgin Mary holding the Baby Jesus. Standing about three feet tall and carved from some type of pink marble, there was something unusually beautiful about the sculpture. Lydia found many of the images of Madonna and Child to be cold in their religiousness, as if the emotional bond between mother and son had been forgotten. As if His sacred destiny made it that He was never Mary's child. But He was once just a baby boy adored by his mother, wasn't He? This had always bothered her about religion. It seemed to Lydia that someone had taken all the humanity out of it. But the face of this Virgin statue was etched with motherly adoration, a loving smile playing on her lips, her eyes brimming with emotion at the baby nestled secure and sleepy in her arms.

"This statue is remarkable," said Lydia.

"So I'm told," answered Juno. "My uncle, the priest who heads this parish, is a sculptor. He mainly works in wood. There's a case at the back of the church that holds the crucifixes and rosaries he makes most often. The statue was a bit of a departure for him. He made it when we had the garden built."

Though beautiful, the garden seemed neither as fecund nor otherworldly as it had in the dark or in her dream. But the flowers were meticulously tended, with not one weed pushing its way through the dirt. The earth looked as if it had been recently turned, as it was wet and black as tar.

"This garden is quite lively for something found in the fall, not to mention in the desert."

"We have volunteers that tend it with great attention. I understand they do a phenomenal job. Though, of course, I've never seen it myself. Their scent provokes in me the imagination of color. So wonderful."

He looked almost rapturous for a moment. Lydia found herself assailed by a flash flood of doubt. She was always suspicious of euphoria. She considered it a state natural only to psychotics and idiots. And he did not seem to be either. But, she considered, he was a blind man of tremendous faith who had likely never strayed far from the church or the yard where they stood. The world was probably quite a different place for him than it was for her. She wondered what it was like to have such faith, to be moved to joy by the imagination of color. She couldn't remember the last time she had felt joy—in fact, wasn't sure if she ever had in her adult life.

"Have you lived at this church all your life, Mr. Alonzo?"

"Yes, I was raised here by my uncle. Our quarters are behind the church. I suppose it's an unusual situation, but I help him with the business of the church and accompany him with my guitar at mass."

"And heal the sick?"

It was a guerrilla tactic, she knew, to lull people into security with innocent questions and then drop from the trees with something more direct. Juno laughed a little and shook his head. It was a laugh of resignation, with just a hint of annoyance.

"Like I said, Ms. Strong, there are people who believe I have that power."

"What do you believe?"

He leaned against the doorjamb and appeared to be looking above her for the answer. "I believe that God can heal. People have claimed, though I myself am unconvinced, that my touch has helped them. But I believe that if even one in a million people are helped or believed they are helped by my touch, what right do I have to turn anyone away? There are far fewer people who come now. And you are the first writer I have spoken to in over a year. Only to say what I have just said to you."

"How can it be that you don't know if you have this power or not?"

Juno paused, as if considering whether to answer her or not. Lydia knew reporters had tried and failed to get him to tell them as much as he had already told her. Maybe he had sensed that her interest as a professional wasn't in his curious abilities, and that is why he was so open. She didn't think she would get any more from him and was surprised when he then went on to tell his story.

"One afternoon, after my tasks had been completed, I was reading the Bible in my room when I heard the sound of a woman's faint sobs from the church. The sound was so hopeless, so despairing. I closed the book and rose quietly and walked toward the sound.

"The air in the church was hot and thick, and the afternoon sun, burning over a hundred degrees that day, was beating in through the west windows. When no one acknowledged me, I continued toward the pews. I could tell from the direction of the sound that the woman was sitting in the first row. I walked over and sat beside her. I could feel her misery as if it were my own. It seemed to radiate from her like a fever.

"It was Allison Drew, a young woman I had known for years through the church. The same age as I am, she had attended almost every Sunday mass with her father since she was ten years old. She had also come for the catechism classes my uncle conducted following the noon mass. She had been in a car accident that was a result of her drunk driving. The other driver had been killed and Allison was badly injured. Charges against her were pending. She had lost her vision but, according to what her father told us, she would probably gain it back. That had not happened yet.

"I did not ask her any questions but slid closer to her and put my arm around her shoulder. She leaned her head against me, and wept. She sensed that there was no need for her to speak, and there wasn't. I could feel her pain, her shame, her hopelessness for the future, her sorrow for the life she took. I knew no words would comfort her. So, instead, I kissed her forehead gently and breathed into her all the love and forgiveness I knew God would offer her.

" 'God has already forgiven you, Allison. Forgive yourself,' I told her.

"Four days later, Allison regained her sight. She told people that I had healed her, that I had told her of God's forgiveness. She told them that I knew her feelings without words. People believed. They began to seek me out for guidance.

"I was very uncomfortable with this new role. But I didn't have the heart to turn them away. I thought, *Maybe God is helping people through me, maybe this is why I am on this earth.* And I found that, somehow, my words had the power to help people solve their problems. When people spoke to me, they felt understood. Maybe it was just because I listened.

"Several months after I saw Allison, a couple who had traveled from several towns away brought their autistic son Morgan to me. I was reluctant, but agreed to spend time with him, though I was not sure how I could help the child. In my heart I knew I hadn't healed Allison, even if she had convinced herself and others that I had. While I did not mind counseling people who sought my advice, I did not want them to be deceived into thinking that I could heal their sick. But the couple seemed so desperate, so needy, I couldn't say no."

Juno had stuck both his hands in his pockets and had turned his eyes toward the ground. He wore a confused and sad expression, as if he still didn't quite believe what had happened to him. He seemed to be offering the story to her, not quite expecting her to make sense of the events as they had played out, not quite able to make sense of them himself.

"I brought him into the church recreation room where

catechism classes were held while his parents waited, praying in the church. The boy sat on a chair silent and perfectly motionless, smelling lightly of soap and talcum powder. I touched his hair, which had been close-cropped for the summer months. It felt like the bristles of a brush, hard and fuzzy at the same time.

"Thirty minutes passed. The boy was a locked box. Whatever was happening inside his head, there was no energy leaking out for me to feel or recognize. *The boy's soul is on inside out,* I thought; *he's sealed inside himself.* I had the sense that Morgan's life was playing on a movie screen inside his head, two-dimensional and distant. Morgan was a witness to what went on around him but could not participate.

"Suddenly, while I was speaking to him, telling him the story of Noah's Ark, the child issued a brief, blood-curdling scream. Then he sat still again, as if he had never opened his mouth. He frightened me and I moved away from him and began to play my guitar, not knowing what else to do.

"After a full hour, I took Morgan back out to his parents. I told them I didn't think I had helped their son. They thanked me for my efforts and left solemn and disappointed.

"As I heard them drive away, I felt angry with myself for not being able to reach the boy, for being so inept in the face of Morgan's obvious need. I wondered if it was God's intention for Morgan to remain as he was, or if I had failed in a task set before me.

"But several weeks after Morgan's visit, the rumor spread throughout the congregation that I had healed the autistic child. It was said that four days after his visit, Morgan began talking and interacting like a normal child. I wanted to believe them but I knew in my heart that it wasn't true. I tried to find out Morgan's last name so that I could call his parents and see if what people were telling me was true but no one seemed to know them. When people asked about it, I replied, I did not heal that boy. If he grew better, it was God's will.

"But my replies were interpreted as modesty, as a deference to God," he said, finishing his story, "and I found that no matter what protestations I made, I could not move people from what they wanted to believe. Even the truth could not diminish their faith in me."

"But then people lost interest when the boy you visited in the hospital died hours later from a failed transplant."

"So you already know all of this?" he said, clearing his throat. And for the first time since she arrived, he seemed uneasy, began unbuttoning and buttoning again the cuff of his immaculately cleaned and pressed denim shirt.

"What time was it when you found the dog?" asked Lydia, changing the subject.

"It was about six o'clock in the morning. I had risen early to practice my guitar, but was distracted by an odd smell coming from the garden—the door was open. As I neared, I heard a rustling. But when I called out, no one answered. I walked out into the garden and slipped in the dog's blood. It was very disturbing."

"Who removed the dog?"

"The police came and took some photographs. Then they took the body away."

"Did anybody else see it?" she asked, hoping someone could tell her exactly how the dog had been mutilated, since obviously Chief Morrow wasn't going to turn over photographs he'd claimed he didn't have.

"Only my uncle."

The hairs on the back of Lydia's neck rose as she had the sudden feeling that someone was watching. She looked around behind her but beyond the garden was nothing but a dirt road, traveled only by a tumbleweed. She looked at the flowers again and flashed on the image from her dream, when they'd mocked her cruelly.

"Is your uncle here now?" she asked.

"Yes, but he is preparing for mass. If it's not urgent, perhaps I could have him call you."

"That would be fine." She pulled a business card from her purse and handed it to him. He slipped it into his pocket and began to move away from her, then stopped.

"What are the reasons for your questions, Ms. Strong?"

She realized she didn't really know how to answer. What was she supposed to say? *I've watched you. I've had a dream about you and my dead mother. Also, I have this morbid curiosity that leads me to ask difficult questions so that I can write twisted books about horrible crimes. I am always following a trail, looking for the monster in the dark, and I think there could be something really sick—sicker than is obvious—behind the mutilated dog you found in your garden.*

Instead she said, "Were you born blind, Mr. Alonzo?"

He paused before answering. "Yes, I was."

"Do you think it's easier? I mean, never having had sight as opposed to being blinded by an accident."

"I'm sure I wouldn't know. But I don't feel disabled in any way, if that's what you mean. Though I might, should I suddenly be paralyzed. I'm not sure where you're headed with these questions."

"I'm not headed anywhere. I'm just curious."

"I find that hard to believe. Your reputation precedes you."

"How's that?"

"I doubt you'd waste your time here just out of curiosity about a dead dog and a blind man."

"Well, Mr. Alonzo, I won't waste any more of *your* time," she answered as she walked past him through the doorway. She was not ready to reveal anything to him about her suspicions and she did not enjoy lying. So it was better to say nothing at all.

"Ms. Strong, will you stay for mass?" Juno asked, as he followed her back through the doorway.

"Please call me Lydia. No, thank you. I have to meet a friend at the airport and I should go."

He had walked her out to the front of the church as they spoke and now they stood facing each other in the arched doorway.

"The door to this church is always open to you. I hope you will come to a service. I'm sure your mother would be happy to know you had come home to God."

"What?" She felt like he had slapped her in the face.

"My sight is a different one from yours, Lydia."

He smiled gently and walked away from her, closing the door behind him.

She was stung by his words, riven with guilt and a deep sadness. She walked slowly to the car, her mind racing, blood rising to her face, a pounding in her ears. She spun around suddenly to run after him, to ask him what he had meant by that, to ask him what he knew about her and her mother. And how he had come to visit her dreams. But she was paralyzed.

Sitting in her car she reached with a trembling hand for a cigarette—her eternal crutch. If he had been bluffing, trying to convince her of his power, he had at least succeeded in reaching into the heart of her somehow. Maybe that was his technique . . . to deny his powers and then to pull some kind of mind-reading stunt, catch people off guard.

As she unsteadily started the engine, she became aware again of the shadow of a feeling that had started in the church garden. She felt like someone was watching her. She could see no one but she backed up quickly and drove away. In her rearview mirror, she caught a glimpse of movement in the garden.

As she drove, memories of her mother washed over her again.

For Marion Strong life had been a series of disappointments, some mundane, some catastrophic. Maybe her expectations were too high, her dreams unrealistic. But perhaps, as Marion believed, fate had been stingy with her, denying her everything but her beautiful, intelligent daughter.

Marion was a serious woman, for life was not a matter to be taken lightly. No one had ever accused her of being frivolous. She was severe, tall and athletic. Square-jawed and unsmiling, with blazing green eyes, she was a striking figure. Her black hair, streaked with gray since her late teens, was eternally pulled back into a tight bun worn at the nape of her neck. She considered herself sensible, frugal. She had been accused of being inflexible, unyielding, hard. These were the favorite criticisms of her ex-husband, who had left just before Lydia was born. But she knew she had to be that way; otherwise life had a way of whipping the reins out of her hands, running wild, rushing headlong into consequences as unforgiving as a stone wall.

But Lydia knew another place inside her mother as well. In the evenings, after the dinner dishes were washed, after homework was completed and checked, Lydia joined Marion in her bedroom. In the upper right-hand corner of the mahogany dresser was a sterling-silver, soft-bristled brush and a matching box for hairpins.

Lydia's mother didn't allow her to touch these things when she was not present. Eager to show her mother how responsible she could be, she removed them from their place with care, feeling Marion's watchful eyes on her. Carefully she pulled the heavy drawer out by its wrought-iron rings. She removed the brush and box, handling them gingerly, as if they were glass, placed them on the dresser-top and then quietly slid the drawer closed. Her mother hated loud, sudden noises.

Marion sat at the foot of the bed and Lydia sat behind her, legs crossed. She removed each pin from her mother's hair and placed it in the box. Then Lydia untwisted the long plait, careful not to pull it but to unravel it like a spool of silk. It was naturally wild and curly and thick like a cloud when it was free from its knot, reminding Lydia of a caged animal released.

Then slowly, gently, Lydia ran the brush through the beautiful tresses of her mother's hair that grew almost to the small of her back. With each stroke the tension of Marion's day, of her life, seemed to wash away. Lydia could see her mother's face in the dresser mirror that hung directly opposite the bed. The deep furrows, which seemed permanently etched on her brow when she came home, disappeared. Her eyes closed and a half-smile graced her beautiful, full lips. After Lydia had completed fifty strokes, she'd return the brush and pins to the drawer as carefully as she'd removed them. Then she lay next to her mother on her bed.

If she had done her job well, her mother was pliant and relaxed. Here her mother could be soft, indulgent, laughing at Lydia's jokes and listening intently to the events of her day. Lydia knew that this was the true woman. Later, after her mother had been killed and Lydia grew older, she had wondered how her mother's life would have been different had Marion shown that part of herself to the rest of the world, rather than saving her most beautiful side for the hour before the sun set. Had her hardness made her unhappy, or had her unhappiness made her hard? Had her father known this side of his wife, or did he leave because Marion was too cold, never satisfied? If her father hadn't left them, would her mother be alive today? Lydia's thoughts on this subject were a downward spiral, questions without answers on and on.

Lost in thought, Lydia absently glanced into the rearview mirror and saw with fright her mother's furrowed brow. She had slammed on the brakes and spun around in her seat, expecting to see a ghost, before she realized the brow she had seen in the mirror was her own.

"Such an idiot," she said aloud, letting out a sharp sigh. She rested her head against the steering wheel. The highway was empty. And her convertible black Mercedes Kompressor stood alone with miles of highway ahead of her and behind her, surrounded by desert and sky. In the distance a hawk called.

Her mother would have said, *Lydia, you're letting your imagination run away with you again. Get yourself on track. Here you are, sitting in the middle of a highway at a dead stop while that boy is waiting for you at the airport. You're always getting distracted from the real world by these crazy fantasies.*

And how right she would have been.

She hit the gas. She was fifteen minutes late to pick up Jeffrey and the airport was still twenty minutes away. He was used to waiting for her. But now that she was focused on the present, anticipating the sight of him, she couldn't drive fast enough. The distance seemed terribly long, suddenly, and way too short.

By the time she had reached the airport, she'd convinced herself that Juno's comment could have had significance to a thousand people. It was open to infinite interpretations. But the most disturbing possibility lingered, dwelling in the same place in her mind as the memory of her dream.

chapter nine

When he saw her today she filled his senses. She had stood so close to him, yet had no idea he was there or how she affected him. He could smell her perfume, light and floral. He could hear the mellow, rhythmic cadence of her voice.

Soft, vanilla flesh. How good it would feel under his hands, in his mouth. He had quivered as he imagined her beneath him, her neck and back arched in pleasure, grabbing at him with her fingernails, leaving red marks that bled ever so slightly. He had put his hand on his erection and began to release his desire, his breath sharp and hot.

As he climaxed silently, he had imagined himself straddling her, covered in her blood, her lifeless eyes staring up at him, her mouth parted in a scream that never managed to escape her lips. He felt a flash of rage, of shame. *Don't you judge me, bitch.* But then in the next second, he had to bite down hard on his tongue to keep from laughing; he hadn't wanted to give himself away.

But, of course, she had a larger purpose in his plan, in God's plan. As much as he would like to have her in that way, it was not for him to decide. He must bend to the will of God. Her role in his plan was fated. It was so perfect, it could be nothing else but Divine intervention. How she had come to him, how she had appeared just weeks after he began reading her books. And how she had come again so close to the culmination of his plans. It was pure poetry.

The room was dark now except for the moon streaming in through the window and glinting off the metal table. He sat in the corner, legs stretched out and crossed at the ankle, a beer in one hand, a cigarette in the other. This morning the ghost of his son had visited him. He had been just waking up when he heard his son's sweet voice.

"Daddy?"

A halo of light glowed over the child's strawberry-blond curls; he looked thin and pale but at peace and smiling. He wore baggy Baby Gap jeans and a crisp blue-and-white-striped T-shirt, odd attire for an angel.

"Daddy, you're so brave. God loves you."

He jumped up to take his son in his arms, smell his hair and little-boy skin so soft and sweet, to embrace that tiny little life again. But by the time he reached him, he was gone. He fell on the floor where the boy had stood and sobbed into the dirty carpet.

It was a sign, he knew. He was doing the right thing, he was sure.

In the cool, quiet bathroom, Maria Lopez applied her makeup in the mirror. Tapping her foot to the Muzak that filtered in through the speakers, she smeared on foundation and powder, trying to cover her flawed skin. The fluorescent light was unflattering but she didn't much care. She knew it would be dark in the bar.

She teased her black curls with a hot-pink plastic comb, closing her eyes as she spritzed it with hairspray. When she was done, she stood on her tiptoes to see more of herself in the mirror over the sink. The tight, black cotton knit dress clung to her small body. She wore gold hoop earrings and a small gold cross hung around her neck. She blew a kiss at her reflection.

She didn't consider herself a prostitute, only someone who took money when it was offered for something she likely would have done for free. Why should they get what they wanted while she was left with nothing but an empty feeling in her stomach and a fake telephone number? At least she could pay her bills and have a little left over. Everybody knew minimum wage didn't cut it anymore.

One day her life would be different. She would meet someone, she knew that; have a family and leave this place behind her. Maybe it would be Mike, the man she met last week. He had called her and even brought flowers to her job. She was meeting him at the bar tonight. Who knows?

"You look good, girl" she said to herself in the mirror. She waved good-bye to her boss as she walked out the door in the cool night air. She did not see the minivan following behind her as she strode up the street, hopeful for what that evening would hold.

The Albuquerque airport was never crowded like O'Hare or JFK; it was smaller and yet more spacious. Today it seemed like a ghost town, inhabited only by the echoes of greetings and farewells. As she walked briskly down the long corridor, her footfalls echoed loudly. She passed by empty gate after empty gate. Her stomach fluttered with nerves, with the excitement of seeing him, and she braced herself against the wave of happiness and relief she always felt the first moment she saw him. When she arrived, he was waiting for her, sitting on the window ledge, his back against the glass, his arms folded across his chest.

"How is it that I always find myself waiting somewhere for you?" he asked with a half-smile.

He was unshaven, his thick, dark brown hair tousled. His muscular chest and arms pressed against his navy-blue T-shirt. Slightly wrinkled gray chinos hung elegantly from his narrow hips and tight stomach. His face was strong and angular around his nose and mouth but soft and laughing around his sweet blue eyes. "You have my favorite face," she said as she slipped her arms around his waist. She could just faintly smell his cologne, lightly sweet and musky. He kissed her on her forehead and pulled her to him gently, until he could feel almost every inch of her body on his. Lydia felt the seductive wash of safety and comfort.

"I've missed you, Jeffrey," she whispered, though there was no one to overhear her. "I have so much to tell you."

chapter ten

As they walked through the parking lot to the car, Jeffrey noticed that Lydia looked thin. She had always been on the lean side, but with solid muscle tone, full hips and breasts, as well as a pink fullness to her face. But she was beginning to look a bit gaunt around the cheeks, and her jeans bagged a little around her thighs, and sagged at her backside. Under her eyes there was the slightest hint of blue fatigue. He put a protective arm around her shoulder and she felt small and fragile. Generally, touching Lydia was like grabbing a live wire; you could feel the energy pulsing through her, feel the strength of her body and her mind.

She could feel him assessing her like a parent would, trying to gauge her physical and mental well-being by how much weight she may have lost. She knew she didn't look well, that she looked drawn and tired.

"It's getting harder," she said, answering the question he hadn't asked, as they reached her car.

"What is?"

"The anniversary of my mother's death. It seems to weigh on me more every year." Her voice was a sliver, almost carried away on the wind.

"We've talked about this. You need to see someone."

"I've talked to plenty of doctors about this. No one has helped me."

"They haven't helped you because you don't let anybody in. You go once, you decide the doctor is an idiot, and then you leave and never go back. That's not therapy. It's like some kind of psychiatric hit-and-run."

Lydia sighed and he could feel his blood pressure rise. He hated it when something hurt her that he couldn't fix; and her way of acknowledging her flaws but refusing to change was exasperating. But he kissed the top of her head and put a hand on her shoulder. She didn't look up at him, kept her eyes level with his chest.

"What can I do, Lyd?"

"You're already doing it. You're here."

"So that's what you wanted me to look into?" he asked as he took the keys from her hand, threw his bag into the trunk of her Mercedes, and climbed into the driver's seat. "Your twisted psyche?"

"Possibly," she answered, smiling. "Possibly something a lot more twisted than that. Why do you always have to drive?"

"I don't know. I just like it."

"You just like being in control," she said, fastening her seat belt.

"And you only mind because you like to be in control."

"Whatever."

As they drove, heavy cumulus clouds gathered above them and the sky darkened. Lydia recounted for Jeffrey the events she'd come across in the paper, her conversation with Chief Morrow, and Juno's history. She omitted her dream and the strange end to her encounter with Juno. "The way I see it, there's potentially a serial killer roaming around."

"Whoa, wait a minute. That's an awfully big jump. No one's even been killed."

"Look, we've got three missing persons. Not to mention the animal mutilation and the arson."

"Yeah, but it sounds to me like those people were flight risks to begin with. And the whole triad thing, the arson, animal mutilation, and bed-wetting, are childhood signs of a future violent offender. People don't generally leap from that straight into murders."

"I just have that feeling," she said, looking out the window.

He had to admit that in all the years he had known Lydia, rarely had her instincts been off.

Lydia was so young when they first met, just fifteen years old. Even so, there had been a bond between them from the first night. It would have been inappropriate then for him to have a friendship with her, but he kept in touch with her through her grandparents. Lydia's grandfather, especially, had taken a liking to Jeffrey and was impressed by his concern for Lydia. And Jeffrey made a point to head up to Sleepy Hollow to see Lydia and what remained of her family whenever he was in New York City on business.

Initially, Lydia's grief, her tragedy, had haunted Jeffrey. He kept in touch with her because he felt responsible for her somehow. But as she got older and seemed to adjust to her mother's death, he came to see her more as a young friend, or a little sister. When she moved to Washington, D.C., to attend Georgetown University, Lydia's grandfather asked Jeffrey to keep an eye on her, which he did gladly. During their regular Thursday evening dinner and movie "date," he observed her closely, making sure she was well and happy.

But even though she seemed to have adapted to university life well and was thriving academically, there was always something about her that worried him. An inner silence, the merest hint in her voice and her eyes that there was more pain in her still than she would admit to anyone. He noticed over time that she didn't seem to make friends easily, was more focused on her role as the school newspaper editor than she was on parties and boyfriends. She just didn't seem to ever have any fun.

"You should get out more, Lyd. There's more to life than going to class," he suggested one night over pizza.

"The paper takes up a lot of my time. I'm busy," she said, avoiding eye contact.

"There's more than the paper. College is about letting go, getting to know yourself. You'll never have so much freedom again. Take advantage of it. I mean, what about guys? Do you date?"

But he was glad when she told him that she wasn't seeing anyone. He suspected that few men her age were worthy of her, would handle her as gently as she needed to be handled. "They're all so shallow, so arrogant. Even the ones that pretend not to be," she'd said.

After nagging her a couple of times and watching her withdraw from him, he let her be. After all, he had never listened to anyone when he was her age either. But he kept a careful watch on her, always ready to come to her rescue should she need him—even if that just meant a late night beer when she was stressing over finals.

But toward the end of the last semester in her senior year, she called him very late, her voice sounding small and scared.

"What's up? Are you okay?" he asked.

"Yeah. There's something weird going on in my building. I think someone's been murdered."

A few nights earlier, as she sat studying, she had heard what she thought was the quick staccato of gunshots. But since she had never heard a gun fired before, she couldn't be sure. She had looked out the peephole of her door but saw nothing. A few minutes later her phone rang and she forgot about the incident. But she had "a feeling" about it, she told Jeff.

"What kind of feeling?" he asked.

"I can't explain it, Jeffrey, except to say that it was the same kind of feeling I had in the parking lot that day when I saw the man who killed my mother."

Over the next few days, she had noticed that the mail belonging to the woman who lived across the hall was piling up in her box. And on the night she finally called Jeffrey, she could hear the woman's cat crying mournfully. She knew in her heart that her neighbor had been killed.

She lived alone off campus in an apartment in Georgetown. It was a nice building in a good part of town. But since she never overreacted to anything, he went right over, much to the displeasure of the woman sleeping in his bed—who left, incidentally, and never spoke to him again.

When Jeffrey arrived at Lydia's apartment, they knocked on the neighbor's door. Even as he stood outside, he caught the unmistakable smell of death. Since this was not an FBI case, Jeffrey had no right of entry. They called the local police.

The police arrived and Lydia's fears were confirmed. The woman had been shot in the head, had been lying dead on her floor, her hungry cat gnawing on her fingers. Rather than being terrified and upset, as Jeffrey had expected, Lydia began asking questions of the police. Were there signs of forced entry or a struggle? How long did they think she had been dead? She intended to cover the story for the Georgetown University newspaper. Jeffrey was more worried about her lack of emotional response than he would have been if she had had a breakdown. That, at least, would have been more normal.

Jeffrey brought her back to his apartment. She hadn't said a word on the way in his car, hadn't shed a tear. She just stared out the window. Once she didn't have anything to say professionally about how she would cover the story, or questions to ask of him about the possible motives, she had nothing safe to say at all.

"Are you all right?" he'd asked as he closed the door to his apartment.

"I'm fine," she said.

"I thought you would be more upset than you are."

He knew as soon as he said it that it was the wrong thing to say, that it sounded judgmental, accusing. She turned on him.

"What did you expect? Do you want me to curl up into a ball and start crying for my dead mother? You know, I've been on the receiving end of every fucked-up thing this world has to offer. I have my own way of dealing with things." She did not yell but her voice was a white flame, sizzling with anger.

Then she sank into the couch and put her head in her hands.

"I didn't mean that the way it sounded."

"I'm sorry, Jeffrey," she said. "I'm so sorry."

He sat down next to her and put his arm around her. She looked up at him; he saw the same look he had seen when he had first met her on her mother's front porch. But these were the eyes of a woman, a beautiful, grown woman.

She wound up selling the story to the *Washington Post,* tying the story to a larger feature about women who were murdered by ex-boyfriends, as had turned out to be the case with her neighbor. Lydia graduated a month later and was offered a staff writing job at the *Post.* That night was the beginning of her career, and of Jeffrey's love for her.

Since then most of her instincts had been dead-on. Still this all seemed like a reach. She was so intense, so wound up about it. Usually she maintained a cool air of disinterest, of objectivity about her work. She could be like a dog with a bone about a story or a case, obsessive and unyielding, going days with minimal sleep and food. But that was not the same thing as caring personally about the outcome. As she recounted her findings, she spoke rapidly, gesticulating passionately. When she recounted the stories of the missing persons, her voice was angry. He could see she was dangerously *in it*. And that concerned him.

"What did Chief Morrow say?"

"That man is an idiot, but even he knows something is going on."

"Did he tell you that?"

"No. But I could sense that he was hiding something from me. He told me that there were no pictures taken of Lucky in the garden. But Juno told me that the police took photographs while they were there."

"Well, that might be something," he said, more to quell the intensity with which she was trying to convince him of her theory. He wondered if she was just in trouble emotionally, needed him to be here for her, and had created this whole scenario subconsciously because she was too stubborn to admit that she needed anyone. Or maybe he was only hoping that was the case.

"Jeffrey, trust me."

"You know I trust you."

As they pulled up her drive, the clouds had not delivered on their threat of rain and had cleared to reveal a blanket of stars visible through the treetops. An amber light clicked on as they reached the garage door.

"Motion sensors. I like that. Very secure," he said as Lydia opened the garage door by remote control. "Maybe you're learning a little caution in your old age."

"It's really more for convenience, Safety Man," she answered, smacking him lightly on the leg, and added, "I just had them recalibrated because they were turning on every time a squirrel ran across the drive."

"Did you have that alarm system put in that I recommended?"

"Actually, yes," she answered as she punched in the numbers on the keypad beside the door leading into the house from the basement.

"Impressive. The fan club finally getting to you?"

"Oh, come on, they're not so bad," she said, taking his bag from him and walking upstairs to the guest room.

Lydia's first book, entitled *With a Vengeance,* had been about Jed McIntyre and his thirteen murders, her mother included. Tracing McIntyre's history, detailing his crimes and his motives, had comforted Lydia somehow, had given some order to the chaos of her pain. She was able to understand him, see how the horrible events in his life had made him what he was, though she still felt nauseated by the sound of his name or any name that resembled it.

The book was a narrative account of Jed McIntyre's crimes, featuring Jeffrey as the main character. Lydia had conducted interviews with the victims' families; McIntyre's psychiatrist; Jeffrey's former partner, Roger Dooley . . . anyone who would talk to her. Jeffrey compiled his notes for her, along with files, videotaped interviews, transcripts from the trial.

What resulted was a detailed, graphic true story that read like fiction. The book raced to the top of the best-seller lists, and Lydia, a previously little-known writer for the *Washington Post,* was catapulted into the national spotlight. A fan club of dubious distinction formed. Psychotics, angry victims, criminals, the world's unsavory began to deluge her with mail. She was forced to change her e-mail accounts and phone numbers frequently because somehow they always managed to get out. Though Lydia's physical safety had never been threatened, Jeffrey believed it was only a matter of time before some psycho's attraction turned to obsession. He had encouraged her to secure the Santa Fe house because it was so isolated, but had assumed she would ignore him.

The desert air was cold that night, so when she returned downstairs she made a fire in the living room. Jeffrey had opened a bottle of Clos Pegase chardonnay he'd found in the kitchen. They both lay on their stomachs, facing the fire, resting on fat, cotton-covered down pillows.

"How's your shoulder?" she asked.

"Good as new," he lied. He didn't like to talk about his pain, didn't like to seem weak or vulnerable—especially to Lydia. He never wanted her to think he couldn't be strong for her, *with* her.

"Yeah?"

"Yeah."

He sat up and faced the fire. He didn't want to look in her face when he was lying to her. She always knew.

"I'd expect nothing less," she said.

He smiled. "Well, it gets a little stiff."

She sat up and moved behind him, began gently massaging his shoulder. "You haven't said what you think about all of this."

"I don't know what to think. It seems pretty thin. But I believe you, you know that. We'll check it out."

"Good enough."

She didn't blame him. She realized her ideas must sound crazy to someone like him, so solid, so grounded. She knew he needed hard evidence to be convinced of the truth. She also knew that sometimes the truth left only a scent on the wind.

She rubbed his shoulder carefully with the flat of her hand, feeling the tense muscle relax slightly under her touch.

Jeffrey could feel the heat of her body against his back. Only the gravest discipline kept him from turning around, carrying her to bed, and making love to her until the sun came up. He knew about discipline, about control. He hadn't survived this long without it.

Jeffrey was an army brat, raised on military bases across the country. Because his family had moved almost every two years and because he was an only child, Jeffrey had learned to rely on himself at an early age. His father was a hard man with no time for tears or tantrums. A high-ranking decorated officer, Jeffrey Mark Sr. was a man of honor. Jeffrey remembered his father with respect but not affection.

When Jeffrey and some of his friends stole his father's car and were brought home to their parents by local law enforcement, Jeffrey's father decided to send him away to military school. In spite of the hysterical protests of his mother, Jeffrey left his parents' home the following fall. He was glad. He wanted to get away from both of them.

At school, the regimen, the high academic standards, and the constant physical exertion relaxed and exhausted him. He excelled there and went on to West Point. But he knew before he graduated that the military life was not for him. He liked the order and the discipline, but he craved risk, danger. He wanted a steady diet of adrenaline.

But lately thrills like those he sought when he was younger were becoming less appealing, especially since he had been shot. The pain in his shoulder as Lydia worked the muscle, her closeness, reminded him of the way he ached for her when they were apart. He was forty, with nothing in his personal life to show for it. He realized that Lydia was the only woman he had ever loved. There had been other women, but his job, his schedule, made relationships hard to maintain. And he had never felt so kindred with anyone. He was alone, except for Lydia. And even *with* her, the way they were now, he felt alone.

"What are you thinking about?" she asked, sensing that he was far away.

"Just about how I've missed you the last few weeks."

"I've missed you, too. But you're here now."

But for how long? And then how long until I see you again? I don't want to hold you down. I want to be your home. I want to be the place where you come to hide. "I'm glad," he said.

"Does your shoulder feel better now?" she asked, changing the subject.

"Much. Thanks."

She moved away from him, afraid to have her hands on him any longer. She sat in the overstuffed chair by the hearth, folding her legs beneath her. There she was cast in darkness. He couldn't see her face anymore.

Silence was usually a comfortable place for Lydia and Jeffrey. They meshed, wrapped around each other like wicker. But tonight the air between them was charged, electric with desire and fear.

She reached for a cigarette in the small drawer in the table by the chair. She lit it and took a deep drag.

"I thought you quit," Jeffrey said, disapproval in his voice.

"I can't quit."

"Please. You have a stronger will than anyone I know."

"Fine, then, I don't want to," she said stubbornly.

"I fail to see how you can run as much and as far as you do and still suck that poison into your lungs. It's physically impossible."

"For me, it's the same drug."

"Are you going to explain that?"

"No."

She wasn't oblivious to what was between them. She knew what he wanted. She wanted the same thing, more than she admitted to herself. But something powerful held her back—a dark fear dwelled in the pit of her stomach that somehow for her, love and death would be inextricably linked.

"So maybe we should pay a visit to Chief Morrow tomorrow, Lyd. What do you think?"

"Yeah, I guess so. You know he'll be glad to see me."

"Because you're so charming."

"Right."

She rose from the chair. He was always surprised by her beauty, amazed by the power of his desire for her. Bathed in the orange light from the fire, she was radiant as she raised her arms above her head and stretched, exposing flat, supple abs as her shirt lifted a bit.

"I'm going to go to bed," she announced.

He nodded toward the pile of clippings and the information Lydia had printed out from the Internet. "I think I'll sit up for a while, look over those articles."

"Good night, Jeffrey."

"Good night, Lyd."

chapter eleven

"*You can make a murder into art,*" Sting and the Police sang from the car radio. The irony was not lost on him but the heat was cranking and his legs were getting cramped. He rubbed his eyes and put the copy of *With a Vengeance* by Lydia Strong in his lap. The cover was bent and cracked and the pages coming loose from the binding, he'd read it so many times. But he had been looking at the same page for the last hour.

He knew that for many killers, Jed McIntyre included, stalking was half the game. But he hadn't been enjoying it. He found it boring. He'd been waiting in front of Maria Lopez's small dilapidated apartment building in the barrio for almost three hours and he was starting to lose his patience. He stared at the plastic Madonna and Child his wife had stuck to his dashboard years ago.

" 'Please God,' " he said, " 'how long must I wrestle with my thoughts and every day have sorrow in my heart. How long will my enemy triumph over me?' "

He turned off the ignition and was glad for the silence. A moment later, like an answer to his prayer, he saw the man that the whore Maria had taken home leave through the front door, get into his black pickup truck, and speed off. He waited a few minutes, let the adrenaline stream through his veins. Then he donned a pair of surgical gloves and a black ski mask. From a plastic bag on the passenger-side seat he took a terry washcloth that had been soaking in chloroform. He patted his pocket, checking for the scalpel and the picklock he would use to get in the building door.

But when he got to the building, the door had been left ajar so there was no need to pick the lock at all. He walked up the one flight to her apartment, and then knocked lightly on the door, knowing she would assume it was the man who had just left.

He stood to the side.

"Forget something?" she called, and flung the door open carelessly. He grabbed her by the throat, almost lifting her small body off the ground with one arm and shoved the washcloth covered in chloroform over her nose and mouth with the other, before she even had a chance to scream. When he felt her body grow limp, he uncovered her face. But it must not have been for long enough because her eyes fluttered, she saw him, and she started screaming and thrashing. He threw her hard through the imitation Oriental screen that separated her bed from the rest of the small studio apartment. But she got up and scurried away from him as quickly as a mouse, her face a blank mask of terror.

chapter twelve

Maria Lopez had fought for her life. With every inch of muscle, every ounce of strength she possessed she went down fighting. And it showed. But her body was nowhere to be found.

The white-and-blue checkered curtains and their fixtures lay in a heap on the floor. A white ceramic lamp shattered next to the toppled table on which it had sat. The imitation Oriental screen that separated her bed from the rest of her small studio apartment looked as if someone had been thrown through it, a large hole pouting in the center panel. The checkered sheets of her bed, which matched the curtains, were drenched in blood, soaked through to the mattress.

This is where he got her, thought Chief Simon Morrow, as he touched a gloved finger to the blood. A sharp instrument to a major artery—the throat, the leg . . . he couldn't be sure. He could imagine the faceless killer on top of her, his knee on her chest. He winced at the image in his mind, in spite of having seen worse. Her fear echoed in the tossed-up room.

He got down on his knees, tucked the bedskirt up between the mattress and the box spring and shone his flashlight under the bed for anything that may have fallen under there in the struggle. He reached for a small wooden crucifix he saw there. He could see where it had fallen from, by the bare nail and the cross-shaped clean space on the dirty white wall above her bed.

"Jesus Christ. Shit."

He wondered how long the neighbors had heard the screams and the banging before they called the police. How he had got her out of the apartment after that. There was no way she walked out, not with all that blood on the bed.

One of the uniformed officers walked in the front door.

"Anybody see anything?" the chief asked, knowing the answer already.

"No. No one I spoke to saw or heard anything, Chief. But some people didn't open their doors."

"Figures. I'll send a detective out in the morning. In fact, page Keane right now, tell him to get over here."

Morrow knocked on the wall with a pudgy callused hand.

"These apartments might as well be separated by cardboard. Jesus Christ," he muttered.

If there had been any doubt in his mind that the two prior missing-persons cases on his desk were somehow connected, and connected somehow to the dog and the surgical-supply warehouse, he was sure now. The other cases on his desk were cold. No leads. No witnesses. No family or even friends to interview. Those people had dropped from the face of the earth, leaving no trail behind them to follow. But Maria Lopez had made sure her departure was not silent like the rest. There had to be something in this mess. Hair, fibers, prints, something—anything. She had to have been cut very deeply with something razor-sharp for that much blood to be spilled, possibly with a surgical implement. Maybe the same type of instrument used to slice up the German shepherd and remove its organs, an act that had been completed with precision.

Lopez was the fourth person missing in two months in a sleepy town that saw little violence. Something was definitely going on.

Morrow still had the crucifix in his hand, was clenching it so hard the edges were hurting him through his latex gloves. He'd found one of these in the home of each of the missing persons—a detailed Christ figure, highly varnished wood. Did it connect them? He couldn't be sure. People were very religious here—especially those who had little else to live for.

"Call in Homicide and Forensics from State," he said to the uniformed officer standing closest to him. "We need to treat this like a murder, with or without a body." If these cases were connected, he was going to have to call in the FBI. If he did it too soon, he'd look like a yokel who couldn't handle a few missing persons. If he did it too late, if someone else disappeared . . .

He'd had to make this call before and things had turned out badly. When he was the St. Louis police chief, three prostitutes had turned up dead in a five-month period. He had been reluctant to call it a serial murder case, because johns killed whores all the time in big cities. So when Lydia Strong had paid him a visit to inform him of the striking similarities to unsolved cases in Chicago, he'd disregarded her as a flake. She had told him about an alleged white-slavery ring that an escaped prostitute had reported to her and which she was investigating for an article for *Vanity Fair*. But he basically shut the door in her face.

He had been unaware of her reputation and her connections at the FBI. By the time the Bureau finally got involved, two more women had turned up dead. The early St. Louis cases provided key evidence in solving the crime. It turned out that the Russian mob was bringing girls into the U.S. illegally, promising them careers as models. When the girls arrived, they were held prisoner in whorehouses and forced into prostitution. Morrow's failure to report the murders to the FBI was a blunder that took on national significance due to the article subsequently published. He resigned from the St. Louis police force.

He'd been drinking then. Heavily. Maybe that's why he didn't pay much attention to the prostitute murders. Maybe that's why he ignored Lydia's warnings until it was too late. Maybe. Six months in rehab and some therapy had helped him deal with his mistakes. He'd been the police chief in Santa Fe for over five years now and done a competent job. Of course, nothing ever happened here. Until now.

Lydia's presence in town gave him an ugly déjà vu. He hated that she was here now, of all times. It was like some kind of fucked-up karma. He knew once this hit the papers, she'd be all over him.

He left two uniformed police officers to guard the scene until the detectives arrived. "Nobody touch anything until they get here. Don't make a sandwich, don't make a phone call, just stand at the door," he barked as he put the cross in a plastic bag, careful to note in his log where he found it. "Tell Keane to look for an address book. I didn't find one."

He looked around the tiny apartment again, noting there were no photographs. He was fairly sure that when the detectives started looking through drawers and in closets, they would find no address book, no letters, no photo albums. This was the apartment of someone utterly alone. Someone unconnected. The furniture was cheap and temporary, looked like the kind you would assemble yourself.

He pressed the redial button on the telephone. *"You have reached Psychic Helpers. Welcome to your future!"*

He hung up. Then he pressed *69, the sequence which would tell what the last incoming call was. He dialed the number and got a recording from the electric company telling him to call back during business hours. He placed the receiver down gently, though he wanted to slam it.

He thought about the others. It was the same with them. Christine and Harold Wallace didn't even have a phone. Sad people. Lonely lives. If a life is lost and no one mourns it, is that death still a tragedy? Regardless, this death was still a crime.

He stripped off the rubber gloves and shoved them in his pocket.

"Tell whoever comes from State to be in my office by noon with whatever information they are able to gather by that time."

He walked to his son's room and pulled on a pair of scrubs over his bloodied clothes, then he removed a clean scalpel from the tray. He regarded Maria's lifeless body, her open mouth, her glassy eyes. He wiped the hair away from her face.

" 'An oracle is within my heart concerning the sinfulness of the wicked. There is no fear of God before his eyes.' "

" 'The path of the righteous man is beset on all sides by the treachery of evil,' " he said, cutting away Maria's bloodied nightgown. His voice was thick with passion, growing louder as he spoke.

" 'Blessed is he, who in the name of charity and goodwill, shepherds the weak through the valley of darkness, for he is the finder of lost children.' "

He cut into Maria's chest with the scalpel, pushing through the intercostal muscle, and made an incision down to her navel.

Lisa Miscione

Then he picked up the small saw and turned it on. Its frenetic whir and the high-pitched scream of metal against bone as he cut away her rib cage was virtually orgasmic. Sweat beaded on his brow and his hands quivered with excitement.

" 'I will carry out great vengeance on them and punish them in my wrath. *Then they will know that I am the Lord when I take vengeance upon them.*' " He was nearly yelling as he made the final cut.

Lydia sat on the plush couch in her living room and watched as the sun rose over the mountains. When she had opened her eyes in bed earlier, she felt warm and safe, remembering that Jeffrey was in the guest bedroom down the hall. His presence had eased the restless, wandering feeling that had plagued her in the days before his arrival. The next thought in her head was about Shawna Fox, wondering if she had ever risen feeling safe and warm. Or had she always felt alone in her foster homes, never fitting in, forever missing her mother? The grainy photo of Shawna in the paper, a school portrait, had made Lydia sad. She wondered who would want that photo, if it would go in someone's photo album; if anyone would remember Shawna five years from now, ten years from now. What about Christine and Harold? Was anyone lying awake at night worrying for their safety? Is it possible to live a life that touches no one, that no one remembers? Lydia needed to know the answer to that question.

Usually when she was working a case with Jeffrey or writing something, she wanted only the details of a victim's life: what he did for a living, who he knew, what his habits were. But she wanted as little personal information as possible. She didn't want to get to know them, feel their personal essence. Like turning off a television screen to escape a violent image or suppressing

86

a traumatic memory, she shut them out. She didn't want to feel even the slightest twinge of pity or sorrow. She didn't want even the smallest part of their tragedy to become her own.

She knew that the people she interviewed, families, loved ones, were often shocked by her lack of concern for the victims of the people and crimes she wrote about, insulted by her refusal to even pretend to want to know about them. Her manner was always clipped and professional. People couldn't believe how little she cared. But in fact she cared too much. The sight of grief, the thought of people being violated, dying in terror and unspeakable pain, was more than she could bear. It cast a light on her soul that crept into dark crevasses where even she was afraid to peer.

But she felt differently about Christine and Harold, and especially Shawna. It was as if their memories were orphans that no one would take in. As if the worried question "Where are they?" had not been asked by anyone who cared about the answer. She felt a fierce need to shelter and feed these lost souls, to know who they had been. It was a sensitive business, sorting through the debris of an abandoned life. The layers needed to be peeled back with gentle fingers one after another, like the skin on an onion, to reveal the essence of a person true and ripe. She certainly didn't trust a hack like Morrow to do it properly.

She wondered if the police had connected the disappearances to one another, if she was the only one who could see the shadow of something sinister behind the collection of strange events. Jeffrey certainly wasn't convinced by what she'd told him. But this did not deter her; she trusted herself. She just needed more information on the victims, to find out what they had in common, where their paths had crossed, what experiences they might have shared. At the intersections of their lives, she suspected, she would find a madman.

She began plotting in her mind the various ways she could gain access to the information she wanted—some more legal than others—if Morrow wouldn't cooperate. She believed her best bet was to see if Shawna's boyfriend was willing to talk.

Jeffrey was watching her from the second-floor balcony that looked down onto the living room, smiling to himself. He could almost see the wheels turning in her mind. She sat on the living room sofa, her back against the armrest, legs tucked up beneath her. She stared absently out the window, biting on her thumbnail. Dressed in black leggings and a pink T-shirt, with her hair wet and no makeup, she looked like a teenager.

"What are you scheming, Lydia?" he asked.

She was too cool to be startled; turned her eyes up to him slyly, catlike. "I'm thinking about what you are going to make me for breakfast."

"You know," he said dryly, "you've never once made a meal for me in all the time I've known you."

"That is patently untrue," she answered with mock indignation. "I cooked dinner for you every night after you got shot."

"You ordered in," he said, smiling as he walked down the spiral staircase.

"Whatever."

"Do you have anything in this house besides coffee and cigarettes?"

"Eggs and wheat bread. Maybe some milk."

"Great," he muttered, walking into the kitchen.

Lydia pulled on her sneakers to walk to the mailbox for the paper. Outside, the morning was crisp, the sky blue and close. That was one of the things she loved most about New Mexico.

Almost thirteen thousand feet above sea level, you dwelled in the sky. It was all around you, not just above. She took the clean air into her lungs, thinking she needed to run later. She would avoid the church.

She was halfway back up the driveway with the paper in her hand before she glanced at the headline.

BLOODBATH IN THE BARRIO:
Woman Missing; Presumed Dead

Lydia ran the rest of the way up the drive and burst in through the front door. Jeffrey was standing at the stove, scrambling eggs.

"Look at this," she said, throwing down the paper.

He turned off the stovetop, took his glasses from his shirt pocket, and scanned the article. The fact that this event had taken place in the late-night hours and was in the first edition of the morning newspaper, coupled with the fact that the police had "no comment," indicated this story had been leaked to the press. Someone at the crime scene had a contact at the paper and had called the story in—always a bad thing when hunting a serial killer, not that he was convinced that they were in fact looking for a serial killer. In spite of the glaring headline, the article contained few details. A late-night anonymous call to the police had led them to the apartment building. The door had stood open, so they could easily see the blood and signs of struggle, and had probable cause to enter. The missing woman was a waitress at a local restaurant near Angel Fire. She had a short rap sheet for solicitation. Her name and picture had not been released because relatives had not yet been located.

"Do you think this ties in with the others?" he asked, trying not to sound skeptical.

"It could," she answered.

"What makes you say that?"

"Because now there are four missing persons. In a town this size, that's an anomaly. There was obviously a mortal struggle. And the body was removed from the scene."

"But there was no sign of a struggle or foul play with any of the other missing people."

"That only means that this situation got out of control. If this woman had been killed and her body found in the apartment, then I would not be inclined to think that it was connected. But someone took her body. For what? If someone was trying to hide the crime, he would have cleaned up the scene . . . or at least closed the door. The most important thing to him was to take her with him. It's a signature behavior. He has another agenda. He probably just did a cleaner job of it with the others."

Lydia and Jeffrey sat at the kitchen table with the newspaper between them. She had leaned across the table, looking at him intently. He had to admit, she did have some good points.

"All right, I think I'm going to talk to Morrow. Maybe he has some missing pieces that will help us determine if there is something here."

"Alone?"

"I just think it might be best."

"Bullshit, Jeffrey. I didn't ask you to come down here to play the Great White Hope. I need to be a part of this."

"You are. I just think Morrow will cooperate more readily without you there at this stage."

"Why?"

"Because you have a bad history with him. And . . . you have a way of putting people on the defensive."

"The only people who are defensive with me are people who have something to hide."

"Come on, Lydia. Charm isn't going to work on me," he said, a sarcastic smile on his face. He reached out for her hand, which she pulled away. She wanted to kick him in the shin. But she knew he was right.

She crossed her arms across her chest and glared at him. "Fine. But you have to swear to tell me everything. Every last detail."

"I promise. Did you pitch this story to someone already?"

"No."

"Then why are you so worked up? I've never seen you like this."

"I just need to know what happened to these people." She turned her gaze away from him and looked out the window.

He kept his hand outstretched on the table for hers.

"I won't do another thing without you. Just let me go there alone first, okay?"

"All right," she said, and gave him her hand, grudgingly.

He squeezed it and then stood up from the table and started clearing the dishes he had set out for the breakfast they were not going to eat now.

"Leave them. I'll take care of it. You just go talk to Morrow," she said.

He placed the dishes in the sink and walked from the kitchen. "Don't be angry," he said over his shoulder, without waiting to hear her response.

She took a pillow from the window seat and threw it at him. It missed its mark by a few feet and lay soft and harmless on the Italian-tile kitchen floor.

She sighed. The thought of sitting and waiting for him to come back was unbearable for her; the hours stretching before her were heavy with boredom and anticipation. She needed to do something.

She walked into her bedroom, pulled her hair back in a ponytail, put on a pair of running shorts and an old T-shirt, and slid three quarters into her jog bra. She put on her Nikes at the door and was gone, running down the driveway toward the road.

From the window on the second floor, Jeffrey watched her go. He hated it when she left without saying good-bye. She seemed so ephemeral at the best of times. Watching her run away, he wanted to throw the window open and call her back. But he couldn't—not now, not ever. He just had to hope she'd come on her own. He watched her until he lost sight of her.

She counted her breathing in time with her footfalls on the dirt road. Running was painful because she had bad knees and she was smoking more now than she had in months, but still it set her free. Her form was perfect, shoulders straight but relaxed, abs tight, heels landing firmly on the ground with each stride. Here, it was enough to think of nothing. She could focus on nothing but driving herself to go one more foot, one more mile, before she could go no farther. Soon her worries would seem imaginary and far away. Soon she would be submerged in her effort and in enduring the pain of her joints and in her lungs. She took a masochistic pleasure in it. But today she didn't seem to be able to run far enough or fast enough to silence the thoughts inside her head, or to quiet the emotions that simmered inside her chest.

She was angry at Jeffrey for wanting to see Morrow alone. On an intellectual level, she recognized that he was right. Jeffrey had a bad history with Morrow, too; but Jeffrey hadn't created a national scandal by writing an article in *Vanity Fair* that had exposed Morrow as the alcoholic, chauvinistic incompetent that he was. Jeffrey going alone was probably the best bet they had to get Morrow to let them in. He probably wouldn't even *see* Lydia if she were to show up there. But she had called Jeffrey for his help and for his support, not so that he could take over. Sometimes she felt like he was Superman and she was just Lois Lane. He was leaping tall buildings and deflecting bullets and she was just hanging on for the ride, then writing up the story when it was done. She knew it was irrational but it still made her angry. Plus his closeness was so unsettling now. They hadn't slept under the same roof since he was recovering from being shot. And it felt so good, so safe to have him in her space. The restlessness she dreaded had subsided. She had what she needed, the real thing. She didn't need to go looking for cheap imitations at the Eldorado.

She had meant to avoid the church today. But in spite of herself she saw it rising before her and she felt powerless to turn around or veer off in another direction. She was drawn to it, drawn to Juno.

"Your mother would be glad to know you have come home to God."

On the day her mother had been murdered, Lydia had known she was in trouble. The principal had caught Lydia smoking in the bathroom and had punished her with a detention. The principal also had called her mother at work to let her know of Lydia's infraction. On top of that, she had missed the school bus and had to walk more than a mile and a half home.

It was September 5, a brisk and clear fall day. The leaves were changing and the air was clean and smelled like cut grass. Lydia sniffled as she walked home carrying her heavy bag. She could envision the scene that awaited her as if it were already a memory. Her mother would be waiting for her at the kitchen table. She would ask Lydia calmly, "How was your day?" Then: "Do you have something to tell me?" Then there would be an unbearably long lecture that would last at least an hour and maybe the whole evening, depending on how angry her mother was and how much energy she had. Then Marion would be distant and silent, and speak to Lydia only when she absolutely had to, with politely cold directions. "Please do the dishes," or, "Make sure you're in bed before ten."

It would be better if her mother yelled. Then Lydia could yell back. Instead she would have to eat her own guilt, feel ashamed and sorry. She would have to wait for forgiveness.

Lydia would always remember what she had been wearing that day: a red plaid, pleated skirt; white tights and black loafers; a white cotton shirt and black suede vest—her favorite outfit.

She hadn't even entered the house before she knew something was wrong. She stood at the end of the driveway for a moment and stared at her mother's car. The door was open. She walked to the blue Chevy and saw her mother's purse sitting on the passenger's seat. She could hear music sounding loudly from inside the house.

Her mother was a precise woman, with predictable habits. She was orderly, nothing ever out of place, no action ever spontaneous. Even if she had heard the phone ringing in the house, she never would have left the car unlocked, never mind with the door wide open and her purse sitting there. Even though they lived in a safe, small town, Lydia's mother had been raised in Brooklyn. She had let Lydia know that the world held dangers she could not yet imagine. No ground-floor window was ever left unlocked at night. When Lydia let herself in on most afternoons, she was to lock the door behind her and not open it for anyone except the police or the neighbors. Her mother was quite strict on these points.

Lydia took her mother's purse and closed the car door. She

walked slowly to the front door of the house and found that ajar
as well.

*"If you ever come home and find the doors open or a window
broken, don't even go inside. Just run to the neighbor's, call the police,
and then call me at work."*

"Yeah, okay, Mom. God."

"Mom?" she called from the front steps. "Mom?"

She was not sure how long she stood there debating what to
do next. Finally, she pushed the door open and walked inside,
dropping her schoolbag and her mother's purse on the floor. She
left the door wide open, the outside seeming safer than the inside
at that moment.

There were no lights on inside. And when she turned off the
blaring stereo, the silence of an empty house greeted her.

"Mom?"

She walked from room to room downstairs, seeing nothing.
Then she climbed the stairs. Her mother's room was dark, the
shades pulled down sloppily below the sill in a way her mother
never would have done. When she flipped the light on she saw her
mother, a sight she had tried to bury deep inside herself but which
she had never forgotten. Bound to the headboard, her dead eyes
were rolled up in her head, her mouth parted in a silent scream.
Lydia ran to her mother, began shaking her, screaming at her.

Then she backed away, stunned and bloodied. It was impossible for her mind to process what she had seen and she was reduced
to an organism reacting to horror. She ran to her neighbor's door
and pounded with both fists, unable to accept that there was no
one home to answer her cries. Her mind was racing as she willed
herself to wake up from her nightmare. A neighbor across the street
finally heard her and called the police. They arrived within min-

utes. Lydia had exhausted herself by then, sat breathing heavily on her front stoop, staring blankly as shock set in.

She could remember refusing to be moved from the front stoop of her house. A female officer sat beside her, trying to convince her to move into the house out of the cold. But Lydia wouldn't, thinking inanely that she should be there to stop her grandparents from seeing what she had seen when they arrived from Brooklyn. She sat there, shivering, wrapped in a blanket, trying to imagine how this wrong could be righted.

It was while she was sitting on that stoop that she first saw Jeffrey. He pulled up with another man in a black car. He walked toward her, his eyes on her the whole time. He looked strong and important to her, like someone who would have rescued her mother if he could have. He knelt before her and asked the female officer to leave.

"Hi, Lydia," he said softly. "I'm Agent Mark. I know you're really scared and sad right now, but maybe you can help me find the person who did this to your mother."

He put a gentle, sympathetic hand on her shoulder and she nodded, then started to cry. He gave her his hand, helped her stand up from the stoop, and led her inside.

Lydia slowed to a halt in front of the church and stretched out her back. She wiped the sweat from her face with the bottom of her shirt. The church looked like it was waiting for her. Even in the throes of the restlessness that beset her as her mother's anniversary approached, she had never reflected on the details of the day she found her mother's body. *Why has this come back to you now? Why is the pain so fresh?*

Her head was so crowded with thoughts and memories, she could barely hear her own voice through the cacophony. It reminded her of something a meditation teacher had said to her once: "Your mind is like a roomful of monkeys. You can barely quiet one before another starts shrieking. You must breathe to quiet your monkeys. Only then will you find inner peace." Lydia had been as big a failure at meditation as she had been at therapy. She walked in a circle with her hands on her hips now, catching her breath before she went inside.

She knew she had come to see Juno. *Do you really think he's going to heal you, Lydia?*

She walked up the steps and pushed open the heavy wooden door. A mass was in progress; the priest stood at his pulpit, about twelve people in the pews before him. She slipped in quietly, unnoticed, she hoped, staying to the back of the church. She dipped her right fingers into the holy water by the door and crossed herself, more out of a reflexive respect than anything.

She discreetly reached for the three quarters she had placed in her bra and dried the sweat off them on her shorts. Placing them in the box provided, she lit three votive candles.

"Let us pray," she heard the priest say.

The silence was so heavy it was almost sound. She sat in the backmost pew, then knelt as the others did. She wondered what they were praying for. Wondered what she should pray for. Ridiculously, she began to wonder, if she found a genie's lamp on some deserted beach and was granted three wishes, what they would be. Right now, a cigarette would do.

When she opened her eyes and sat back, she saw Juno at the altar. He began to play his guitar. The acoustics of the church carried the music on the air and filled the room. His fingers were sure and every note was perfect. But it was him and not his music that captivated her. She had to know if he was truly what he was said to be.

She watched him carefully, considered moving closer, but not wanting to call attention to herself, remained seated. He did not look like other congenitally blind people she had seen. She had always thought that the signs of blindness could be seen in a physical deformity of some kind: sunken eyes, an especially large brow, eyes without pupils. Juno looked like someone who had been sighted once, but had lost his vision through some cruel twist of fate. He was peaceful, rapt, moved by this music written for God. She stared at him shamelessly, taking advantage of his blindness, and that all but the priest had their backs turned to her. When his song had finished, the priest said some parting words and the parishioners filed out. They all looked at Lydia in turn, curious, perhaps, at her inappropriate attire. The priest said a few words to Juno and then disappeared behind a doorway. Juno remained, putting his guitar in the case.

She walked toward him, making noise on purpose by clearing her throat.

He looked up. "Hello?"

"It's Lydia," she answered.

He smiled. "Lydia, how are you?"

"Curious."

"About?"

"About what you said the last time I was here." She was speaking softly because his demeanor, his church, demanded it. But she was feeling like herself again, not afraid, not ashamed like an intruder. She was angry. She felt tough, aggressive. And she felt familiar with him, like she had known him for years.

"We talked of many things."

"You know what I mean. You said my mother would be happy to know I had come home to God."

"It's true, isn't it?"

"Yes, it is. But how did you know to say that? I mean, what do you know about me? What do you know about my mother?"

"Perhaps we should sit down. You're upset."

She preferred to stand away but sat beside him in spite of herself. "Just tell me what you meant."

"Lydia, you have conducted a number of interviews on National Public Radio where you were quite candid about the death of your mother and how it affected you. I could sense when you came to see me that she was very much on your mind and the church had some strong connection to that. I was only trying to help you. I didn't mean to cause you any more pain."

She scanned her mind for what she had said in interviews on the air. Would she have mentioned that her mother was a religious person and that she was not? Any moron could have made the inference he made from a statement like that. But she couldn't remember.

Juno had his head cocked to the side and a questioning look on his face as he waited for her to respond.

Why are you here? She asked herself not for the first time.

"I dreamt of you," she found herself confessing. She revealed the details of her dream to him.

"Others have claimed to dream of me and a loved one. Some claim that I help them communicate with people on the 'other side.' I can't explain that. But maybe your mother is trying to tell you something."

This answer annoyed her because it managed to be vague and presumptuous at the same time.

"What do you think she is trying to tell me, Juno? And what do you have to do with it?" She knew that she sounded belligerent.

"Maybe she is trying to tell you to let go of the past," he said, calmly, not even responding to her angry tone.

"I *have* let go of the past."

"Running away from the past and letting go of it, moving forward, are two different things."

His words were sincere, and they touched her because she knew he was really trying to help her. He was not trying to manipulate her, but she felt invaded, felt herself edging away from him inside, bringing down walls to protect her truth. She wasn't responding any better to this "psychic healer" than she had to any of her shrinks. *Go figure.*

What do your dead parents tell you, you smug bastard? The words were poison darts, waiting to be thrown. But she held her tongue, knowing they were vicious, designed to hurt deeply.

"You don't know me," she said weakly.

"That's true . . . in a way. But then why have you come here?" he asked calmly, unflappable.

"I'm sorry. I don't know," she answered. She honestly didn't know. She had planned to avoid the church, yet she had carried quarters to light the votive candles. Instead of turning away from the church, she ran right to it. Was it something outside herself or inside her that had led her back here?

She rose to leave. "I'm sorry," she said again.

"Please don't be sorry, Lydia. I understand you." They were simple words, easy to say. But he meant them and they touched her, even if she wasn't sure they were true.

"When you're ready, you'll be back," he said. He rose also, and finished putting his guitar away as if their conversation had never interrupted him.

She paused and looked at him. He looked so normal, so earthly now. He no longer seemed angelic to her, as he had while he was playing his guitar during mass. He was flesh and blood, like she was. How could he exert so much power over her emotions?

"When I'm ready for what?"

"To come home to God, of course."

"But why you?" she asked. "Why were you in my dream?"

She knew what he was going to say before he said it and was disappointed at the cliché in advance.

"The Lord works in mysterious ways, Lydia."

She walked up the aisle, more confused than she had been when she entered. But something that had been like a stone in her heart had shifted.

chapter thirteen

Before Jeffrey headed to the station house, he called the New York office to check in and to let his partners know that he was unofficially looking into something with Lydia. As Jeff walked the perimeter of Lydia's house, making a security check, he spoke to Jacob Hanley on his cellular phone.

"You want us to send some guys down?" asked Hanley.

"I don't think so. Not yet, anyway. I'm not convinced there's anything going on here."

"Well, it does sound a little weird. And have you ever known her to be wrong?"

"That's the only reason I'm here at all."

"Yeah, right."

"What's that supposed to mean?"

"I wish you two would just get it over with."

"Mind your own business, Hanley."

"I mean, you need to just take control of the situation. Force her to realize that she loves you, man. Give her an ultimatum."

"I think you've been watching too much daytime television. Fuck off, Hanley."

"Don't get your panties in a twist. Meanwhile, why don't I run a few checks up here for you. . . . What were those names again?"

"Do that. Make yourself useful, for once." He gave Hanley the names and hung up. *Believe me,* he thought, *no one would like to get it over with more than I would.*

As far as the security of Lydia's home went, he was happy except for the fact that the breaker box was outside the house. It was in a locked, weatherproof yellow case, but if the power for the alarm system was located in there, it wasn't ideal. He wasn't overly concerned, though, because the system, he knew, was designed to default to alarm. In other words, if the power went out, a signal still went to the local police. But he would need to check with Lydia about the setup later.

He got into Lydia's Kompressor and headed to the station. He thought about calling ahead to let Morrow know he was coming but decided to keep the element of surprise on his side. One could never be sure how local law enforcement would react to private investigators, particularly ones without actual clients. Jeffrey wanted the facts as they existed, not narrated or colored by someone else's agenda—whatever that may be. He expected Morrow to be wary of him after their last meeting in St. Louis. Jeffrey had been sure that was the end of Morrow's career, whether he deserved it or not. Jeffrey wondered if Morrow was still drinking.

He walked into the small precinct house and was greeted by a burly, redheaded desk sergeant who eyed him suspiciously.

"I'm Jeffrey Mark," he said, flashing his private investigator's identification out of habit. "I'm here to see Chief Simon Morrow."

The desk sergeant never took his eyes off him as he picked up the phone and dialed.

"There's some private investigator here to see you, Chief." He paused. "Okay." He said to Jeffrey, "What is this regarding?"

"Just tell him Lydia Strong asked me to talk to him about Lucky."

The sergeant repeated the information into the phone and paused before putting the receiver back in the cradle. "Have a seat. He'll be right with you."

"Thanks, I'll stand."

When Morrow walked out from a door behind the desk, he did a double take as he recognized Jeffrey. But he recovered nicely and offered his hand. Jeffrey took it and felt that his grip was strong but somewhat clammy. He thought Morrow was sober; his eyes were clear and his breath smelled of peppermint and coffee. But he was definitely guarded, looking Jeffrey up and down uneasily.

"Agent Mark, what can I do for you?"

"I'm not with the FBI anymore, Chief. I have my own investigation firm now."

"Then what brings you to New Mexico?"

"I was wondering if you have a few minutes to talk to me about your missing-persons cases."

"What's your interest?"

"Let's just say I know a thing or two about missing persons and would like to offer my help."

Jeffrey was a man's man, most often liked and trusted right away. His manner was understated, respectful. But his handshake was steel, and his eyes revealed a hard edge other men immediately recognized. He was amiable, but not to be fucked with.

"Well, I don't know how much there is to look into."

"Really? Well, you have four missing people, one of them presumed dead. Is this normal for your jurisdiction? Or maybe some of these people have turned up safe and sound. Or maybe all you have in the barrio is a prostitute killing."

Jeffrey's not-so-subtle reference to Morrow's unpleasant past caused him to flush. He felt his cheeks burning. Morrow remembered that Jeffrey had treated him with respect in St. Louis, but brought him down just the same. In fact, their first meeting had been eerily similar to this one. Morrow had knots in his stomach.

"Come with me," said Morrow, leading Jeffrey to his office.

Seated, Jeffrey waited while the chief got him some coffee. The office was a mess, files stacked in every corner, a half-empty cup of coffee and a stale Danish on the desk, an ashtray piled high with cigarette butts. The blinds over the windows behind the desk were covered in a thick layer of dust and hung unevenly. The white walls were gray with age. A typewriter sat by the desk on a rickety old table. Jeffrey rose to look at it; he hadn't seen one quite like it in years. *This thing must be an antique,* he thought as he fingered the round black keys. It wasn't even electric.

As he was inspecting the typewriter, he caught sight of something out of the corner of his eye. It was a photograph, a picture of a mutilated German shepherd. The dog had been sliced open from stem to stern. Its body cavity looked to have been partially gutted and the ribs had been sawed off.

He looked up to see Simon Morrow standing in the doorway, a cup of coffee in each hand.

"Lucky, I presume," Jeffrey said, raising the photograph with a slight smile.

"Yes," Morrow answered, clearing his throat. He handed Jeffrey a cup and seated himself behind his desk, the old chair creaking beneath his weight.

"I have to admit, Morrow," Jeffrey began, "when Lydia Strong told me of her suspicions about some of the recent events down here, I was skeptical that there was anything to worry about. The crimes seemed rather random, petty. The missing persons seemed like typical runaways. But looking at the facts, an arson, the mutilated corpse of the dog, four people missing now—one of them presumed dead if the paper is to be believed—I'm starting to wonder. Some would say these are classic indicators of a maniac on the loose—possibly even a serial killer."

"Maybe. But nothing until the murder, or supposed murder, this morning really clinched it for me. Look at it from my perspective. As far as the arson goes, out here, there are a lot of old structures, like the barn, that are burned down by kids making mischief or by people trying to defraud insurance companies.

"The seventeen-year-old girl who went missing has run away from various foster families three times. The missing couple—well, people take off. It was suspicious, they took nothing with them, but that's not a crime. Besides, I figured if something had happened, the husband probably killed his wife, hid her body, and ran off. He'd been beating her for years. We've brought him in at least a dozen times over the last five years.

"But around three A.M., when we got the call from Maria Lopez's apartment building, I started making connections. I mean, four people missing in a town this small—it means something. I'm just not sure what. I'm not sure I'm ready to say there's a serial killer out there. That's why I haven't called the FBI. I don't want to involve them unless I have to."

"What about the surgical-supply warehouse and the dog?"

"The supply house seemed strange. I mean, whoever did that stole enough stuff to set up a small hospital. And it seemed even stranger still when the dog turned up." He motioned to the picture still in Jeffrey's hand. "But there was no *evidence* connecting those events. Either thing could've been kids, pranksters."

"You must have some pretty sick kids in this town."

"Hey, don't you read the news? Kids in a rural area are restless, looking for kicks. More and more there's a lot of methamphetamine around—that's some dangerous shit, turns normal people homicidal. I guess Nintendo doesn't cut it anymore."

They laughed. Like people laugh at a funeral, uncomfortably, hushed.

"So what are you thinking now, Chief?"

"I don't know. I've got detectives and Forensics from State at the crime scene right now. They'll be here by noon with whatever they've gathered. I just don't know. After what I saw this morning, I'm starting to think something very ugly may be going on. But I'm really reluctant to call in the feds. Things always get messier when they're around. No offense."

"None taken. I know what you mean; it's part of the reason I left to start my own firm. Too much bullshit from the top. I started to worry more about public relations than about doing my job," he said, partly to put Morrow at ease, to create a sense of camaraderie, and partly because it was the truth. "I think you can avoid calling them in. After all, the only reason to do so would be if you can't solve the case yourself, if there is one."

"That's true."

"Whatever your opinion of Lydia and of me, you must be aware of our track record. If you let me take a look at your files and let me know what the guys from State find at the scene . . . If there really is a serial offender, maybe we can give you a hand. The feds never have to be involved until it's over. Until your department has solved the case. We're ghosts, me and Lydia, you never even have to let anyone know we were here."

"Why are you interested in this?"

"Let's just say I'm doing a favor for a friend. And in doing so, I could do a favor for you and your department. It wouldn't be the first time since I started my firm that I've worked with the police—confidentially, of course. Otherwise I have a good contact in the Behavioral Sciences Department who I'm sure would be happy to give his opinion if I called."

Chief Morrow rubbed his balding head. He honestly couldn't tell if he was being offered a helping hand or if he was being threatened. Was Jeffrey saying, *Let us in or I'll call the FBI myself*? Whether it was a threat or not, if Morrow could avoid involving the FBI, even if it meant working with Lydia Strong, he would be happy. He was smart enough to know that trouble was brewing and neither he, nor anyone in his department, had ever handled a serial case. Hell, he had to go through the state police department to gain access to VICAP and the other FBI databases.

"I'll send everything over to you later today. Where are you staying?"

"With Lydia. Do you know where her house is?"

He nodded.

"In the meantime," Jeffrey said, "make sure no one else talks to the press. There's already too much information out there."

"One of the cops guarding the scene leaked the Lopez story to his girlfriend, who is apparently a reporter trying to make a name for herself at the local paper. He's being reprimanded. But they don't know everything."

"Like what?"

"This, for starters," he said, handing Jeffrey an evidence bag that contained a hand-carved wooden crucifix. "At each of their homes, I found one of these, different shapes and sizes. It might not mean anything, though. People are pretty religious around here."

"Left there by the perpetrator, or as part of the victims' belongings?"

"Part of their belongings."

"What else?"

"Lucky, the dog. The paper mentioned that the dog's organs had been removed. Well, we found most of them in a pile by the body. It looked like whoever was performing the 'surgery' was interrupted when the blind man came out into the church garden."

" 'Most of them'? What didn't you find?"

"The heart."

Lydia expected boxes of files to be carried in by the cop that arrived at her house later that afternoon. But instead there were just four moderately thick manila envelopes. The lives of Shawna Fox, Christine and Harold Wallace, and Maria Lopez had been reduced to a few piles of documents. What kind of life, Lydia wondered, leaves only a paper trail in its wake?

There were voices inside the files, though. Voices with stories to tell, with secrets to reveal. Voices that had been silenced. Lydia regarded the files and paused before opening the one on top, as if it were the lid to Pandora's box. She looked over at Jeffrey, who was sitting on her couch, feet up on the coffee table, reading through his notes from Morrow's noon meeting as if he were reading the newspaper, cool, disinterested. She envied him. She was about to step through a portal to another time and place, about to take a journey into some dark and unknown world, while he could remain here on earth, a beacon for her safe return.

"Let's make the boards," Jeffrey said, putting down the notes. "I can't think straight without them."

Lydia slipped three 4- by 10-foot pieces of corkboard from behind the bookshelves and Jeffrey pulled easels from the closet to the right of her desk. They set them up in front of the plate-glass window-wall. They wrote the names of each victim on index cards and made columns for each on one board. On the other they pinned a map of the area. And on the third they pinned newspaper articles, clustered together by subject.

"Let's see what we have here," said Lydia, opening the first file.

Shawna Fox had been trouble for just about everyone she met: her teachers, her foster parents, her counselors. She was a discipline problem, a poor student, a runaway. A ward of the state since her parents had died when she was five, Shawna was a child who had never known a happy home. She had been arrested three times—once for driving drunk without a license in a car stolen from her boyfriend when she was fourteen; once for selling marijuana to another minor; and once for prostitution in Albuquerque.

A psychologist's evaluation read: "Shawna is reticent, unemotional and yet prone to violent outbursts. She seems to have no remorse for anything she has done. Is not able to see that her behavior is self-destructive. When asked why she behaves the way she does, she replied, 'I do what I have to do to stay alive.' She would not elaborate. More than likely the victim of abuse from one or more of her foster parents. A tragic case, seems that there's little hope for a turnaround."

Unlike the last three times Shawna ran away, the final time she took nothing with her and stole neither money nor possessions from her foster parents. An ongoing investigation turned up no leads. An anonymous tipster told police he had seen a lone girl walking on the highway toward Albuquerque. When he had pulled over to ask her if she needed help, she ran into the desert. He drove on. It was dark so he could not be sure if she matched the description he read in the paper.

The police also had had a visit from Shawna's boyfriend, Greg Matthews, an eighteen-year-old dropout who worked at his father's gas station. He insisted that Shawna never would have run away without telling him; that she loved him and was going to marry him. Greg had had a rap sheet of his own as a juvenile, but had been clean since working with his father for over two years. He had been investigated as a possible link to Shawna's disappearance but no evidence of any foul play was uncovered. He provided a color photograph of Shawna, a close-up of her pixielike face, framed by short-cropped boyish blond hair. She had sparkling green eyes, and a pug nose, pierced with a small gold hoop. She wore a bright smile and a look in her eyes that told Lydia she was in love with whoever had snapped the photo, presumably Greg. Photographs of living people now dead always made Lydia angry. They were cold, eerie reminders of how easily life was lost, how vividly alive people remain in the memories of those who loved them, and how grief is the slick-walled, bottomless abyss between those places.

A month after her disappearance, Shawna was still missing. There were no leads.

"So why are we assuming that this girl didn't just run away again?" asked Jeffrey.

"One: She didn't take anything with her like before; she had a habit of stealing from her foster parents before taking flight. But this time, nothing of theirs and not even her own belongings. Two: She had a boyfriend who clearly loved her. Show me one damaged teenage girl who runs away from love, probably more love than she's ever had."

"What makes you think he loved her? Maybe he beat her. Maybe he killed her."

"Maybe, but it says here he visited the police station three different times to check on progress, insisting that she wouldn't have run away."

"A lot of serial killers insinuate themselves into an investigation."

"He's too young to be a serial killer. And he doesn't fit the typical profile. Not smart enough, not antisocial enough."

They pinned Shawna's picture on the board, and below it they placed index cards listing everything they knew for a fact to be true about her, vital statistics, date last seen, address. On the map board they placed a red pushpin at her last known address.

Christine and Harold Wallace had had a troubled marriage, according to a state-appointed abuse counselor. Both frequently unemployed, both recovering methamphetamine addicts, their life together had not been an easy one. Pulling each other back and forth into and out of addiction, their relationship had been violent, ranging from a slap in the face to a brutal beating which left Christine in the hospital for three weeks, to a stab wound that just missed Harold's vital organs.

In the ten years they had been together, only three years had seen both of them out of prison or rehabilitation clinics at the same time. But at the time they went missing, they both had been off drugs for a year, both were holding down work-fare jobs cleaning the park in the middle of town, and there had been no incidence of abuse in more than eight months. Christine was studying for her GED.

When they did not show up for work that first day, their supervisor did not call it in to the welfare board. He liked them and didn't want them to get kicked out of the program that had been helping them move forward in their lives. But after the second day, he had to call it in. When counselors went to the Wallaces' home in the barrio, a small two-room house, they found the door standing open. All their possessions remained; no evidence of struggle or forced entry. They were simply gone. Calls to each of their parents revealed that both had been estranged from their families for over ten years. No one was interested that they were missing and could offer no information.

The last entry the social worker made in her file, a week before they disappeared, read: "I am so pleased with Christine and Harold's progress. They are both working, drug-free, and seem to be healing their relationship. During our last session, they were holding hands."

The only pictures available of Christine and Harold were their respective mug shots. Though no one expects mug shots to be flattering photographs, it was clear that neither Christine or Harold were particularly attractive people. Both were painfully thin from years of drug addiction, with scraggly, longish hair, Christine blond and Harold brown. Harold had small brown eyes, a beakish nose and thin lips, protruding cheekbones, and one missing front tooth. Christine had a similarly gaunt face, but with big blue eyes that were moist and sad, and full pouting lips. She might have been pretty once, but years of abuse and self-neglect had ravaged her face and she just looked broken.

"So again, why are we assuming that these people are not holed up in a crackhouse somewhere?" asked Jeffrey.

"Again, because they took nothing with them. Their bank accounts have not been touched since they disappeared. They really did seem to be back on track."

"So then we are assuming that our alleged serial killer killed or abducted both husband and wife from their home. There's no precedent for that."

"Son of Sam."

"David Berkowitz killed couples in their cars with a gun and ran away. He didn't break into people's homes, incapacitate or kill both of them, and then remove them somehow from the scene—leaving no evidence. That's a huge undertaking, highly organized and taking tremendous motivation. Whatever this guy wants, he wants it bad enough to take outrageous risks and perform complicated assaults and abductions. He must have un-questioning faith in his agenda to have such a high-maintenance signature."

"So if you were going to kill or abduct a couple how would you do it?"

"I would stalk them to determine when they were the most vulnerable. Wait for the perfect opportunity, neutralize the greater threat, and then overpower the weaker. Man first, woman second, under normal circumstances. I would have a van or truck parked close to the point of assault because dead or unconscious people are very heavy."

"So you'd have to be smart, organized, and fairly big and strong."

"I'd say so."

"Well, I guess that rules you out as a suspect."

"Very funny."

Maria Lopez had been picked up twice for prostitution. But she hadn't walked the streets in years and was a waitress at a local restaurant called Blue Moon Café. Last night, she had left work at eleven P.M. dressed to go out. She went to Smokey's Sports Bar on Highway 434 that she frequented more or less nightly. She left with a man named Mike Urquia, who the police had picked up that afternoon and was being questioned as Lydia and Jeffrey spoke.

Hair, fibers, blood samples, and fingerprints had been col-lected at the Lopez scene and sent to the state lab for analysis. But it would take at least twenty-four hours for any results to come back. Even then most of what had been found would only be use-ful to eliminate or confirm suspects. Unless they got very lucky, for example, a carpet fiber that came from a very rare rug, only sold in a certain location . . . something like that. Or in the best case scenario, the offender had a prior record and the prints could be matched to someone already entered in the FBI database. DNA results could take months, not like on television where they came back in hours.

"So it may be that Mike's our man," said Jeffrey.

"I don't think so."

"Why?"

"I just don't."

"Well, okay, then. Maybe you should get a job with Psychic Helpers."

"For starters, he's Hispanic. There aren't too many Hispanic serial killers."

"Richard Ramirez."

"It's not him." Lydia was firm, and Jeffrey had only been playing devil's advocate.

She placed the final index cards on the board and the final red pin on the map.

She stood back and looked at them, wondering what it was they had in common. The problem child. The abuser. The abused. The prostitute. She could catch the scent of these lives, but their life force, their personal essence remained elusive.

"It's hard to really get a sense of these people. Whoever gave the cops their information was distant, on the outside looking in, neighbors, bosses, social workers. No intimates, no friends except for Shawna Fox's boyfriend, and no families. It's almost like there's no one to say who they really were."

"It's a start," he answered pragmatically.

She paused, leaning forward on the desk, picking up a crystal paperweight and holding it up to the sun streaming in the southern window. Rainbow flecks of light danced on the wall behind her.

"I wonder . . ." She drifted away, staring into the facets of the object in her hands.

"What?" He hated it when she started a sentence and then let it float off into space, leaving him waiting for the finished thought.

"I wonder if the lack of information is something in and of itself. Not even an incompetent like Morrow would fail to interview people close to the victims—especially a juvenile."

"So, what are you saying?"

"I'm saying maybe there was no one close enough to give a true picture of these people. Maybe that's significant." She walked over to him and sat close to him on the couch. She pulled her feet up beneath her and let her legs rest on his thigh. She looked up at him. "We're going to need to do some digging on our own. Nobody leaves this world without showing someone their truest heart."

Her gray eyes stared past him at the boards then, her body leaning into his. She could feel his strong quadriceps beneath the soft rust-colored corduroy pants he wore, could smell the faint musk of his cologne.

Really? Who have you shown your truest heart to? He put his arm around her and rested his chin on her head.

"In fact," she mused, "it's really the only thing that connects them."

"What is?"

"That no one seemed to care when they were gone. That and poverty."

"And religion."

He handed her the picture of the crucifix that Simon Morrow had showed him. He had told her about the crucifixes when he recounted his conversation with Chief Morrow, but her jaw dropped when she looked at the picture. The crucifix was large, made of a highly varnished red wood—the Christ figure intricately detailed. The feet were neatly folded over one another, nailed viciously to the cross, a single drop of blood falling like a tear. The knees were bent together to one side in a feminine, almost demure manner, like a curtsey. The rib cage and collarbone strained against taut flesh and the neck was arched in agony and the face uplifted, contorted in an expression of profound pain and anger. It was just so human, so emotional, just like the statue of the Virgin Mary in the garden at the Church of the Holy Name.

"What's wrong?" Jeffrey asked, peering at her over his Armani eyeglass frames.

"I'm so stupid," she said. "I didn't even think of it when you mentioned the crucifixes. When I went to the church before I picked you up at the airport yesterday, I saw a statue of the Virgin Mary and Baby Jesus. It was remarkable for its humanism and Juno said that his uncle had sculpted it. He mentioned that his uncle carved wood crucifixes and sold them to parishioners. Looking at this picture . . . it must be the same person, the same artist."

She walked over to the map. "All these people, they all live within five miles of it. The church is the connection." She was excited but not really surprised. She felt the pieces start shifting into place like the squares on a Rubik's Cube, though the puzzle wasn't close to being solved.

"Wait a minute. Let's not get ahead of ourselves. We still don't know for sure that these people have been murdered."

"Jesus, Jeffrey, what do I need to convince you?"

"A body for starters. Any body. Have you lost all perspective on this, Lydia? We're nowhere yet."

She sank into the chair across from him, as distant as she was close a moment earlier.

"I need evidence. We can't conduct a murder investigation without a body," he continued.

"Spare me the FBI rhetoric," she said sharply.

"It's not rhetoric, Lydia. We have four missing people . . . one of them probably violently murdered, I'll give you that. If their crucifixes all came from your church, then okay, that's weird. I'll give you that, too. But there are no bodies, no actual proof of anything. I'm not with you on this. Do you *want* there to be a serial killer running around? Are you going to be happy if it turns out you're right?"

"Of course I'm not going to be happy. I also don't want to be sitting on my hands while he's picking his next victim. I thought this is why you left the FBI in the first place. Because you didn't want to always play by the rules that sometimes allow people to be killed in the name of protecting civil rights.

"Remember when families had to wait twenty-four hours before reporting a child missing? Remember when women had to wait to be assaulted or killed before anyone did anything about their stalkers? Serial killers don't always advertise. We're not hurting anyone by looking into this. We may be killing someone if we don't."

It was an old argument that never ceased to infuriate him. Lydia had a knack for pressing his buttons and making him more angry than anyone else he had ever known. One moment they could be as close as it was possible for two people to be. Then, in a heartbeat, they were spitting fire.

Suddenly she jumped up and ran from the room. In the distance he could hear the phone ringing. He sat and stared at the sunset, the sky painted in brilliant pastels, the sun dipping below the mountains in the west. He became aware of a powerful, irrational feeling of jealousy that she had gone to the church yesterday and again today. *Why did she go there? To see the blind man? The one she dreamt about?*

A moment later she was standing in the door.

"Well, you got your wish," she said, smug and smiling bitterly. "They found Maria Lopez's body."

chapter fourteen

Someone had gutted Maria Lopez like the dog Lucky. It was a disturbing sight for the hunters who found her, in an open body-bag, sloppily half-covered with the dirt and sand from the ground around her, deep in the woods at Cimarron Canyon State Park. *I guess you thought the animals would get to her, you cold bastard,* thought Morrow as he stared down at her decomposing body.

"Cover her up," he said to the uniformed officer standing beside him. He felt badly for her. No one had come to the station to report her missing, no one could be found to notify about her death. And there was no one to question about her life except her boss at the restaurant and Mike Urquia, who was the last person to see her alive. He was the prime suspect, only because there were no other suspects. But there was no evidence so far to indicate that he had done anything but sleep with her, and looking into his eyes, Morrow knew it wasn't him. This was something much bigger than a good fuck gone wrong. Something so much uglier.

He took the number Jeffrey Mark had given to him and called from his cell phone. The phone rang a couple of times at Lydia's before she picked it up.

"You and Jeff might want to meet me at the station. We think we found Maria Lopez's body."

"I want to see where he dumped the body. You didn't move it yet, did you?"

"No, but . . ." Morrow didn't really want her at the crime scene. He didn't want her to have a front-row seat to this investigation, even though he'd agreed to have them on board.

"Good," she said, like she was talking to a student. "Tell me how to find you."

He told her to take Highway 64 north for thirty miles and that he would have a squad car waiting for her at the park entrance so she and Jeffrey could find the way to the remote spot in the woods.

"Fine, we'll be there." She hung up the phone without another word. A little civility was perhaps too much to ask from someone like Lydia Strong.

An hour later the pair arrived at the crime scene. Lydia brushed by Chief Morrow without a word and walked straight to the covered body. She asked the uniformed officer for a pair of surgical gloves, which he handed her, and she removed the light plastic tarp from the victim's body.

"Was this tarp sterile?" Morrow heard her ask the officer. "Because if it wasn't, you just contaminated the crime scene."

"Yes ma'am."

" 'Yes ma'am,' what?"

"Yes, it was sterile."

That was exactly why Morrow hadn't wanted her here, looking over his shoulder, second-guessing every fucking move he made. Waiting for him to screw up again so she could ruin him for good.

"Hey, Chief," Jeff said as he approached Morrow. "Who found the body?"

"Some hunters from New York were looking for big game and they came across the body instead." He motioned to a group of men, who for all their weathered toughness, rifles, and orange hunter's attire, looked pale and shaken.

Lydia regarded the grotesque body of Maria Lopez. Throat slashed, a gaping wound from her sternum to her belly, eyes wide and glassy, skin tinged black-and-blue, the naked body lay discarded by the killer without regard. Lydia could tell instantly by the careless disposal that the killer did not care for Maria, had not known her in life. She was less than trash to the person who had killed her. Lydia wondered if the killer was becoming disorganized, descending into a careless rage to murder Maria so brutally and then dispose of her like a hated piece of furniture. Or maybe he was becoming cocky, having killed, presumably, three times without even raising suspicion.

She did not feel moved by the body. Life had abandoned it. It was nothing more than an object, arousing only wonder in her, as if she had spied a single shoe lying dirty and flattened in the middle of a city sidewalk. She stood up and circled the body. This was a dump site and not a true crime scene. He had not killed her here. There was not enough blood. He had carried her here in the body bag and opened the zipper, hoping, probably, that the scavengers would find her before the park visitors did.

It had not rained since Maria was taken from her apartment, but the ground was soft and damp so maybe they would get lucky—footprints, tire tracks. He could have driven only part of the way to the dump site. He would have had to then park the car on the dirt road below and carry her up the incline that Lydia and Jeffrey had just ascended, moving through the trees. Had he known this area well? Or had he just driven in during regular park hours and dumped her, hoping he wouldn't be seen? It was very risky behavior, if that's what he had done. Maybe, more likely, he had come and stayed at one of the campsites and done his deed under the cover of night. She wondered if there was a visitor registry or a list of license-plate numbers of park visitors.

"Lydia, check this out," Jeffrey called.

Lydia walked over to where Jeffrey stood. He pushed aside some weeds, revealing a partial footprint. The rest of the area was more exposed to the wind, but the weeds had preserved the top half of a large boot. Lydia glanced over at the hunters.

"It could belong to one of them, or to another hunter. We should check their boots before they leave."

"Gentlemen, could you help us out over here?"

One by one, each man removed his right boot and compared the tread to the track in the ground. There were no matches.

The crime-scene photographer came over and took some shots as Jeffrey directed.

"Chief, can you get someone over here to take a mold?" Jeffrey inquired.

"I don't know how well a mold will take. The ground is pretty soft," Morrow replied.

"We should at least try," Lydia snapped, annoyed by what she considered to be his laziness.

"Fine," Morrow replied curtly, angry at her tone but feeling powerless. He walked off to the squad car to use the radio.

"He's right, Lydia. There's no need to be so hard on him."

"Back off, Jeffrey." Lydia was still angry from their argument earlier in the afternoon. She always held a grudge for a little while, at least, and didn't like being criticized at the best of times.

"Fine." Jeffrey walked off toward the squad car as well.

You're the most popular girl at the crime scene, she thought.

Lydia walked back over to the body and scrutinized it for anything she might have missed before. Around Maria's neck hung a small gold cross. Lydia bent down, covering her mouth and nose against the stench, and leaned in to get a better look at it. It was plain, thin and light, a cheap piece of gold if it was gold at all. Had she seen something like this in the case at the church? She couldn't remember. She checked Maria's earlobes. They were pierced but she wasn't wearing earrings. Lydia was reminded of the earrings Jed McIntyre had stolen from his victims. She noticed that Maria's right hand had a deep, wide gash, probably a defensive wound, and that she appeared to have blood beneath her fingernails.

Lydia approached Jeffrey and Morrow, who were conversing with the hunters. She eyed the strange men one by one, envisioning each of them as the killer, trying to imagine them stalking and murdering their victims, then removing their organs. But they all seemed too dimwitted, too simple. She was sure they would offer nothing by way of leads or evidence. She waited for a pause in the conversation.

"Morrow," she interrupted, purposely neglecting to use his title, "will you make sure that you get that gold cross off her neck? And we need to talk to someone who administers the park to find out if there is a camera at the entrance, or a register of vehicles that have entered the park since Maria Lopez went missing."

"Yeah, no problem," he answered, silently kicking himself for not thinking of that first.

She turned to Jeffrey. "Unless you think I should stay, I'm going to speak with Greg Matthews and then go to Smokey's, see if anyone's talking, maybe run into Mike Urquia."

"You want me to come with you?"

"No, I think I should go alone. Sometimes people are willing to say more to one person than they are to two."

"I'll go with Morrow and follow the body to the Medical Examiner's office and see what the autopsy turns up. On the way out, we'll stop at the guard on duty, find out what the procedures are for logging in visitors."

Lydia looked at Jeffrey, and smiled slightly, lowering her eyes in a silent apology. She raised her hand and quickly smoothed the collar of his leather jacket, a gesture he knew meant peace. "I'm sorry, too," he said and her smile widened.

"The results from the Maria Lopez apartment could arrive as early as tonight," Morrow interjected. "I have a contact at the state lab who promised me a rush."

"Great," Jeffrey answered Morrow. Turning to Lydia, "Just be careful. I'll get a ride back to the house from Morrow or someone."

He watched her walk back to the car, her hands in her pockets. She paused before she was out of sight and looked back at him, saw he was watching her, and smiled again. She looked at him with equal parts apology, laughter, and wistfulness. He took a breath at the intensity of his feeling for her, at the magical quality of her beauty in the early-evening light.

Lydia knew about isolation, the lure of it, the seduction of having only yourself to answer to. She knew about the craving for a silencing of all voices but one's own, about the urge to escape the gaze of others. In fact, she had constructed a life where isolation had become as comfortable as down, solitude as welcome as sleep. She was alone, had taught herself not to need anyone, and somewhere along the line loneliness just became familiar. And she had grown afraid of everything else. She had started to fear intimacy the way some people fear being alone. She had driven people away all her life with her coldness. She had no friends; her relationship with her grandparents, who still lived in Sleepy Hollow where they had moved from Brooklyn after Marion was killed, was loving but distant. The only significant person in her life was Jeffrey, and she kept him always at arm's length.

But she also knew that beneath that desire to alienate the world was another, more ardent wish to be understood and recognized, a desire bound and gagged by the hopelessness that such a thing was possible anymore.

That was the look she saw in Shawna's eyes, and the image she carried in her mind as she drove up the winding road toward the garage where Greg Matthews worked. Lydia pulled up slowly, the gravel and sand on the unpaved road crackling beneath her tires. The garage looked more like a shack than a place of business but the large, painted sign above the roof reading JOE AND GREG'S AUTO REPAIR told her she was in the right place. As she got out of the car, a young man emerged from beneath a red pickup. His curly hair stuck out from beneath a plain red baseball cap, its team logo, whatever it had been, long since fallen away. He stood up, wiping his hands on his overalls and squinting into the dusk, then shielding his eyes as he strained to see her.

"Are you Greg?" she called as she walked toward him.

"I sure am," he said amiably. "What can I do for you?"

"I would like to talk to you about Shawna's disappearance."

The friendly smile dropped from his pink lips and his face seemed to age. Big, light-blue eyes swam with emotion in a galaxy of freckles. His hands were square and strong, with black grease wedged beneath his fingernails. He smelled of soap and gasoline, and beneath his baggy coveralls, he was large and muscular like a bodybuilder.

"I've already spoken with the police and nobody has listened to a word I said," he said quietly. "Short of accusing me of hurting her, they basically have done nothing to try to find out what happened to her. I'll tell you what I told them, my girl did not run away. Unless you're going to tell me something I don't already know or are going to try to do something to find out what happened to her, I have nothing to say to you, ma'am."

He turned to walk away from her but Lydia gently grabbed his arm.

"Greg, wait. I don't think Shawna ran away, either. I'm an investigator. My name is Lydia Strong and I do want to find out what happened to her."

He looked her up and down suspiciously. She was conscious that she didn't look the least bit official in her faded blue jeans, lizard-skin boots, and cream suede jacket. She began to reach for her ID, but he spoke before she could present it.

"All right, then, come on inside."

She followed him behind the garage and the adjacent office to a small apartment. Run-down but clean and orderly, it smelled of burnt coffee and cigarettes. Lydia sat down at a faux wood Formica card table on a wobbly, green vinyl-covered chair, while Greg made coffee.

Her eyes scanned the room, soaking up details. The appliances, an olive-green stove and matching refrigerator, were old but seemed to be well maintained. The countertop, made of butcher block, was well scrubbed but riddled with scratches and deep, black burn marks. Some of the Formica tiles on the floor, featuring a gold and brown floral pattern, were buckling. The orange sun coming in from a dirty window over the stainless steel sink lit the dust particles that fell like snow through the air. The room was overly warm and Greg turned on an air-conditioning unit over the door that protested, then reluctantly groaned to life.

She could see two orderly bedrooms from where she sat at the table. One, presumably Greg's, had a wall covered with posters of motorcycles and a shelf filled with books about hot rods, mechanics manuals, and luxury car magazines. On the bedside table was the picture of Shawna that she recognized from the copy in her file.

These were the rooms of hard-working people of small and honest means. If she had to guess, Lydia would say that Joe Matthews, Greg's father, was a former military man who conducted his business and his home the way he had been taught in the barracks. Greg's mother had either left them or died young because there was no feminine warmth in any of the rooms, and Greg seemed fairly self-reliant in the kitchen, not like a mama's boy used to being coddled.

She tossed it out. "You live here alone, Greg?"

"No, with my dad. My mom passed on when I was ten from cancer."

"I'm sorry."

"Me, too. But my dad took real good care of me. A little strict, though," he chuckled without much mirth. "But what do you expect from a former Marine?"

"Mind if I record our conversation?" Lydia asked, pulling a small tape recorder out of her bag and laying it on the table. She never went anywhere without it but almost always forgot to use it, relying more often on pen and paper.

"No. How do you like your coffee?"

She looked over at him and noticed that he was peering into an empty refrigerator. *So much for light and sweet.*

"Black," she answered. " 'No,' you don't want me to record this? Or 'no,' you don't mind?"

"I don't mind, Ms. Strong. I've got nothing to hide."

He sat down across from her, placing a chipped white cup in front of her, filled with coffee so black it looked like tar. The chair creaked beneath his weight and screeched against the floor as he pulled it toward the table.

"Your name sounds familiar," said Greg.

"Well, I'm a writer."

"I'm not much of a reader. Is that why you're here? You're going to write about Shawna?"

"Not exactly. I also consult with a private-investigation firm."

"Did somebody hire you to look for Shawna?"

"Not exactly. Let's just say I've taken a personal interest in this case and I have the time and the resources to see what I can do to further the investigation. Shawna is not the only person missing."

"You mean that other woman who went missing yesterday?"

"Yes, and others, too." She didn't want to be the one to tell him that Maria wasn't missing anymore. He'd read about it in the papers soon enough.

"Why are you interested?"

She considered her answer before speaking. "I lost someone once, too, Greg. A long time ago. And even though I know what happened to her, I still don't know why. So I guess I'm always looking for answers, in a way."

He nodded as if he understood that. Lydia wasn't even sure why she said it that way, having never vocalized the thought to anyone. She'd never revealed anything about herself to a stranger before, especially someone she was interviewing. But the fact that she'd shared something personal with Greg seemed to have put him at ease and he began to speak.

"Most people just assumed Shawna ran away, Ms. Strong. And while she might have run away from her foster parents, she never would have run away from me. We were just waiting for her to turn eighteen so that we could get married and live here. I was going to keep working for my father and someday we wanted to buy a house."

Greg's eyes glistened and Lydia felt him searching her face for faith and compassion. He had paused, waiting for her to question his words, offer judgment, but she nodded her head and remained silent.

When he didn't continue, she encouraged him. "Tell me about the night she disappeared."

"She called me on the phone about eight on Sunday, August fourteenth. She was real upset and said she was on her way over. I told her to stay put, that I would come and get her. But she said no, she had to leave the house that second. It was a short walk, about a mile, and she needed the time to cool off. She had had another fight with her foster parents. They are good people but they were strict with Shawna and she was headstrong, so they were always going at it.

"I told her to get moving because it was getting dark. I waited about a half an hour and then I set off to find her down the only road she would take. I went all the way to her house and knocked on the door. Harden, her foster father, told me she had left. I didn't believe him, so I pushed my way into the house and ran up to her room. She was gone but it didn't look like she had packed anything.

"I was angry. She had promised me she would try to get along with them because we only had four months to go and I didn't want her to be sent away. I got back in my truck and drove home fast, hoping I would find her there. But the house was empty. I swear to God, as soon as I walked into this kitchen and didn't see her where you are right now, smoking a cigarette, I just had a feeling in my gut that something wasn't right. I don't know how many times I drove up and down that road looking for her.

"She's gone," he said, voice trembling, betraying a boyishness that his physical bearing did not. "Something terrible happened to her that night. I can just feel it, you know?"

Lydia was thinking of Maria Lopez's gutted body rotting in the woods.

He paused and looked away from Lydia. His voice was softer, almost a whisper when he began speaking again, and she noticed his hands were shaking slightly.

"I would have made her stay put if I could have. But no one could tell Shawna what to do, not even me. She had a real problem with authority. I wish she had listened to me only this once."

She didn't have to be a mind reader to see how much Greg had loved Shawna, and that he would rather be dead than ever hurt her. There was no way to fake grief like that. Lydia hated to probe further, knowing that the more he had to recount for her, the more painful this conversation would get, but she needed to know who Shawna was, where she had spent time, what her routines were.

"Greg, tell me what you can about Shawna, what she was like. I need to get a sense of who she was."

"Other people only saw the worst of her, her bad temper, her lack of interest in school, her rebelliousness. But to me, she was an angel. God, she was sweet. Loving, thoughtful."

The earnestness in his voice moved Lydia more than she liked. She steeled herself against the wave of sadness and sympathy that welled within her.

"No one I know had a harder life than Shawna. Her parents

both died in a plane crash when she was five and she was turned over to the state because she had no living relatives. A lot of people who take in foster kids do it for the money. They don't really care about the children; some even resent them. Shawna had a real run of bad luck when it came to that. Most of the time she wouldn't even talk about it. But she had scars all over her body—cigarette burns, a long gash on her back. If you raised your hand too fast, too close to her, she'd flinch. If I held her too tightly, too close to me, she'd panic, fight to get away like a coyote in a trap.

"Meg and Harden Reilley, her foster parents up the road, never hurt her, she said. But she was more than they could handle, stubborn and wild. They tried to love her, I think. But she wouldn't let anyone close to her but me. She distrusted everyone—for the most part."

" 'For the most part'?"

"She loved to go to church. She said it was the only place that gave her peace, the only place where she didn't feel like a black sheep. She was close to Father Luis and his nephew Juno at the Church of the Holy Name. She helped out with things like the bake sale, bingo night, the Christmas party. She said they accepted her without judgment, like I did. Trusted her with responsibilities that no one else would dream of. They made her feel special, trustworthy. It was very important to her—the church. But she kept it a secret. She would sneak off there, like she was going to do something wrong. I asked her why she didn't want anyone to know. She said she was afraid someone would take it away from her. She wanted to guard with her life the things she loved, always afraid of losing them. It broke my heart."

"So she spent most of her time at the church, at school, or with you. Was there any other place she hung out regularly?"

He shook his head. "She didn't really have any friends. She

wasn't one to go to the mall. She didn't care much for movies. We stayed around here mostly."

A silent tear traveled down the landscape of his face. He put his head down in his hands and sat, his breathing shallow and quick. She wanted to reach out and touch his hair, or take this boy in her arms and tell him that the pain goes away—that it fades like the memory of Shawna's face will fade. But she was locked up tight inside, unable to give him what she was still unable to give herself. And besides, maybe it wasn't even true. Maybe his pain would never go away; maybe every woman's voice would echo Shawna's for him for the rest of his life; maybe he would keep thinking he saw her in crowds; maybe the color green would forever remind him of Shawna's eyes.

Lydia sat across the table from him, watching his big shoulders tremble. She was not at all surprised to learn of Shawna's connection to the church. Since a few hours ago, when they'd put everything together, she expected each of them to have left a silken, spider's-web thread leading her back to Juno. She just needed to find the point at which it all converged and the killer would be there, waiting for her.

"I'm sorry," Greg said finally, raising his head and wiping the tears from his eyes.

"Please don't be. I understand."

"You're the first person to hear me out that hasn't treated me like a criminal or a fool whose girl ran away from him."

"In the days preceding Shawna's disappearance, did you notice anyone strange hanging around or did she tell you of anyone bothering her?"

"No, not that I remember. And I think I would remember. I was pretty protective of her."

"Just think for a minute. Anything she said, even in passing, someone she found creepy or didn't like?" She saw something flicker in Greg's eyes.

"Well, it's pretty stupid. I'm sure it doesn't mean anything."

"What is it?"

"The day before she disappeared we had a good laugh because Shawna made me promise never to buy a minivan, no matter how many kids we had. She said the past couple of days, she'd seen a green minivan a couple of times. She said, 'Once you buy a minivan, you can kiss your youth and any hope you ever had of being cool again good-bye.' But she never said where she'd seen it, or that she felt she was being followed."

"Did you see any other cars on the road that night when you went looking for her?"

"Not one. Do you think someone was following her, Ms. Strong?"

"It's possible."

"Either I or her parents drove her almost everywhere."

"But she walked here often? From her house?"

"Often enough."

Lydia pulled a card from her pocket and handed it to Greg. "If you think of anything else that might help, call me day or night."

She stopped the tape machine and put it in her bag, rose, and took his outstretched hand. There was a warmth and gentleness to his grip. It was easy to see why Shawna loved him. He was a protector.

"Do you think she's dead, Ms. Strong?"

"I don't know, Greg. I wish I did."

He nodded, closing his eyes. "Thank you, Ms. Strong."

He walked her to her car and opened the driver's seat door for her. "You'll keep me posted?" he asked.

"Of course."

———

As she did a U-turn and drove up the road away from him, she saw him in the rearview mirror, just standing and watching her drive away. He looked so sad and alone, so powerless, like a child who had lost his grip on a helium balloon and was watching it float into the sky.

She gripped the wheel so hard her knuckles turned white. She was angry, so fucking angry. She'd never admitted to anyone, not even Jeffrey, how furious she felt after interviewing the grief-stricken loved ones, the other victims of murderers. They had to live with what had been done to the person gone, they had to try to keep from imagining what that kind of pain and fear must be like, to keep from wondering what the last moments were like. When someone you love dies in a car wreck or a plane crash, there is always the possibility they died instantly, that they never knew death had come for them, that one minute they were on their way for milk at the store and the next . . . nothing. The families of murder victims didn't have that luxury, that chance for peace. They were haunted always, forever altered.

Who are you? And what do you want? she thought as she turned onto the main road and gunned the engine.

They always wanted something; these kinds of killers always had an agenda. The pedophile, the rapist, he was driven by an urge he couldn't control. Nature or nurture, biochemistry or psychosis, whatever compelled him was as much a part of him as the blood running through his veins. But a serial killer like this always had a reason—vengeance, fame, punishment.

Jed McIntyre had wanted to destroy lives. The killing of his victims, though he enjoyed it very much, was only a means to achieving an end goal, which was to destroy the life of the child left behind. Just as Jed's life was destroyed when his father had killed his mother in front of him and was sent to the electric chair.

Jed was alone with his rage for so many years, so isolated by his circumstances, by the horror he witnessed, by the impenetrable loneliness that surrounded him. He watched people go about their lives, fellow students, then co-workers, knowing that their perception of the world was so vastly different from his, knowing always that his life was forever cast in the shadow of his past. And as he grew older, his fury and his misery grew, too, and twisted like a vine of thorns, choking him and carrying him over the edge of sanity.

In a way, Lydia had grown to see him as someone fighting isolation, someone trying to create a community for himself, a brethren of misery. He had come to symbolize pure human evil to her. Not Evil in some cosmic sense, not the embodiment of Satan, but evil born of unspeakable psychic pain and cruel injustice, the victim become the victimizer with a vengeance.

But this killer . . . what was his agenda? What did these people mean to him? She was driving fast, taking the winding roads too hard as the faces of Shawna, Christine and Harold, and Maria swam in her mind. Usually it was so easy for her to see, like in the case of the Cheerleader Murders. All the girls were similar physically and, they later found out, just wicked, nasty young people. Once she knew what they shared in common, it was easy to deduce what type of person would want them, or want to be rid of them. But with these victims, even though she was sure that the church would be the point at which their lives intersected, she just couldn't see what characteristic they shared, what attracted the killer to them.

A deep fatigue was setting in behind her eyes as she relaxed her grip on the wheel. Her hands felt cramped from gripping it so hard. She sighed, rolling her neck from side to side to relieve the tension gathering there. She had never denied being obsessive about her work. But this case was different; it was her heart and not her brain that was driving her. Maybe that's what Jeffrey was sensing when he said he'd never seen her like this. She'd never felt like this. Rather than trying to solve something that had already happened, she felt inexplicably that she was racing to *prevent* something. Not only another murder, which was highly possible, but something even more than that. And that if she failed . . . well, she couldn't fail. Failure was not an option.

chapter fifteen

It was nearly ten o'clock when Lydia's Kompressor pulled into the dirt parking lot of Smokey's Sports Bar. The dilapidated building was a caricature of itself, of a dive bar by the side of the deserted road. The gray wood building sagged and was covered with graffiti. A wide variety of pickup trucks, with shotguns mounted on the back windows, sat waiting for their drunk drivers to try to get them home in one piece. *God, how grim,* Lydia thought as she eyed the flickering neon sign. Most of the letters had gone dark and not been repaired, so the sign just read, "m. .e. .s . . . S."

"Mess is right," muttered Lydia as she sat mustering the strength to enter. She was stepping out of the car when her cell phone chirped.

"What's up?" she answered, sinking back into the leather interior.

"I was just wondering where you were."

She smiled to hear Jeffrey's voice, hoping that he wasn't angry with her anymore. She knew she could be a bitch and she was eternally grateful that he always forgave her.

"I'm at Smokey's Sports Bar. I thought I'd have a few drinks and see if I couldn't get any action."

"Sounds like it's right up your alley. You still mad at me?"

"No. Are you still mad at me?"

"You know I can never stay angry at you. Besides, you were right."

There was a moment of silence before he said, "Her heart is missing, Lyd. Removed with surgical precision."

"Like Lucky."

"Yeah, except everything else is still intact . . . more or less."

"Did you come up with anything out there?" he asked, changing the subject.

"Yeah, I think so. I talked to Greg. Turns out Shawna was involved with the Church of the Holy Name. He also said that she had seen a green minivan a couple of times in the days before she disappeared." She could hear him flipping through the pages of a file.

"He never said anything about that before."

"No, he said it was just something she mentioned when they were kidding around. It's probably nothing but if we came up with a green minivan entering the park, we might have a lead. Any luck with the security guard?"

"The good news is there's a log, the bad news is that security guards seem to have really bad handwriting, and that a hundred and twenty-three vehicles have entered that park in the last twenty-four hours. We sent detectives over to the airport rental car offices to get a list of their customers since the afternoon before Lopez was murdered, just to cover all our bases. We also got the airport to release their security tapes."

"You don't think it's someone local?"

"I don't know. Like I said, just covering the bases. Tomorrow we'll have someone start punching license plate numbers into the DMV database, do some cross referencing with VICAP. If a green minivan pops up, we might get lucky."

"We should get a list of parishioners and volunteers at the church, too."

"Good idea. You almost done out there?"

"I'm just about to go into this bar and talk to Mike Urquia."

"They talked to him for over four hours today."

"Well, they talked to Greg, too, and they didn't get the information I got. Is the autopsy done?"

"Almost done. Morrow and I are waiting to meet with the ME. He told us already that he thinks she's been dead for more than fifteen hours, out there for ten."

"The killer didn't do a very good job of hiding her. Do you think he wanted us to find her?"

"He didn't stage the scene, there were no anonymous tips to lead police to the body. He didn't leave any messages or clues. He just dumped her. Maybe he just didn't care. Maybe he's that sure of himself."

"Did anything else turn up at the scene?"

"Well, the body bag, which was the best hope for prints, was totally clean. We are working to match the semen and pubic hair to Mike Urquia. All physical evidence indicates that the intercourse was consensual, and Urquia admitted to sleeping with her. We also scraped under her nails and hope there's DNA evidence, but that will only help to eliminate or confirm a suspect. And obviously results will take a while to come back."

"So, nothing?"

"We're waiting for toxicology to come back—things are slow as shit in these backwater jurisdictions," he said.

"All right, well, I'll meet you back at the house."

"I have an ugly feeling about this, Lydia. Watch yourself."

She laughed at his paternal concern. "I thought you didn't believe in feelings."

He didn't answer her.

"If you don't think I can handle a few rednecks then you don't know me very well," she said, trying and failing to lighten the mood.

"That's not what I mean," he answered quietly.

"No. I know. Don't worry. I'll see you later."

The bar was dark and Led Zeppelin's "Stairway to Heaven" blared from the jukebox in the corner behind the pool table. A few warped cues hung on the paneled wall next to a plastic Marlboro clock. It was like a million other dives in small towns across the country. Dirty and full of smoke, inhabited by overweight, flannel-and denim-clad men who looked like they knew no more familiar sight than their own reflection in the mirror behind the bar.

She perched herself on a stool near the window and waited for the bartender to notice her, which she thought wouldn't be long since all eyes had been on her from the moment she walked through the door. The bartender, a small woman with teased blond hair and an excess of blue eyeshadow, walked toward Lydia, her eyes narrowed with suspicion. She wore tight, tapered acid-wash jeans, and a cut-up white sweatshirt over a black tank top, *Flashdance*-style. The eighties had been an ugly decade.

"What can I get for you, honey?"

"Guinness on tap?" Lydia asked hopefully.

"'Fraid not. Coors or Bud on tap. Or Pabst in a can."

Of course. "Coors, then. Thanks."

When the bartender returned with her beer, Lydia asked, "Do you know where I can find Mike Urquia?"

"I haven't seen him tonight." She glanced at the clock behind her. "He's usually here by now."

"Do you know where he works or where I can find him?"

"Are you with the police or something?"

"Not exactly."

"Then what do you want with him?"

Lydia worked hard to conceal her rising annoyance with the woman and put on her best charming smile. "It's rather personal, but if you must know, I think he may be the father of my child."

Lydia suppressed a belly laugh at the woman's shocked expression. She was glad Jeffrey wasn't here to see this; he always hated it when she fucked with innocent people. She could imagine him getting up and walking away so the girl couldn't see his face.

"I'm sorry, honey. I don't know anything about him."

"He's here every night but you don't know anything about him?"

"Look, I just serve beer to the customers. I don't get involved in their personal lives. Are you sure you're not with the police? You're not from around here."

"No, I'm not. Look, let me give you my number . . ." Before she could finish, she noticed the woman was looking past her to a man walking in the door.

"Hey, Mike," called one of the barflies.

Lydia turned around to see a tall, dark-haired man with a mustache amble through the door. He was entirely clad in denim, with a sizable belly straining against the mother-of-pearl buttons on his shirt. Cowboy boots added about two inches to his already large frame. She didn't get a good look at his eyes as he walked past her. He gave his hand in greeting to the man who had called his name.

"Hey, Rusty. How you doin'?" he asked amiably.

Rusty raised his glass. "Can't complain, can't complain."

"There's your man, honey," the bartender sang. Lydia ached to smack her, for no good reason, imagining that many people shared her feelings.

Mike had seated himself, back to the wall at a small table near the jukebox. Lydia walked over and sat down across from him like she'd known him all her life. He looked sullen, tired. But he perked up considerably when Lydia joined him.

"Are you Mike Urquia?" she asked, in a tone she knew would immediately dash whatever hopes he had—official, cold.

"I am."

"I'm Lydia Strong. I have some questions about Maria Lopez. Do you have a few minutes to talk to me?"

He looked over at the other people at the bar and then leaned in close to her. "Look, lady, I don't want any more shit from you people. I had nothing to do with her death. Sure I fucked her and I was there the night they say she was killed, but I didn't do it. If you want to ask me any more questions, you're going to have to arrest me."

"Mr. Urquia, I know you didn't do it but I want to find out who did. As far as I understand, you were the only person close to Maria and you were the last person to see her alive. I want to find out about her, about who she was."

"Close to her? Lady," he said, and chuckled, "I wasn't that close to her. To these people, 'close' means I fucked her more than once—twice in my case. Look, I got a wife and two kids living about twenty miles from here. I come here to blow off some steam. When she came on to me, I took her home. Some of the guys around here said she gave good head, sometimes you had to pay her a little something. She was attractive enough—what can I say? But I don't know a thing about her. I'm sorry if something bad happened to her, but I didn't even know her last name until the police came and questioned me."

She looked at him and felt a little nauseated by him, by people's ability to use one another so cheaply. "Did you talk at all? Did she say one word about herself to you? Anything about someone who had been bothering her, following her?"

He looked like he wanted to say yes, to get the heat off of himself for a moment. "No, we really didn't have . . . you know," he paused, searching for the right words, "any conversations."

"So, basically, what you're telling me is that you took her home because you heard she gave good head, threw her down, fucked her, and then left. And the only time she opened her mouth was to put your dick in it?"

He leaned back in his chair, put his thumbs through his belt loops. "Basically, yes," he said without a trace of shame, a wide grin across his face.

Sadly, Lydia could see that he was telling the truth. "One more question. Did you see any vehicles on the street when you left Maria Lopez's apartment that night?"

"The cops asked me that question."

"And what did you tell them?"

"It was dark."

"Think for a second, Mr. Urquia. Did you see *any* vehicles?" Lydia was careful. There was a fine line between leading someone to tell you what you want to hear and jogging their memory.

"There were some cars parked but I didn't notice what make and model."

"Cars only? Could there have been anything larger—say, an SUV or a van?"

"Actually, I think there *was* a van," he said, casting his eyes down and to the right. "I couldn't say a color exactly because it was dark but maybe blue, or black. It wasn't a van, though. It was one of those minivans."

"When you exited the apartment, was the car to the left or to the right of the front door?"

"To the right."

She pulled her card from the inside pocket of her coat and slipped it across the table. "Please hold on to this, Mr. Urquia. If you think of anything else that might be helpful, don't hesitate to give me a call."

She got up and strode out, throwing a ten on the bar as she left.

At midnight, the coroner's office was dead quiet. Maria Lopez's autopsied body lay covered on the metal examination table. The fluorescent lights buzzed quietly, flickering slightly every few minutes, casting the stark room in a cold eerie light. A leaky faucet dripped rhythmically into the aluminum sink. The sound was measured, not actually distracting, but it was annoying Morrow, who had gotten up from his seat at the conference table in the next room twice to try to tighten the spigot.

The conference room was bathed in the same cold harsh light. Jeffrey, Simon, and Henry Wizner, the chief medical examiner, sat slouched around a conference table littered with their notes, photographs, and the empty wrappers from the meal they had eaten while working. Long hours of poring over the same material had wearied each of them and it showed in their wrinkled shirts, loosened ties, and the dark circles forming under their eyes.

Henry Wizner stood over six feet tall, and was so thin as to be gaunt. With ivory skin, large dark eyes, and hair as black as coal, he looked like a ghost of himself. Soft-spoken with a British accent, Wizner exuded the quiet authority of a man who knew he was the best of his profession. His intelligence and wit were as sharp as the scalpel he used to do his job.

He took pleasure in his work, always marveling at the damage people do to each other and to themselves, at what the human body could endure—and what it couldn't. Twisted bones, broken flesh, disembowelment, decapitation . . . he'd seen it all and then some. It had taken on a cartoonlike unreality for him, something that allowed him to sleep at night.

Maria Lopez was a mess. He'd seen worse cases, but nothing quite so intriguing in a while. "Well, it's interesting," remarked Wizner, "because this almost looks like the work of a surgeon. It's no hack job. It's not like someone just reached into her chest cavity and ripped the heart out."

"And according to your report," interjected Jeffrey, "she was dead before the incision was made and the organs removed. But alive when he slashed her throat . . . ?"

"Yes."

"Because of the rash around her nose and mouth, you believe that he used chloroform to subdue her."

"Yes."

"Where does one obtain chloroform?"

"You can get it easily enough over the Internet . . . if you know where to look. You can also make it by mixing bleach and acetone and distilling it. Chances are, if he knows how to use a scalpel, he knows how to get or make chloroform. It was once used as an anesthetic and they probably still say a word or two about it in med school."

"So you think this guy has a medical background."

"It would be a reasonable guess."

"And where the fuck is her heart?" said Morrow.

"A couple of years ago, I don't know if you gentlemen remember," began Wizner, "an American tourist was beaten to death in South America. She was there to pick up a child she had adopted. The natives had been spooked by a rumor that Americans had been abducting children then stealing their organs for trade on the black market."

"I do remember. The Bureau had some men down there," Jeffrey said, glancing up from the picture of Maria's body at the crime scene. Lydia was in the shot, and he'd been looking at her, half listening to Wizner.

Morrow had no idea what they were talking about so he kept quiet, not wanting to seem uninformed.

"Of course, UNOS was outraged and went to great trouble in publishing reports about these supposedly unsubstantiated claims, claiming it was an urban myth with no evidence to support it. But meanwhile the reports kept coming in; there were television shows airing in Europe; *Dateline* did a show here featuring a man who claimed his corneas were stolen."

"You can't be suggesting that this is actually happening here. It's impossible," said Jeffrey, incredulous. "You can't just take any organ out of some random person and plug it into someone else. There are strict time constraints, batteries of tests that need to be run. You're a doctor, you know this."

"Clearly it wouldn't be safe. But I'm not sure it's as impossible as UNOS makes it sound. It would just take a little corruption and a little organization."

"That's ridiculous," Jeffrey said, too tired for some far-fetched theorizing when he was lacking what he really needed—cold, hard, undeniable facts.

"Look, all I'm saying is the Lopez heart was removed with skill; it is currently nowhere to be found. One can only hope that it is being put to good use. Don't look so green, Mr. Mark." Wizner was smiling and it made him look like a ghoul.

Jeffrey hated the glib indifference he found so common to those professionals accustomed to the unspeakably grotesque. He had managed to keep his humanity over the years, in spite of the horrors he had witnessed. He wondered why others had not.

Nonetheless, what Wizner said made a sick kind of sense. But it was too out there at this point to bear any real looking-into.

He began to roll down his sleeves, which had been pushed up past his elbows. He was getting ready to call it a night. "Morrow, first thing in the morning we should head over to that church. Lydia said the Fox girl had some involvement there, and she seems sure that the crucifixes you found came from there as well."

"Most people in this town have some connection to that church. People are pretty religious here, like I said. And that blind healer is a local celebrity. The priest there, Father Luis, is a bastion of this community," Morrow said.

"Whatever, it still bears looking-into. If all the victims attended that church, which we don't know for sure that they did, then it's possible the killer is connected to it, too. It would really help if we could come up with another body. I suggest you have some of your men comb the park where we found Maria Lopez and see if they turn anything up."

Wizner quietly began gathering his notes and photographs with his thin, delicate white hands. He placed the papers in a manila envelope, which he slid under his arm after donning his brown cotton jacket. "I hope you'll keep in mind what I said, Mr. Mark," he said, walking out the door without pausing for an answer.

"I will. Thanks for your help," Jeffrey said, not noticing that Wizner was already down the hall.

In silence Morrow and Jeffrey gathered the rest of the materials scattered on the table. Photographs of the missing people, now presumed murder victims, hung on a bulletin board in the corner of the room, similar to the one Lydia and Jeffrey had set up back at the house. Jeffrey paused to look at them again.

In high school, Jeffrey had always been troubled by *The Bridge of San Luis Rey*, the novel by Thornton Wilder. Several people crossing a bridge are killed when it collapses beneath their feet, sending them all plummeting to their deaths. Their lives were not extraordinary, neither especially wicked or divine. Their deaths seem just a random selection of fate. What worried Jeffrey was thinking that maybe there was no order to the universe after all—just a series of accidents, lucky or unlucky, determining the course of lives. Not very comforting. Especially in his line of work.

"Jeff, are you coming?" asked Morrow, after waiting politely for Jeffrey, who'd been standing in front of the bulletin boards for over five minutes.

"Yeah, yeah . . . sorry."

Lydia sat in her car in the driveway leading into her garage. She could see by the absence of lights on inside that Jeffrey was not there. She wasn't afraid to go inside, she just didn't want to. A temporary depression had seized her, and instead she sat and smoked in the dark car, feeling like a hole had been cut in her chest and a cold wind was whipping through. She felt exposed, unprotected: the same familiar feeling she suffered every year as the anniversary of her mother's death approached, but as disturbing as if it were the first time.

The New Mexico night sky was riven with stars, close and bright, like diamonds scattered on velvet. She peered at them through her sunroof, her head resting on the seat. The silence was a presence. The shadows of mountains rose around her.

She thought about Mike Urquia and Maria Lopez's sad union. She had been so judgmental of him, wondering how he could be so glib and cold. But then it had occurred to her that if her Italian friend from the Eldorado had turned up dead somewhere, she would have had less to tell police about the man she'd slept with less than a week earlier than Urquia had had to say about Maria. She was no better than Mike Urquia. The thought made her sick.

She wondered if Jeffrey would even want her anymore if he knew about this side of her. She imagined trying to tell him about her little sexual assignations, so tawdry and meaningless. Her pathetic attempts to stave off loneliness, her quest for closeness to someone she wasn't afraid to lose. Jeffrey was so honorable, so upright, how could he ever understand? They never asked each other about their personal lives as far as dating was concerned. It was an understood taboo between them that neither one could stand to know if the other was seeing someone. Jeffrey had had a few relationships when Lydia was in college. She never paid any attention to any of the women in his life because she knew they wouldn't last. Maybe she'd always known they belonged together and that someday they would be. She couldn't think about this now, though, with a serial killer on the loose.

She considered heading over to the church to talk to Juno again, maybe have a word with Father Luis, whom she had yet to meet. A glance at her watch told her it was approaching one A.M. Too late for a visit. But she'd have to go tomorrow; the answer was there somewhere, somehow. Did they know their parishioners were missing? Had they missed Shawna? They must have. Could they somehow be involved? *A blind, psychic healer/serial killer, that would be a first.* She began to laugh and couldn't stop. It felt like hysteria, the tension she had felt for the last few days catching up with her. She was still laughing when Chief Morrow and Jeffrey pulled up behind her. She stepped out of the car to greet them, wiping her eyes and chuckling.

. To Jeffrey it looked like she was sobbing. He pushed the door open and jumped out of the squad car before it had fully stopped moving. "Lyd, what's wrong?" He grabbed her by both arms, and looked into her eyes.

"Nothing, nothing, Jeff. I just had a funny thought and couldn't stop laughing. I think I'm a little punchy."

"Oh. You scared me." He spoke slowly, unconvinced.

"Is everything all right?" said Morrow, stepping out of the car. Lydia thought how he looked a little like "the Commish," and she almost started laughing again but controlled herself.

In an unusually pleasant tone she answered, "Yeah, everything's fine. Have a good night."

"I'll pick you up at eight," Morrow said to Jeffrey.

"Thanks, Chief."

Morrow got back in his car, glad to be on his way home. He wondered as he pulled away, not for the first time, if Lydia Strong wasn't one card short of a deck.

"We really need another body to turn up if we are going to get anywhere," Jeffrey concluded after he had summarized the day's findings for her.

"Why did he take her heart?" Lydia wondered aloud. "What do you think it means to him?"

"Well, what does it mean to most of us?"

"Love, metaphorically. Maybe life. Medically it's the organ that pumps the blood, keeps us alive."

"Could he be keeping it as a trophy?"

"No, it's too complicated a behavior for it to be only that. Taking the heart is his whole agenda, or at least a significant part. He obviously has a place somewhere dedicated to its removal. We know that Maria was subdued with chloroform, so we know he did not intend to kill her at her apartment. He wanted to kill her at another location and remove her heart. It may be the whole reason why he kills them."

"Or how he kills them."

"The medical examiner said the incision was made after she died."

"But he didn't expect to kill her so soon."

"So what does it mean, then, to lose your heart or to have your heart taken?"

"To lose someone you love. To lose hope. To lose faith."

"Perhaps each of these people offended him or slighted him in some way. Perhaps he was attracted to the women—say Harold was just in the way—and each of them turned him down or was rude to him, in his perception. He took their hearts, the way they took his."

"But all the women are so different. Usually when that's the case, the killer has one physical type that attracts him. There's one woman in his past that has deeply traumatized him, usually his mother, and he kills her over and over again."

"Okay, so let's think about it—why *their* hearts? I mean, assuming that we eventually discover Shawna, Harold, and Christine in the same condition we found Maria. What was it about these people that made the killer want to take their hearts?"

He was tapping his pen on the kitchen tabletop, a gesture Lydia had picked up from him years ago. Lydia was curled up in the window seat, wearing a thick gray sweatshirt, black leggings, and white socks. She arched her back and moved her head side to side to relieve the tension that had settled there. The teakettle whistled hysterically and Jeffrey rose to make them some chamomile. She liked to watch him in the kitchen, his strong shoulders and big hands dealing not with guns and fistfights but kettles and potholders. He looked sweet and somehow irresistibly masculine. She smiled to herself.

"I heard back from Jacob a little while ago."

"I didn't know you had spoken to him."

"Yeah. I called him after you left this morning. He ran some checks on Christine and Harold. No activity on bank accounts or credit cards. He checked some rehab clinics around the area but nothing there, either. No arrest records in surrounding towns. I guess I was really hoping you were wrong, that these people were just going to turn up. I should know better than to question your instincts."

"I'm sorry about today, Jeffrey."

He paused, surprised that she had apologized. "It's all right, Lyd. I'm sorry, too," he answered as he put honey in the tea, keeping his back to her. "I know you're worked up about this."

"Still, I shouldn't have bit your head off."

"Which time?" he asked, smiling.

"Any time," she answered solemnly.

He placed the tea in front of her and touched her face with fingers warm from the cup he had just held. She reached for his hand and put her mouth to his palm. It was a warm and passionate gesture. He stood still as she held his hand to her mouth, wanting so much but too afraid to touch her for fear the moment would pass too soon.

Inside, she struggled against herself. *How close he is this moment, how easy it would be to surrender.* But she released his hand finally, stared down at her teacup. He sat in the chair across from her, not wanting to speak, afraid his voice would fail him.

"They were alone," she said, slicing the tension between them.

"Who?"

"Maria Lopez and the others. No one cared about them."

"I know. It makes you think, you know? Well, it makes me think."

"Think about what?"

"About loneliness."

She looked over her teacup at him with surprised, questioning eyes. "Are you lonely, Jeffrey?"

"Aren't you?"

She rose quickly from her seat and walked over to the refrigerator, opened the door, and looked in for nothing except an escape from his eyes.

"What does this have to do with anything?" she said defensively.

He took off his glasses and rubbed the point on his nose where they rested and leaned back in his chair. "I'm so fucking sick of this."

"Of what?"

"Of this little dance we do. I approach you, you back away. You come back a step, I move in again, you take two more steps back. Who are we kidding?"

"What are you talking about?" she asked the milk carton.

He got up and gently turned her around from the refrigerator. The frustration that had been building inside him was reaching a level that was getting hard to ignore. "Oh, come on. Are you going to pretend there's nothing between us? Are you going to pretend you don't know how I feel about you?"

"Jeffrey, please . . ." she said.

He looked into her eyes and saw fear there and he instantly hated himself. He pulled her into a tight embrace which she returned with equal passion.

"If we . . . I couldn't . . . Oh God," she said into his shoulder.

Suddenly the dim kitchen was flooded with light, startling them both. The outside floodlights, triggered by the motion detectors that surrounded the house, had turned on. He walked over to the window and peered out to the driveway. Had someone just stepped out of his sight? Or was it his imagination?

"Do you still have that Glock?"

"Yeah . . ."

"Go get it."

She ran quickly to her office, punched a code into the keypad lock on the safe beneath her desk, and withdrew the heavy semi-automatic pistol. Beside it was a .38 Special, a revolver favored by older cops, less powerful but more reliable. She had been trained to use both during her stay at the FBI academy but had never fired them off the range. She liked the way the Glock felt, cool and heavy in her hand. She returned to the kitchen, where Jeffrey had turned off the light and was peering out the window. She handed the gun to him.

"Loaded?"

"Of course."

"Stay here," he said sternly, knowing her instinct would be to follow him.

He walked out onto the driveway, gun level. He heard nothing but he sensed a presence, something or someone, waiting. He walked toward the trees that edged the house, his ears pricked for even the slightest noise. He could see nothing through the trees, just an impenetrable darkness.

"Do you see anything?"

He spun around to see Lydia standing directly behind him, hugging herself against the chill, still in stocking feet. A less-experienced marksman would have discharged his gun from the jolt she gave him.

"Jesus Christ, Lydia, I told you to stay in the house."

"There's no way I'm letting you come out here alone."

In the next instant Jeffrey heard someone cut and run into the woods. He was after him in a heartbeat, following the large, dark form through the thick trees. The intruder's flight was panicked, clumsy, but he was oddly fast for someone so large. Jeffrey could feel the distance between them growing and he picked up his pace, pushing aside the branches that slapped at his arms and face.

"Jeffrey!" Lydia yelled after him, then ran into the house to get her shoes and her other gun.

His call of "Freeze, motherfucker—" shot like a bullet through the night air, but it only served to urge the intruder on with greater speed. Jeffrey had been in law enforcement far too long to shoot a fleeing suspect in the back.

Suddenly he lost sight of the form in the darkness. Jeffrey stopped when he realized that whoever it was had eluded him unexplainably. The night was alive with mysterious noises and bright stars above, but Jeffrey was alone with the sound of his own breathing, labored from the chase. He searched the area for any sign of the intruder's escape route, but he was impeded by his poor eyesight, his glasses still sitting on the kitchen table. He sensed that he was alone, that no one was waiting in ambush for him. In the far distance, he heard the sound of a struggling ignition.

He slipped his gun into the waist of his jeans and began walking back toward the house. He could not be sure how far he had come and he could not see the lights through the trees. The shapes around him were difficult to discern. His heart was still racing from adrenaline and exertion as he wiped the sweat from his brow with a quick, aggravated gesture.

"Shit," he muttered.

He was more than a little annoyed that the intruder had slipped away. It never would have happened a few years ago. Another reminder that he was getting older. Who was it? One of those kids Morrow was claiming caused so much trouble? A common burglar, vandal, vagrant? Even as the multitude of possibilities turned in his mind, he knew the answer. This case, which he had at first regarded with skepticism, was starting to take shape like the trees around him when the moon passed from behind the clouds. He had the sense of something sinister, something twisted, something connected to Lydia.

Darkness, solitude; the two places where thoughts turned most often to her. Tonight his thoughts were edged with worry. Who was hiding in those trees? How long had he been there? Had he been waiting there when Lydia had come home alone?

Jeffrey made his way more steadily now, feeling his way in the moonlight, treading carefully toward the gleam of the houselights he now saw in the distance. An anxiety, a fierce need to protect Lydia arose in him. He could see the look in her eyes just a few minutes before, feel her in his arms. He would die for her. If he could have caught his breath enough to break into a run to her, he would have.

A perfect circle of light bounced before him. He was struggling to see what it was, straining his weak eyes in the darkness, when he heard Lydia calling his name.

"I'm here," he called, "stay still. I'll come to you."

"You're not hurt, are you?" she called.

"No, just old, winded, and blind."

When she finally saw him, she ran to him but stopped herself from throwing her arms around him. Instead she touched him tenderly on his bad shoulder. He could see she had a .38 in a holster at her waist.

"Did you see who it was?"

"No. He got away. I don't know how. . . . He was big and clumsy. But he was ten feet in front of me one minute and then it seemed like seconds later that I heard an ignition struggling a mile away."

"I called the police."

"All right."

She slipped her arm around his waist and he draped his arm across her shoulders in return. She leaned in close to him as they walked. "Who do you think it was?" she asked.

"Who do *you* think it was?" he answered, knowing from her tone what she suspected but did not say.

"It was him."

"You don't know that."

"I can feel it."

"You say that like it's proof."

"It is for me."

They were silent as they walked toward the house, which was visible now through the trees.

"What do you think, Jeffrey?"

"I don't know."

But she knew him too well, knowing his heart and his meaning more by what went unsaid than by the words he uttered, understanding more from the protective tightening of his arm around her shoulder. She stopped walking and faced him, put her fingers to the rough stubble on his face.

"Seems like you're always rushing to my rescue."

"God knows you've come to my rescue a thousand times."

"You're always here when things get out of hand."

"It's my honor, Lydia."

"I don't know what to do, Jeffrey. Give me time."

"How much more time do you need, Lydia? What are you so afraid of?"

He pushed the hair out of her eyes and tilted her face upward with a featherlight touch under her chin. The yearning of years ached inside of her like a hunger she had never been able to sate, that made her weak and unsteady on her feet. He pulled her in close. There was no truer home to her than the one she knew in his arms. That was becoming more clear to her every day. She shivered as if someone were walking over her grave. Her desire and fear seemed almost audible, like sirens in the distance, moving closer from opposite directions, warning of danger.

"Lydia."

The tone in his voice was a confession, mirroring her own. And in the second before his lips touched hers, the quiet night was pierced by a cacophony of sirens and the chaos of red-and-blue flashing lights on the street. In what seemed like seconds, the forms of at least ten police officers filtered in through the trees like wraiths.

"Over here," Jeffrey called out to the cops, supporting Lydia as she leaned against him, shaking her head against his chest. "We're over here."

They walked onto the drive. Jeffrey borrowed an officer's cell phone to call Morrow to tell him what had happened. While she was giving her statement to a young female officer, something near the front door to her house caught Lydia's eye. She stopped speaking in midsentence and walked toward it. Jeffrey saw her and followed behind. Sitting on the low stone step before the door, was a box wrapped in newsprint.

chapter sixteen

Lydia lay on her king-size bed, her body wrapped in soft white Egyptian cotton sheets and a rose-colored chenille blanket, the down comforter in a twisted mound on the floor where she had tossed it during her restless night. What would it be like to wake up beside him every morning? What would it be like to wake up one day, have to wake up with the knowledge that he would never lie beside her again?

"Anybody who ever said it's better to have loved and lost than never to have loved at all is an idiot," her mother said to her once on a rare occasion when they'd discussed her father. "You can't miss what you never had."

Lydia had met her father only once, on the day after her mother's funeral. She sat alone in the living room staring out the bay window at the woods behind her house. The day was cool and sunny in cruel contrast to the way she felt. She heard the doorbell but paid no attention, assuming it was another neighbor come to offer their condolences. She dreaded having to smile politely, having to say she would be all right. Then she heard her grandfather's voice as he opened the door, then a soft murmuring, then silence. To Lydia her grandfather sounded angry, but she thought she must be mistaken. Then she saw him at the door, his face tight and ashen.

Hovering behind her grandfather, she saw a stranger with her eyes. Tall and slouching, poorly dressed, he held flowers and looked ashamed. He shifted uncomfortably from foot to foot.

"You don't have to see him, Lydia," her grandfather said.

But her curiosity was great. It was the first feeling she'd had other than grief and horror since her mother died. "No. It's okay, Grandpa."

She stood up and her father walked toward her. He held the flowers out to her. She took them, her eyes fixed on him. In all the fantasies she had had about him in her life, none of them had even come close to predicting the ordinary man who stood before her. She had imagined him as a great lover, dark and handsome; a motorcycle daredevil, reckless and brave; an international spy, suave and sophisticated. What other kind of man could have stolen her strong, beautiful mother's heart and left her broken and forever sad? Surely some great danger or some irresistible intrigue had lured him from her mother and their child. In spite of what her mother said.

"Don't fantasize about your father, Lydia," her mother told her numerous times. "He was just an irresponsible man, living for get-rich-quick schemes, always looking for something more than what he had."

She had never believed her mother until this moment, as he stood before her, eyes begging, hands quivering. It was like another death for her.

She let the flowers drop to the floor, turned her back on him, and walked back to her perch by the window. She might have forgiven him for leaving them, for breaking her mother's heart, but she could never forgive him for being so unremarkable. She could never forgive that he had obviously left them for nothing.

There was a soft knock at the door. She closed her eyes and

rolled over, feigning sleep. She heard Jeffrey push the door open and walk into the room. He sat on the bed beside her.

"Lydia?"

"Hmm?"

"You want to get up? Morrow will be here in an hour to go over to the church."

He touched her shoulder tenderly. His hair was lightly tousled. Unshaven, clad in a white T-shirt and faded blue jeans, he seemed irresistible. But she resisted him.

"Okay."

"I'll make some coffee."

Even in this moment she knew she could call him back to her.

"Jeffrey."

"Yeah."

"Make it really strong."

"You got it." He answered without looking at her as he eased the door shut.

But in the end, I'm just a coward. What am I afraid of?

It was a question she couldn't answer. She only knew that when she thought of surrendering to Jeffrey, she was a child again standing in front of the open door of her mother's house. That sinking fear, teetering on the edge, mere moments from total devastation. It consumed her, paralyzed her, forced her into loneliness.

It wasn't only him. It had been this way for as long as she could remember, with every person who had ever tried to get close to her. He was the only one who had stayed around, gauging perfectly when she needed him to be close or far. It wasn't fair to him. She knew that.

She flipped the covers back and got out of bed. The clock glowed 6:50 A.M. as she stretched, feeling her stiff muscles warm and relax. Arms in the air, back arched, then torso against each lean, tight thigh, her flexible body energized with each gentle movement, with each deep breath.

She switched on the light and examined her naked body in the full-length mirror. Unlike most women, Lydia loved her body. It was lithe and lean, but muscular and strong, with a womanly fullness around her hips and breasts. She leaned in closer to examine her face, her creamy skin. Tiny lines had started to make their debut on her too-often frowning brow, around her eyes. She didn't much care, wise enough to know the passage of time was one thing she could not control. Her cold beauty was hard-lined and knowing, sometimes brutal. Her gray eyes did not betray the child's fear that lurked some days within her heart, or the fragility of her soul.

"Good morning," she said to the killer, staring at her own eyes in the mirror. "I'm coming after you today."

She thought about the package he'd left for her last night.

"Well, he's fucking with us now," Jeffrey had said, annoyed. "He was right at your doorstep."

He'd been angry last night. Angry that the killer had been right within his grasp and got away, and angry at Lydia for the same reason, she imagined. They had sat again at the kitchen table after the police had left, taking the package to be analyzed at the lab. They were avoiding totally what had almost happened between them in the woods, avoiding Jeffrey's obvious pain and frustration and talking about the "gift" the killer had left.

"He obviously knows you, knows where you live, and knows what you do for a living. He gave it a lot of thought. Which means he gives *you* a lot of thought," Jeffrey had said quietly.

She had nodded, the impact of the visit finally pressing on her. "It means that I am part of his design, that I figure somehow into his plan."

"How did he know you were involved?"

"Maybe that was always his intention, to draw me in some-how. I just beat him to the punch."

"He's watching you."

"Yes, I believe he is."

"You don't seem overly concerned."

"What do you want me to do?"

"I don't know. Maybe we both just need to get some rest."

So they had parted with much unsaid and unresolved between them. She had almost turned back to him as she walked up the stairs. They had been so close. If they hadn't been interrupted by the police, there was little question as to what would have happened.

She was some combination of disappointed and relieved as she walked into the adjoining bathroom and felt the cool hard tile beneath her feet. The room was a study in the varied uses of white marble—the floor, countertop, and sink were all formed of the beautiful stone. With mirrored walls and bright marquis bulbs, no inch of the room escaped reflection except the steam-room and shower, which were enclosed behind frosted-glass doors that reached from floor to ceiling. The countertop was a pretty clutter of the finest cosmetics and toiletries, expensively packaged soaps and lotions, bath salts, powders, fragrances. Lydia loved the smell, the feel of these things. They were a tiny indulgence she afforded herself, in honor of her mother. Marion, too, had cherished the luxury of a beautiful bathroom, filled with products that pleased the senses and soothed the skin. But Marion had never allowed herself the pleasure of the costly items she saw in magazines. Lydia would have lavished her mother with such things, had Marion lived to share her wealth. So in-stead she bought them for herself.

The cold water of the shower braced her skin, shocking the last sleepy cobwebs from her head. She lathered herself with lavender soap, at first enduring and then enjoying the frigid water raising goose bumps on her flesh. She washed her hair twice and then conditioned, letting the cold water beat on her back while she let the conditioner sit, making her hair soft. When she emerged, her body glistening, she dried herself with one of the plush black towels that hung on the wall. Then she wrapped herself in it and brushed her teeth.

Jeffrey placed a mug of coffee on her bedside table. He heard the shower and shivered, knowing that it was ice cold. Cold showers for the morning; hot showers at night. He could hear her saying the morning was the beginning of the day, no time for luxury or relaxation—it was time to get moving. He smiled at the thought, but he held a sadness inside of him, mourning the moment that had passed between them last night. He knew that it could not be recaptured, and could already feel her laying distance between them. He let her do it, aware that she would have to come to him. Like a lunar eclipse, that moment could not be forced—only anticipated. He walked from the room and closed the door as Lydia emerged from the bathroom.

The sight of the steaming coffee at the bedside made her want to smile and cry at the same time.

Lydia and Jeffrey followed behind in the Kompressor as Morrow's beat-up squad car led the way to the church. High winds whipped sand around the car and rushed loudly through Lydia's partially opened window, making conversation between them difficult. Not that there was any conversation. The silence between them was like barbed wire. If he tried to get through it, it probably wouldn't kill him. But it would hurt like hell. So Jeffrey kept quiet, watching the landscape pass and preparing for the interview ahead.

In Jeffrey's imagination, the Church of the Holy Name had taken on cathedral-like proportions. Maybe because of the significance it seemed to hold for Lydia. So, he was a bit surprised when they pulled up beside the tiny adobe church, with its simple wood doors, unassuming bell tower, and cross-shaped windows.

"This is it?" he asked.

"This is it," Lydia answered. She walked up the three small steps and pushed the heavy doors in, followed by Jeffrey and Morrow.

A frail, dark-haired man wearing faded but well-washed and pressed jeans and a white oxford shirt approached them, and Jeffrey was again surprised when Lydia introduced him as Juno. From Lydia's description he had expected to see Gabriel in flowing robes, ensconced in a heavenly light. As he took the hand Juno offered, Jeffrey was delighted by the blind man's entirely earthly, rather plain appearance.

As Juno disappeared through a door beside the altar to get Father Luis, Jeffrey, Lydia, and Morrow moved over to the glass case by the church entrance. Laid out on a red-velvet cushion beneath the glass were two leather-bound Bibles, three rosaries, and a hand-carved crucifix. Morrow removed an evidence bag from the pocket of his J. Crew-style barn jacket and held it on top of the case. The crucifix contained in the plastic bag was identical to the one in the case.

"They're the same," Lydia said, certain.

"Looks that way," answered Morrow, nodding.

Lydia's eyes drifted to the back of the church to the doorway through which Juno had disappeared moments before. Jeffrey noted it was the third time her eyes had followed the path Juno had taken. She wouldn't even glance in Jeffrey's direction and they hadn't made eye contact all morning. She was moving away again, just as he had accused her of doing last night. Maybe it was always going to be like this with her. Maybe it was just time to forget it, time to move on, sad as the thought made him.

Jeffrey sat down in one of the pews and watched as a man in beige coveralls painstakingly polished the long wooden table on the altar. He seemed to make endless small circles with the cloth in his hand and moved slowly and stiffly, as though he were a robot low on fuel. Every few circles, the man would shuffle a few inches to the side and begin polishing another small section. Maybe sensing that he was being watched, he lifted his eyes and looked at Jeffrey with a blank, unseeing stare. Not blind, but uncomprehending. The man was obviously mentally impaired. Jeffrey smiled but the man looked back down at the table, returning to his circles. An old woman kneeled in the first pew, her head bent. Jeffrey could hear the murmuring of her prayer.

Morrow walked around the church, his footfalls echoing loudly as he looked behind some embroidered wall-hangings, and under the pews. He stepped into the confessional, touching the tattered Bible with a tentative finger.

"Bet you haven't been inside one of these in a while," said Lydia from the other side, through the wrought-iron grating, startling him.

"About as long as you," he shot back, more weakly than he would have liked.

Lydia chuckled. He couldn't be sure if she was laughing at him but it was a safe bet. He went back to join Jeffrey.

The wood inside the confessional was spotless—meticulously scrubbed and dusted. The cushion on the small bench was old and worn with bits of white stuffing visible beneath the red velvet cover. Lydia felt uncomfortable, the same feeling she had had in the garden, during her first visit, like somebody's eyes were on her. She peeked through the grating, but Morrow was gone. She picked up the Bible off a narrow shelf. The leather was smooth and malleable from years of use, and the pages, the edges gilded with gold, made a crisp whisper as she flipped through the book absently. She hadn't held a Bible since her mother's funeral.

"Lydia," Jeffrey called.

She walked from the confessional to see Juno and the man who must be Father Luis Alonzo sitting in the final pew. She was introduced to the priest and he rose as he shook her hand.

As Jeffrey told the priest about the recent disappearances and what they had come to suspect, Lydia watched Father Luis's open, earnest face darken with concern. He leaned slightly forward and began knitting his hands. She could see him searching his mind for the last time he'd seen Harold and Christine, Shawna, or Maria. And in his deep, brown eyes, she saw the flicker of something else. Something she hadn't expected and which didn't make sense. Fear.

"Of course I'd noticed their absences. At first I thought nothing of it. It is not uncommon for people to drift away from the church and then return. Then I read in the paper that first Shawna, then Harold and Christine were missing." He shook his head. "I never connected them to each other. Then Maria, may she rest in peace. Even then I never made the connections."

"We've missed Shawna very much," he continued quietly. "She was a great help to us. Maria came to confession every Wednesday and to mass every Sunday. Christine and Harold came to Sunday mass sporadically over the years."

Morrow pulled the crucifix from his pocket and handed it to the priest. "Did you make this, Father?"

The priest inspected it, holding it in a hand that trembled slightly. "Yes, it looks like an older one. Where did you find it?"

"At Ms. Lopez's apartment. One was found at the homes of each of the other missing persons as well."

The priest tapped his foot lightly on the floor. It was an unconscious gesture, the slender black leather shoe rapping a staccato on old wood. Lydia and Jeffrey exchanged a glance. "I have to admit, I never imagined any harm had befallen them. Maria, of course—the headlines were shocking. But Shawna, Christine, and Harold were all troubled people. I thought they had just run off."

"That's what we all thought," said Morrow.

"Not all of us," muttered Lydia. The priest appeared not to have heard her, but Morrow shot her an angry look.

"And it still might turn out, though it's doubtful, that Shawna, Christine, and Harold have nothing to do with our case," interjected Jeffrey. "But, Father, if you know anything that could help us, now would be the time to let us know. Anybody any one of them may have mentioned to you. Someone they were afraid of . . . ?" Jeffrey sat down beside the priest, who seemed to be deep in thought.

"Nothing comes to mind," he said, sighing.

Lydia spoke up for the first time. "Father, it seems obvious, with all of these people being members of your congregation, with the dog's body that was found here, with the crucifixes that were found in each of the victim's homes, that this church is somehow tied in. Has anyone said anything to you during confession that may have sounded suspicious or threatening?" She fixed her eyes on him as if she were trying to read his mind.

"Obviously, I would be loath to violate the sanctity of the confessional. But I can tell you that certainly I have heard nothing of the nature you mean."

"Does the church have any employees other than you and your nephew?"

"No, we have volunteers who care for the church. Some are just parishioners who want to give time to the church, like Shawna. Some do community service here, you know, as punishment for a minor offense of some kind, and some of them come from the school for the mentally challenged."

"The man who is here today, was he from the school you mentioned?" asked Jeffrey.

"I'm not sure who you mean."

Jeffrey looked up and saw that the man was gone. The old woman who had been praying had also left unnoticed. "He was polishing the table."

"We didn't have anyone in today to do volunteer work, as far as I knew." He turned to his nephew. "Juno, did you schedule anyone?"

"No, I didn't. The people from the school are always scheduled because they need to be supervised," he explained. "They usually come in groups. The volunteer parishioners come and go as they please."

"Did either of you see the man I saw?" Jeffrey asked Morrow and Lydia. Both shook their heads. "Morrow, can you go take a look out the door?"

"Sure," he said, rising and walking to the entrance.

"Father, can we get a list of names, addresses, and telephone numbers of your congregation and volunteers?" Lydia asked.

The priest hesitated. "I don't think I'm within my rights . . ."

Morrow returned, overhearing the priest's reluctance.

"Father, this is a murder investigation. If you would like me to get a warrant, I can do that," said Morrow, respectfully but with authority.

"No, no, that won't be necessary." He rose. "I'll just get what

I have from my office. Of course, not all of the people who attend mass give their addresses."

"Of course. What you have will be good enough for now," Jeffrey answered.

When the priest had left, Morrow turned to Jeffrey. "I didn't see anyone out there. There are no vehicles except for ours and the church van."

"I wasn't aware of anyone else being here today, except for Mrs. Mancher who walks here to pray nearly every day," said Juno.

"Did you notice any other vehicles when we came in?" Jeffrey asked Lydia and Morrow.

"No, the lot was empty," Lydia answered, and the chief nodded his agreement.

The priest returned with some xeroxed pages and handed them to Jeffrey.

"Thank you, Father. Lydia, is there anything else you need from Juno and Father Luis at this point?"

"Just one thing. Father, have you noticed that any of your parishioners, or any of your volunteers, drive a green minivan?"

He let out a small laugh. "Well, in fact, *I* drive a green Dodge Caravan."

All three of them looked at him.

"But it's been in the shop for the last week, and I've been using the church van for all my business. My minivan is an older model and the transmission is slipping," he said; then added uncomfortably, "It's a fairly common vehicle."

"What service station is it at, Father?" Morrow asked. "No disrespect, of course, but we'll need to take a look at it."

"It's at the Amoco station in town. I'll call and let them know you'll be dropping by."

"Anyone else you can think of?" asked Morrow.

"No, but I'll certainly keep my eyes open."

The priest was kind and eager to help, but Lydia was sure he had something to hide. The fact that he owned a green minivan had thrown her a bit. She turned the possibilities around in her mind. Was he protecting someone? Was he involved in some way? She looked at him, his eyes filled with emotion and empathy, his large soft hands, the slight paunch of his belly. It didn't seem likely.

"Father, have you noticed anyone strange lurking about the church? Someone who has recently started coming to mass but that you haven't met before?" she asked. "Someone whose behavior has struck you as odd?"

Lydia saw something in the priest's eye—a thought he considered voicing but dismissed.

"No, all my parishioners have been coming here for years, many of them as children themselves."

"The man I saw today?" said Jeffrey. "He was large-framed, with sandy-blond hair. He wore beige coveralls. He appeared to be . . . you know, a bit on the slow side. Does this sound like anyone you know to be a volunteer here?"

"Well, there is Benny. He doesn't go to the school I mentioned. But he is somewhat impaired. According to his mother, he has the intelligence of a twelve-year-old. He does come by occasionally and do some work for us. He loves to work in the garden. In fact, his name and number are on the list I gave you. Benjamin Savroy."

"Thank you for your time, Father, Juno," said Jeffrey, shaking each hand. "You can expect us to be stopping by again."

Lydia said her good-byes as well. "Father, Juno, if you think of anything—no matter how small or insignificant it might seem to you, please call us."

———

The three left and the church was quiet and peaceful again. The air still tingled with her essence, even as Juno listened to their cars pull away. Lydia's scent still lingered, mingling with the odor of wood, candle wax, and incense.

Juno had remained silent throughout his uncle's interview. He felt strongly that something horrible had befallen all the missing people. He had little doubt they had met with a fate similar to Maria's. Juno was not an emotional person by nature and though he was deeply saddened by these events, they failed to move him to tears, as they did his uncle. Juno possessed an unflappable inner peace. Though he had great empathy, and a tremendous capacity to feel, the core of him, his faith in God, in the order of His universe, remained solid. No matter how horrible a tragedy occurred, no matter how people suffered, Juno knew in his heart that he and all people were part of a plan, God's plan. After death, all suffering would fade from memory and the plan would be revealed. This is what his Bible and his heart told him.

And as he had listened to their conversation, something had begun to tickle at the edge of his consciousness. Like a whisper from a distant place, he caught the scent of lavender, of rose, of Lydia. His thoughts had turned to her many times since they had met. To touch her was like an electric shock, blue heat. He had seen her so clearly that first day—her power, her emotion, her fear and vulnerability. The different shades of her, the black and white of her soul and the internal battle that was waged there, intrigued him, excited him. It was so unlike anything he had known in his own inner life.

He realized that his uncle was sitting in the pew in front of him but hadn't said a word since they had been alone. "Uncle, will you be all right?"

The pause was pregnant with sorrow, and when the priest

spoke, his words were taut with tears. "Yes. But it is not for myself that I am afraid."

"Of course."

The priest rose and left Juno alone in the church. In the silence Juno contemplated Lydia and Jeffrey. The rising temperature in the church told Juno that it was nearing noon. Jeffrey's tone had been quiet and professional but the sound of Lydia's name on his tongue was liquid with love. In the way Jeffrey's lips touched those three syllables, Juno could feel his passion for her, taste Jeffrey's painful restraint.

At wedding services, Juno often played guitar. Seated on his wooden stool, he perched at the altar, to the right of Father Alonzo. He could hear the bride and groom exchange their vows, and could sense almost instantly who married for money, for fear, for lack of any better opportunities. On only a few occasions had he heard the sound of fierce, tremulous love in the voices of both being joined before the eyes of God. Only rarely had he heard the melodic pitch of two souls bound long before they had reached the church to exchange their earthly vows.

He detected such a bond between Lydia and Jeffrey. But the chorus of her fears was louder.

Lydia dragged on her cigarette, face like stone, eyes staring at the road in front of her. She drew smoke into her lungs, its drug soothing her, cooling her agitation like ice water in her veins. Jeffrey rolled down his window as he watched her slender arm move from the steering wheel to her lips. It was a graceful, sensuous movement—more so because it was unconscious.

"I want to stop by the station and see what they've come up with on that list of park visitors. I want to cross-check it against that list of volunteers," Lydia said, again driving too fast up the winding road away from the church.

"And I want to go talk to that slow kid," said Jeffrey, forever politically correct.

"So, what do you think?" she asked him.

"I'm not sure. That priest has something to hide, though."

"I picked up on that, too. You think he's involved?" she answered, her words punctuated by a sharp exhalation of smoke.

"He drives a green minivan, he made the crosses that were found at each scene, he had knowledge of and proximity to all the victims. If he wasn't a priest, I might have taken him in," Jeffrey said, only half joking. "I don't think he's involved directly. But I think he knows something. I'm going to have Morrow put some men on the church, have them lurk about, make people uncomfortable, and see what shakes loose. We also need to get a tech out to that minivan."

"Jeffrey?"

"Yeah?"

"How long are you going to stay?"

"As long as I need to."

A leaden silence fell between them. He waited for her to say something to clarify the meaning of her question. But she just reached for the ashtray and stubbed out her cigarette.

"Why?" he asked finally. "Do you want me to get a room somewhere?"

"No," she said quickly, sharply, glancing over at him. "Of course not. Don't you dare."

"Then why?"

"I was just wondering," she said, quickly lighting another cigarette with one hand. After she took a drag, she added, "I just don't think I can get through this without you."

"Well, you won't have to. In fact, you never have to get through anything without me, if you don't want to. As you well know."

He stared out the window as he said this, and she looked over at him, her heart tight in her chest. He put his hand on her knee and she did not remove it. *Why are you more afraid of him than you are of serial killers?*

The minivan lead was a weak one but it was all they had right now. So Lydia sat in an uncomfortable orange plastic chair, in a rickety carrel housing a computer that might have been older than she was. The sun beating in through a window in the police station's computer center warmed her back as she entered into the Division of Motor Vehicles database the license-plate numbers of vehicles that had entered Cimarron State Park in the hours between Maria Lopez's time of death and the discovery of her body.

This was grunt work pure and simple but she had wanted to do it. Jeffrey and Morrow went with forensics to the service station to have a look at the priest's minivan. It was a reasonable thing to do, but it just didn't work for her. She couldn't reconcile the priest she had met with the killer in her mind. However, maybe the killer had access to the van, had been using it without the priest's knowledge. It was certainly worth looking into. But her time was better spent going over what they had. Morrow had been surprised that Lydia wanted to run the lists. But she knew that no one would be more likely to pick up an inconsistency or make a match than she would.

Meanwhile, the only prints recovered from the Lopez crime scene were Maria's and those matching Mike Urquia, who they already knew had been there. The killer must have been wearing gloves. It was also likely that he had worn gloves when delivering

Lydia's "gift" last night, as no prints or DNA had been found. A local homicide detective was visiting area shoestores and searching the Web for boot treads that matched the footprint left at the dump site. In the absence of any substantial physical evidence, the best they could hope for was a lucky break. And that Lydia's "buzz" would lead them to it.

So, she started with the list of 123 vehicles that had entered the park on the day following the Lopez murder. Of those cars, 60 had been rented from Albuquerque Airport rental-car offices, two were school buses shuttling kids in for a nature walk, and the remaining 61 belonged to private citizens in the area.

Going down the list of vehicles, she punched each plate number into the DMV database. On the screen before her a name, picture, and address popped up. She checked each name against the list of parishioners, then plugged it into VICAP, the FBI's database of violent offenders. If the plate was a rental, she would check the lists already delivered from the rental-car offices this morning to find the corresponding driver and go through the same cross-referencing process. She wanted to see faces, look into eyes—even if they were just license photos.

Armed with the list of church parishioners and volunteers, the log of visitors to Cimarron State Park, and lists of rental-car customers, Lydia had felt the "buzz" big time. She had *known* there was something hiding in the lists in front of her. But now nearly done with the list and no minivans, no matches with VICAP, and no church parishioners matching visitors to the park, she was starting to feel tired and frustrated. None of the people whose pictures popped up on the computer screen had a big tattoo on their forehead reading "Serial Killer." *You're missing something. Something so obvious.*

She entered the next plate number and it turned out to be

a rental. She crossed-referenced it with the lists and found that it was a green 2000 Jeep Grand Cherokee picked up at Avis at six P.M. the night Maria Lopez was murdered. It was rented to a Vince A. Gemiennes of 124 Black Canyon Road in Angel Fire, New Mexico. It wasn't a minivan but he was the only local resident to have rented a car that day. She entered his name into the DMV database and was surprised to be informed that there were no matches. *It must be a fake name.* She entered it into VICAP, hoping that it would pop up as an alias but she had the same results . . . no match. She sat for a moment, tapping her pen against the side of the carrel. She reached for her cell phone to call Jeffrey and then changed her mind. Instead, she wrote down the address Vince A. Gemiennes gave to Avis and left the station without a word to anyone.

She felt another momentary pang of guilt as she got into her Kompressor. *You should at least bring a uniformed officer with you,* she thought. But instead, she checked the Glock in her glove compartment to make sure it was loaded, raced out of the parking lot, and headed up Highway 64 toward Eagle Nest Lake alone.

She took the turnoff onto Black Canyon Road—though "road" was a vast overstatement for what basically consisted of a wide dirt trail. Heavily wooded by towering aspen on either side, the road was so dark, Lydia had to turn on her headlights to see the inconspicuous numbers on the widely spaced mailboxes. She was familiar with the road from her property search and she knew that each private drive led to the beautiful custom log "cabins" that were common in the resort area. Most of them had spectacular views of Eagle's Nest Lake and were wildly expensive. She went back and forth up the road looking for number 124 and eventually ascertained that it must be the only turnoff without a number and a mailbox.

She made a right off Black Canyon Road and took the steep, winding drive up until the trees parted and she reached a clearing where the drive ended. It was an empty lot. She took the Glock out of her glove compartment where she had put it as they left the house that morning, placed it in her bag, and got out of the car.

It was so quiet she could hear the sound of her engine cooling. She turned when she heard a quiet rustling and saw a doe staring at her, wide-eyed and poised for flight. The sky was moody, scattered with clouds, and the air hinted of cooler temperatures on the way. She smelled pine and the scent of burning wood as she looked down into the valley, onto Eagle's Nest Lake surrounded by the Touch-Me-Not Mountains. It was a spectacular view and it dawned on Lydia slowly that she had seen it before—had, in fact, been at this very lot.

The real estate agent she had spoken to had shown her this property, thinking Lydia might want to design and build her own house, since Lydia's ideas about what she wanted were so "particular," as the real estate agent haltingly phrased it. And though it was a beautiful piece of property, Lydia hadn't liked that she could see other people's homes from the lot.

Her mind began to race. She looked at the piece of paper in her hand at the name written there. Vince A. Gemiennes . . . There was something about the name, something off and something familiar at the same time. It was too big a coincidence that the address she had found was an empty lot she herself had almost purchased. But if she had been led here, then this man had constructed all of his planning to do that, and it would mean he had been watching her for years. She wasn't sure which of those two possibilities was more far-fetched. Had the killer somehow known she would become involved in the solving of his crimes? Had she somehow been part of his design all along? The thought chilled her as she mentally retraced her visits to New Mexico.

She had first visited the Santa Fe and Angel Fire areas nearly three years ago when she had come to Albuquerque for a book signing. As soon as she first stepped foot off the plane, she felt like she had come home. It was something about the way the air smelled, about the sky and the stars that seemed to wrap around her like a blanket. It was something about the buildings—how they were small and warm, how there was a coziness, a womblike comfort to their interiors. And then there was the terrain, the gorgeous mountains, the hot springs, the trees in the highlands, the desert. It just felt like heaven to her and after she had left, she'd kept longing to return, so much so that she'd bought property here.

The book signing had been held at a Barnes and Noble in Albuquerque. She tried to remember now if there had been anyone there who'd imprinted on her memory as especially odd, but there had been so many book signings between now and then in so many Barnes and Nobles across the country. And there were always one or two freaks that had to be escorted from the signing table. She just didn't pay attention anymore.

She thought about all the various people she had encountered during the purchase of her home: real-estate brokers, mortgage brokers, maid service, lawn maintenance people, locksmiths. She could think of nothing that had made her uneasy, no one who had seemed off to her.

"What do you want from me? And why did you want me to come here?" she said softly. She thought about the pen he had left for her and the note: *Vengeance is mine.* Did he want to wreak vengeance on her? Did he perceive her as having wronged him in some way? Had she written about him and offended him?

She walked the edge of the clearing, peering down a slight slope that led to a heavily forested area. She could see the windows of the neighboring house through the pine glinting in the sunlight. She sidled down into the trees, holding on to branches to keep her balance, her lizard-skin boots not finding much of a hold in the dirt. Once she reached level ground, she walked away from the clearing, her eyes on the forest floor, scanning for anything left by humans . . . a matchbook, a cigarette butt, a soda can, anything. She heard a soft rustle of leaves to her left and turned, expecting to see the doe again but there was nothing there. The sun moved behind a patch of cloud and it became more difficult to see the ground. Then about fifty feet in front of her she saw, mingled in with the green, red, and brown of nature's palette, a square inch of pure white.

She continued to move toward the white patch, when she was startled by her cell phone. "Hello?"

"Where are you? The desk sergeant said you took off out of here like you were being chased by a ghost."

"Hold on a second."

"Lydia . . . Lydia . . ."

His voice was distant as she bent down and started brushing aside the leaves and dirt. Sticking out of the ground was a soft corner of plastic. She moved away from it, not wanting to touch anything and contaminate the scene any more than she already had.

"Jeff," she said into the phone, as she looked around her into the darkness of the trees.

"Lydia, where the fuck are you?"

"I'm at 124 Black Canyon Road, there's no marker, but it's the only drive without one on the street. You better come with Morrow. We're going to need the ME and all the usual suspects."

"What have you found?"

"I think someone's been buried here."

Jeffrey's voice was soft, but authoritative enough to hold rapt the room of men and women gathered to discuss what was now the first serial-murder case the jurisdiction had ever seen. In the room dimmed by pulled shades, Lydia, Chief Morrow, Henry Wizner, and several local police officers sat around the conference table taking notes. The shifting tray of slides in the projector that Morrow operated punctuated Jeffrey's comments. Images of gore and decay reflected on the screen.

"We've asked Private Investigator Jeffrey Mark and Lydia Strong to be involved in what we now consider to be a serial-offender situation, because of their vast experience in this area," Chief Morrow had said by way of introduction between them and his department. "Having them here allows us to conduct this investigation without calling in the FBI, which no one wants. So I will ask that you give them the same amount of respect that you give me, and take their orders as you take mine, and by the time the feds hear about this, we'll all be heroes instead of local yokels that couldn't handle the situation ourselves."

"The bodies of Christine and Harold Wallace were found today," Jeffrey began. "So now we have three corpses missing their hearts. We don't know where the killer is removing them or why. We do know that the locations where he's dumped the bodies are not the locations of the kill. As far as evidence goes, we have turned up nothing except a partial footprint at the Lopez dump site.

"Due to some very unglamorous but very important

legwork—no pun intended—on the part of Homicide Detective Raymond Barnes," Jeffrey continued, motioning to a heavyset man with a military bearing and haircut, "we have determined this boot to be a Timberland Toledo with a rubber lug sole. This doesn't help much because it's a popular boot sold in virtually every men's retail shoestore in the area.

"The bodies of Christine and Harold Wallace were in bad shape. But we are trying to determine at this point whether he removed their hearts after he killed them or before."

"Why is that significant?" asked one officer.

The image of Christine and Harold's gutted bodies flashed on the screen behind Jeffrey. "Because it tells us exactly how sick a fuck we're dealing with."

A ripple of uncomfortable laughter moved through the room.

"Because," Jeffrey continued, more seriously, "the more we know about what he does, the closer we are to why he does it. The more we understand about his motivations, the more we under-stand him, and the better profile we have.

"So this is what we know about him: His MO is to over-power his victims, either incapacitate or kill them, take them alive or dead to another location, and then to dump their bodies in a third location. The killer's signature behavior is that he removes their hearts. For those of you that missed last week's episode of *Profiler,* a 'signature behavior' or 'aspect' is something that an of-fender does above and beyond what he needs to do to commit the offense. It's something he does to satisfy his emotional needs. Removing the heart is one part of it. I believe that what he does with the heart is another part of it. We're in the dark as to what the underlying motivation is at this point.

"But we know enough to draw a decent profile. We know that he is an 'inadequate' type by the way he blitz-attacked Maria

Lopez; he used as much force as he had to subdue her. He forced his way into her apartment and put chloroform to her face. When that didn't work, he killed her there. We know he is highly organized, in that it was necessary for him to burglarize the supply warehouse and set up an operating room somewhere, stalk his victims, perform his sick 'surgery,' and dump the bodies—all without getting caught. He is likely to be white and in his mid- to late thirties, on the older side of the traditional serial-killer profile, because it takes maturity, organization, and skill to do what he is doing. We are probably looking for a person with some medical background but probably not an actual doctor or surgeon. More like a buff, someone that would have liked to have been a doctor but failed in some way. He holds down a job somewhere. He probably lives alone or he has a place separate from his home where he's doing his crime.

"The other notable element is that this killer seems to have an agenda other than the pleasure of the kill. He wants something else. He has a plan—either real or imagined. Ms. Strong seems to be a part of that agenda." A picture of the items the killer had left on Lydia's doorstep appeared on the screen.

"The message he left for her indicates he wants some kind of 'vengeance.' Whether he wanted revenge on his victims, whether he wants it from Ms. Strong, we can't be sure."

A collage of photos of the victims' faces loomed on the screen behind him. "So far, the victims are all different physically, crossing age, gender, and racial lines. But they all attended the same church with varying degrees of regularity. They were all leading somewhat lonely lives with checkered pasts. Christine and Harold had extensive records of drug abuse and domestic violence. Shawna was a chronic runaway and a discipline problem. Maria allegedly accepted money for sex. We can see by the way he disposes of the bodies that he is remorseless. These people are less than trash to him. He did not have intimate connections to them in life."

The image of Maria Lopez's trashed apartment was next on the screen. "We were hopeful that Maria Lopez's apartment would contain some physical evidence. But the only hair we found we matched to Maria Lopez and Michael Urquia, who has been eliminated as a suspect. Same deal with the fingerprints. We found some fibers at the scene, but it takes a while to sort through that, and State is working on it. We found blood and skin underneath Lopez's fingernails that has been sent to the lab for DNA testing . . . we all know that takes forever. Same with the bodies of Christine and Harold—checking for blood or DNA that doesn't match theirs. Again, it's going to take a few days. And then it will only help us if our killer has been entered into the system somewhere for some other offense.

"We don't know for certain if anything was missing from the victims' personal belongings. Shawna Fox, whose body we have not recovered and who may or may not be one of the victims—though we believe she is—took nothing with her when she left her foster parents' home. Neither her foster parents nor her boyfriend Greg noticed anything missing from her belongings. In other words, we're not sure if he's collecting trophies."

Lydia, sitting in a darkened corner in the back of the room, had been listening intently to the facts though she was more than familiar with them at this point, hoping that there was something that she missed. But when Jeffrey mentioned trophies, the image of her mother's garnet earring occupied Lydia's mind again for a moment. She remembered it glittering in the palm of Jeffrey's hand as he'd returned it to her, and she shivered.

"Chief Morrow," said Jeffrey, "this is the plan of attack I suggest. First, you need several stakeouts. One at each site where we found bodies because killers often return to the scene to relive their kill. And one at the Church of the Holy Name because all the victims were parishioners there. And one at the home of Lydia Strong. He has likely developed an obsession with her, and we can expect to see him there again.

"All officers are advised to be on the lookout for someone fitting the profile driving a green or other dark-colored minivan. You can always find a good excuse to pull someone over if you look hard enough.

"Rental-car companies have been advised to alert us if someone using the name Vince A. Gemiennes tries to rent a car. This was the name, obviously a fake, someone used yesterday to rent a 2000 Jeep Grand Cherokee, which has since been impounded. The address that was left led Lydia to Christine and Harold Wallace's bodies today. This could have been a huge break for us but apparently it was a very busy day at Avis yesterday and none of the three women working the counter remember this person enough to give a description. We have them here at the station now, looking over airport security tapes, hoping they will see someone that jogs their memory. Unfortunately, there is no camera directly on the Avis rental desk."

"How did he rent a car? He had a fake credit card and driver's license?" asked one uniformed officer.

"Well, we're not a hundred percent positive. In the file, there is neither the imprint of the card or a copy of the license as there should be. All the girls insist that no one could have rented a car without those things. But the records have disappeared."

"But it's possible that he could be walking around making purchases with a fake credit card."

"Yes, and area merchants are being notified via fax and e-mail to be on the lookout for someone using that name."

Lydia wrote down the name again in her notebook, Jeffrey's voice fading to background noise. It was an odd name, clearly fake since there was no record of it at any of the government offices. She traced the letters. Had she heard it before? Did she somehow know this person? She had the sense she was missing something.

Jeffrey paused and looked down at his notes. "Also, someone should start going through records of local arrests over the last two years. We are looking for sex crimes, domestic violence, pedophilia, animal mutilation. Keep the profile in mind, though. And remember also that we are looking for someone with a medical background.

"One of your people should get online with VICAP and plug in the elements of this case, see if anyone turns up. Though it's highly unlikely, we could have a traveler. Remember Johansen?"

"Yeah," Lydia replied, shaking her head and speaking up for the first time. "The traveling salesman who liked to pick up women in bars. He was an attractive guy. When a woman checked him out, he took her back to her apartment, strangled her, gouged her eyes out, and cut off her breasts. Seven victims, all found in different poses across the country. We finally figured out that he was positioning the bodies in the shape of letters. By the end, he'd spelled out 'FUCK YOU.' "

"That's the one," Jeffrey said, and the local officers groaned.

"Someone else," Jeffrey continued, "needs to start going over the crime-scene notes and photographs. Go back to the locations and poke around, get the feel of them, make sure nothing was missed. Then start going to places like the bar, the restaurant where Maria worked, the church. Observe, ask questions, start making people uncomfortable.

"Does anybody have any questions?"

When no one spoke, Morrow stood up. "Okay. Let's get to

work," he said, as he starting handing out assignments to different officers at the table. In pairs the officers filed out, each with their tasks before them, looking a little overwhelmed, Lydia thought.

"Is there anything else you think I should do, Jeff?" Morrow asked when he was finished.

"Chief, you are the hub of this whole operation. You probably have a better overall picture of this community and its crime activity than anyone does. Spend time thinking back on anything over the last few months or even as long as a year that has struck a chord with you."

"You got it," Morrow said, with alacrity. He walked away feeling like the clumsy kid finally chosen to play on the softball team.

Jeffrey looked around the room for Lydia, then caught sight of her through the window, leaning against her car, smoking and staring off into space. She was waiting for him. He walked out of the station house and approached the car. "I'm not letting you out of my sight until this is over. And don't even think of pulling another stunt like you pulled this afternoon."

"Yes sir," she answered sarcastically.

"Lydia, I'm serious. There's no reason for you to be a renegade. What were you hoping to prove by going there alone?"

"Nothing," she said, shrugging. "I just didn't want to wait for you to get back."

"But you're not going to do anything like that again, right?"

"Right."

"I want to drive," he said, nudging her aside playfully with his shoulder and reaching for the driver's-side door.

chapter seventeen

It was late evening before Jeffrey and Lydia returned to her house. They stopped at the bottom of the drive and picked up the mail, which Lydia sorted through as they pulled into her garage.

"Any letters from the president?" asked Jeffrey, after noticing a prison seal on one of the envelopes.

"The president?"

"The president of your fan club?"

Most of the letters that arrived from her fan club of the world's most sick and twisted Lydia threw away unopened, the way they had been forwarded from her publisher's office, particularly those that came from correctional facilities across the country. Initially she had been interested enough in what these people had to say to her to open them. A lot of them were the incoherent ramblings of damaged minds; some were from families of murder victims. Some were from people who claimed to be serial killers on the loose and she forwarded those to the FBI. But there was a person who had written to her every month since the publication of *With a Vengeance.*

When she received the first letter, in a way, she wasn't even surprised.

Dear Bitch,

I fucked your mother and then I killed her. She was very satisfying.

I liked your book. You really put your finger on it. You really got into my head. But you know that, don't you.

You like being inside my head? It makes you feel like you understand? Maybe you do. Maybe you don't. Maybe I can make you understand a whole lot better one day.

I take great satisfaction in you, too. I made you what you are today. Don't forget it.

Fuck you,
Jed McIntyre

After the first letter, Jeffrey called the publisher's office and insisted that her mail be screened from that point forward. Lydia's editor, appalled by the incident, agreed. But Lydia called her back and asked that they continue to forward her mail unopened.

She wanted his letters. She needed them.

She never opened them. They just sat in a locked drawer in her desk, whispering profanity. But as long as she kept getting those letters with the prison stamp on them, she knew where he was. Locked away, forever. They reminded her that he was a mentally ill man and not a demon. Not a demon with supernatural powers who could reach through the earth from the depths of hell and snatch her away.

Jeffrey never stopped nagging her about the letters. But, as usual, Lydia could not be swayed. And Jeffrey had long since given up, feeling rage rise in his chest whenever he thought about the first letter.

But as they walked in the front door and he caught sight of the letter in her hand—indeed a letter from Jed McIntyre—with the rest of the mail she collected from the box, he felt his throat constrict with anger. He slipped it from the pile when she dropped it on the kitchen table.

"Jesus, Lydia, what the fuck do you do with these?"

"At least I know where he is."

"By not returning these, you're allowing him to perpetuate whatever fantasies he's having about you."

"Jeffrey, don't we have enough to deal with right now without rehashing this?"

He handed the letter back to her without a word and opened the refrigerator, looking for a beer. She stared at his profile cast in the light. She could see the anger in his set jaw. She stood behind him and wrapped her arms around his waist.

"Don't be angry. Try to understand."

He placed his arms over hers and leaned back into her. "It makes me crazy to think of him even *thinking* of you."

"I know but it's all right. He can't hurt me," she said, turning him around.

"Okay," he said, and gave her a sad smile.

She left him and walked up the stairs to her bedroom. As she flipped on the light, she stopped cold in the door frame. Her lingerie drawer stood open and its contents had been cast to the floor. On the full-length mirror that stood beside the dresser was a message written in red lipstick.

o righteous god, who searches minds and hearts, bring to an end the violence of the wicked and make the righteous secure.

Jeffrey came up behind her. "Lydia, did you leave the back door unlocked?" he asked.

"No," she answered, turning to him, her face flushed. A moment passed as she heard him inhale sharply and felt him stiffen as he registered the message on the mirror.

Instinctively, he reached for the .38 he'd been carrying. "Stay right where you are. Don't touch anything," he called as he left the room and began searching the house.

But she knew even as she heard Jeffrey slamming open doors, that the killer was gone. Somehow, somewhere, he had seen her, been close enough to her to want her. He knew enough to know when she would not be here. And he wanted her to know that he had been here. She smiled, in spite of the fear twisting in her belly. The desire to find him, to finish him, was more powerful than her desire to breathe. She leaned against the doorjamb, shaking with an adrenaline rush. *I am not a victim, and I'll be fucked if I'm going to let some backwater psycho turn me into one.*

"He broke into the breaker box behind the house and turned the system off. That's how he got in. But he's gone now."

"I know," she said, pulling her cell phone from her pocket and dialing Morrow from her speed dial. "It's Lydia Strong. We've had another intruder at my home . . . Okay . . . we'll be here."

Jeffrey walked past her and stood staring at Lydia's lingerie. The rage, the fear that churned inside him, blurred his vision. It was clear to him that if he lost her now, all his patience, all his resolve would have been for nothing. His love for her would be a stone swallowed whole, unexpressed, unrequited, sitting in his heart for the rest of his life. If anything ever happened to her, he might as well be dead, too. *"Never love anything so much that if it goes away your whole world turns black."* Too late. Too fucking late.

She could see his face in the mirror that hung on the wall over the dresser. The pain etched there frightened her. "Jeffrey?" Her voice was a plea, soft but urgent.

He turned and walked over to her, grabbed her hard into him, burying his face in her hair. "I want you to leave here until this is over," he said urgently. "Please, Lydia."

"I can't, Jeffrey, you know that."

"Lydia . . ."

She reached up and touched his face, smoothing the anger from his brow, ran her fingers through his hair. And then he was covering her face in kisses.

"I can't do this anymore, Lydia. I can't pretend that I'm going to leave you when this is over and everything is going to be as it has always been. I can't pretend that I don't think about you every day and wish you were beside me every night. I can't hold you like I'm your friend when I've wanted so much more for years. I can't pretend that I'm not in love with you. I'm sorry, Lydia. I love you. I've always loved you."

A thousand thoughts swirled in her head: her mother, her father, Jed McIntyre, the killer they hunted now. All this death and tragedy in her life and in the lives of others. Love had never brought her mother anything but pain. Lydia had lost or been disappointed by so many people, except for Jeffrey. She thought of Maria Lopez, how no one had claimed her body, how she had been disconnected from the world. *How much more connected am I? If you don't love anyone, then you don't lose anyone . . . but nobody loves you, either. Do I keep him at bay because it keeps him loving me and I don't have to love him back? So I don't have to give him my heart?*

She closed her eyes against tears, against the fears. And when she opened them he was watching her, so intently, with so much love. In his face, so beautiful to her, so familiar, she saw home.

"I love you, too," she whispered. "You know I always have. You must know."

His mouth on hers tasted like the ocean, salty, warm. She felt his urgency, his desire on her tongue. "I'm not going to let you move in close and then back a mile away from me again."

"I know. I don't want that anymore either. I'm tired. Tired of fighting everything. Tired of pretending I don't need you. I do. I have, probably, since the first day I met you."

They were startled by a pounding on the front door.

She didn't want to let go of him, didn't want to move from his arms and face the nightmare they found themselves in now. She'd chased this monster and now the monster was chasing her. She hated herself suddenly for inviting this horror into their lives. But there was no choice now but to face it down.

"That must be the police," she said.

"I know. I don't want to let this moment pass."

"It's okay," she said, and smiled. "We have all the time in the world."

Lydia sat on the couch in the living room as Jeffrey let the police in. Chief Morrow was the first person through the door.

"How did he get through the alarm system?" he asked Jeffrey.

"The breaker box is outside the house. He forced the lock and turned off the alarm. These things are supposed to default to sounding an alarm in that case, but this one didn't," answered Jeffrey. "Basically it looks like when the power went out, the house opened wide."

"Shit," said Morrow. "The stakeout starts tonight on the twelve-to-eight shift. I couldn't start it sooner than that. We're short-staffed."

"A day late and a dollar short," said Lydia from her place on the couch. "As usual."

"It's no one's fault, Chief," Jeffrey said quickly. "Let's just make sure we've got someone on this house day and night from this point forward. On foot, on the property, not sitting in a car down at the bottom of the drive."

The chief nodded his head, his face flushed with embarrassment and anger. He followed Jeffrey up the stairs and into the bedroom to inspect the scene.

Lydia stayed on the couch downstairs, her legs pulled up to her chest and her arms wrapped tightly around them. She did not want to be in the room while the police dusted for fingerprints. She did not want to see that message again, which she was sure was from Psalms. *"O Righteous God, who searches minds and hearts . . ."*

She heard Jeffrey's voice but couldn't make out what he was saying. He had his professional voice on—the one that made everyone jump, the one that accepted no excuses and no hesitation. She always envied him that. It seemed to come so naturally to him, as if he were born with an authority that no one questioned.

She was not afraid. It was more like every atom in her body was buzzing with electricity. She scanned her memory for strange faces, things that had caught her attention fleetingly but were dismissed, a car she'd seen more than once. Anything that could have been a warning. But there was nothing. She would not have missed something like that. She knew it. He was watching her from the periphery of her life, just out of sight but close enough to touch. And she hadn't even known it.

She thought about the name again. It had been bothering her—there was something about it. She grabbed a pen and paper from the drawer in the coffee table beside her and wrote the name again; she started rearranging the letters. When she realized, it was so simple, she almost laughed. "Vince A. Gemiennes" was an anagram for "*Vengeance is mine.*"

"Unbelievable," she muttered.

What were the odds? Her mother had died at the hands of a serial killer and now she was being stalked by one. Maybe there was some genetic coding that marked her as a victim. The thought made her shudder. Jed McIntyre had chosen his victims because they were so valuable to the people who loved them—their children, specifically. This bastard chooses them . . . why?

Shawna, Maria, Christine, and Harold were strangers, ghosts in this world. Unconnected. Disposable. But there was some reason the killer had wanted vengeance on them. They were religious people, though. They went to church. But there was something she was missing. Something so obvious. *"O Righteous God, who searches minds and hearts . . ."*

The fact that he had taken such a risk in coming to her house was an indicator that he was losing control of his desires. He would start making mistakes now. And she was there—waiting for him, like he'd waited for his victims. And he'd pay, the way she'd always wanted to make Jed McIntyre pay. *I am nobody's fucking victim.*

But she was so tired. It was too much . . . the anniversary of her mother's death, a second house call from a serial killer, and now Jeffrey. She felt as if her head and her heart were going to explode.

One by one they left, the cops, the technicians, the photographer. Everyone had hoped that the killer had jacked off in the bedroom, leaving behind some good DNA, but no such luck. Lydia remained on the couch in the dark, staring out the window into the black night sky. Finally, when they were alone, Jeffrey joined her. He sat down beside her and opened his arms to her and she slid into their protective fold. She told him about the name.

"I've been thinking," she said.

"About . . ."

"What they have in common."

"And . . . ?"

"Well, they were religious to a degree, right? But they all committed actions that could be considered sins. All of them could have been considered sinful people."

"O Righteous God, who searches minds and hearts, bring to an end the violence of the wicked and make the righteous secure . . ." Jeffrey recited the message on her mirror.

"Yes."

"God forgives sins."

"But maybe our killer doesn't."

"And he takes their hearts because . . ."

"Because their hearts are false, because they are untrue to God."

"Jesus."

"Does he think I am untrue to God? Has he seen me at the church but thinks I write of godless things? That I've done sinful things?"

"I don't know."

"I have, you know."

"It's all right."

"Is it?"

"Yes. As long as I'm alive no one will ever hurt you. I promise you that. I swear to God."

She didn't want to tell him about the things she'd done, the faceless men she'd sought to bring some ridiculous semblance of love into her life. She didn't want to tell him how alone she'd finally realized she was and how much she needed him. And how she still missed her mother every day. How broken inside she felt, and that all these broken people, with their lonely, empty lives, all these people who no one mourned, were like mirrors for her. And how she couldn't bear it anymore, the horrible aloneness of her life. So instead she reached for his face and kissed him gently on the mouth.

With deft fingers he unbuttoned her blouse, his mouth never leaving hers until he slid the garment off her shoulders, let it fall to the floor. He drew in a sharp breath at her beauty and kissed the delicate slope of her shoulder, the soft nape of her neck. He let her pull his T-shirt off, and groaned as her lips glanced his chest and alighted on the scar on his shoulder. He felt her fingers unbutton his jeans and he grew hard for her.

She stood and offered him her hand and led him up the stairs to his bed, not wanting to face the mess in her bedroom. She stripped off the rest of her clothes and stood before him. He traced the lines of her body with reverent hands, kissing her breasts, then running his lips down to her tight belly, then to the sacred place below. Her moans, her hands in his hair, brought him to his knees. Then he rose and lifted her onto the bed. She pulled off his jeans, and touched him with a tenderness he had never known, stroking him, caressing him. His pleasure was so intense, he could make no sound as he entered her.

She could feel the power of his desire as he thrust himself deeply inside her. Slowly, gently at first, then harder, more urgent. His arms held her as close to him as she could be and his lips were on hers with an insatiable hunger. She had dreamed of this but never had she imagined it so beautifully, never had she realized how much she loved him, how strong was her desire—or his. And as he repeated her name over and over like a prayer, she gave in to the building crescendo of her pleasure as they came together.

They lay wrapped around each other beneath the moonlight that slipped into the room between passing clouds, not speaking, not sleeping, but savoring each other.

"I'll never leave you now, you realize that," he said, lifting his head to look into her eyes.

"I know," she said and smiled. "That night in the hospital, Jeffrey?"

"Yeah, I wanted to tell you then. But you stopped me."

"If I had known the sex was going to be this good, I wouldn't have."

Moving past their awe of what had happened between them, they laughed. It was a laughter full of relief, comfort, of homecoming.

chapter eighteen

Even as he knelt before the altar, rosary in his hands, he could not feel the presence of God. There had been times in prayer when Father Luis had felt the presence of the Lord so profoundly that it had made him weep. But today, he was alone. Perhaps, he considered, he had been for the past thirty years. What use would God have for a priest whose whole life was a lie? Who had done nothing but lie since the day of Juno's birth?

In his mind he could argue the existence of God. In his actions, he affirmed his faith in the Church. But his heart seized with doubt in the face of the violence, poverty, and pain he witnessed in the lives of his parishioners, in the news of his world. It was an ache within him that did not begin with the death of his sister but had solidified that day, became like the benign tumor he had on the bottom of his foot which he felt only when it rained, but then every step was agony.

He had prayed feverishly since the police had visited, asking for guidance, for a sign. But no answers came. Rather, no different answers came. Father Luis knew it was time for Juno to know the truth of his past. Perhaps God had abandoned the priest in his prayers because he was really only asking for a reason to excuse further cowardice, more lies.

When Luis looked at Juno, he was sometimes overwhelmed

with feelings of love and tenderness. As a child, Juno was so delicate, so sensitive, the picture of cherubic innocence. Luis wanted only to protect him within the walls of the church. In this, at least, he had not failed.

Juno's blindness kept him necessarily isolated and the church kept him sheltered. Interaction with other children had been limited to mass and Sunday school. Juno had never heard the sound of a television set. His uncle kept an old transistor radio but very few channels came in clearly except a classical-music station and the local NPR affiliate.

Father Luis read to him from the paper, so Juno was not ignorant. He had an awareness of world events, technological advances, famous people. But these things existed in another universe, a place Juno would never visit. Juno was more concerned with his guitar, with the business of the church and the people who sought his counsel, than he was with a celebrity murder trial or the Mars probe. His uncle was secretly grateful Juno lacked the curiosity that could only bring him pain and harm, that could only expose a world far less peaceful than Juno's, a truth more terrible than anything he could conceive.

He had always planned to tell Juno the truth about his past. But when the boy put the inevitable questions to him, Father Luis had woven an extraordinary tale. Juno was nine years old when he heard rumors of how his parents had died. And instead of delivering the truth his nephew deserved, when confronted the priest lied. The story differed little from the Scriptures read to him every day, and Juno never questioned its veracity, even as he grew older. Much as he never questioned the story of Noah's Ark, or the Garden of Eden, or the parting of the Red Sea. For Juno this was truth, history. This was what his uncle and his heart told him.

But the real story of his mother and father and how they had died was not a fairy tale. It was as ugly and real as the world could be. In grief after his sister's death, the priest had written a narrative of the events to share with the boy one day, something he hoped would help him to see into his mother's heart and know the truth of her motivations.

"Care for him and make him know me." His sister's dying words haunted him. He had failed her yet again.

The truth had stayed locked away in the drawer in his desk for the last thirty-five years, bundled by a piece of string with the documents of Juno's life—his birth certificate, his Social Security card. The pages were creased and yellowed and no one had laid eyes on it except the priest. Luis had always told himself, *I have done this to protect Juno. Does he not suffer hardship enough?*

But he could feel the cold eye of God on him. Luis knew he was also protecting himself from questions he could not answer even now.

It was late and the church was dark, with only the light of a few altar candles. The New Mexico night was silent. Juno was asleep. But not for long. Father Luis blew out the candles and walked toward Juno's closed bedroom door. As he reached for the iron knob, he knew that he must wake Juno now and tell him or he never would—that he would lie until the day he died.

He startled at a sound from behind the church. Was it the back door? Had he been careless again and left it open? Grateful for one last delay, he walked back into the church. The door to the garden did stand open. And he could see a light coming in from outside. Not the mounted light, but the beam from a flashlight. It was obvious he should call the police. Yet he didn't. He walked quietly toward the light, hearing as he grew closer the rhythmic sound of someone digging in the dirt.

He tried to peer through the opening of the door. But whoever was in the garden stood beyond the periphery of what the priest could see while remaining unseen. The digging stopped as the priest pushed open the door and stepped out into the garden. The man he saw there, he knew well.

"We've been worried about you, my son. Where have you been?"

"I've been so busy, Father. So very busy," the man answered with an unusual solemnity.

"What are you doing?" The priest looked down at the head of the shovel, and something unspeakable, in the beam of the flashlight. The cold finger of fear pressed into his belly. He took a step backward, the unformed thoughts he'd only vaguely considered when speaking to the police earlier, coming into horrifying focus now. He stared at the man before him and searched his face for the man he knew, and saw no trace. The wild, shifting eyes, the tousled hair, the mouth that twitched horribly between smile and sneer, were the features of a mad stranger.

"My son," Father Luis began, voice quavering, "no sin is so great that the Lord will not forgive you. Come with me."

"I don't think so, Father. I have too much of the Lord's work left to do. I know you could never understand, even though you are a man of God."

In the last moment, the priest tried to run. But the killer was on him with the deadly speed and grace of a lion on a gazelle. The priest's legs buckled and he lay dying in silence with a scalpel to the throat, staring with his dying eyes into the stars. The killer sat on top of Father Luis's chest and watched the blood drain from his neck into the fresh, black earth until he was dead. *"Ashes to ashes, dust to dust."* He waited and was not surprised when the angel appeared to him again.

"Daddy."

He knew better now than to try to touch his son. It only made him go away. He just sat and stared at the beautiful child. The priest held the little boy's hand. The killer was comforted to see how peaceful he looked. Of course, he knew he had had no choice but to kill Father Luis. But still, Father Luis was such a good man. It was a shame he had come outside when he did.

"Daddy, I'll take him to God. It's the only place he ever really wanted to go anyway. You did the right thing. You always do."

"Thank you, son."

They turned their backs on him and walked into the desert night, fading into nothing. He was overcome with fatigue. So tired, but so much work before him. And yet another grave to dig.

But first, to finish the task at hand. He walked away from the priest's lifeless body and returned to the hole he had dug. It was not the first hole he had made in the little garden.

" 'For look, the wicked bend their bows; they set their arrows against the strings to shoot from the shadows at the upright heart,' " he prayed, as he removed Maria Lopez's heart from the jar of formaldehyde and placed it in the black wet earth.

His thoughts returned to Lydia Strong. He remembered the day she had stood in this garden. He could see from the look on her face that she sensed something. Of course she could never have imagined or intuited what was buried there. But she would know soon enough. He filled the hole, replaced the flower that was growing there, packing the earth in around the roots and the stem. He pointed the flashlight and assured himself that the ground did not seem disturbed. Then he walked to the van and took a body bag from the back. He lay it on the ground and then rolled the priest's body into it, zipping it quietly.

chapter nineteen

Greg stood at the sink, washing up the breakfast plates and watching the man standing outside the garage waiting for service. Though the sun was just up, his father, Joe, would have been in the shop already. But he had left an hour ago, heading to Albuquerque looking for some used parts he needed. Greg dried the dishes and left them on the counter atop a tattered blue dish rag, never taking his eyes off the pacing man and his green mini-van. There was something off and edgy about the man. Something that made Greg hesitate before going outside. But Greg decided he was just being silly, spooked by his conversation with Lydia Strong, and headed outside.

"Been waiting long, sir?" he called.

"No, no. Sorry to come at this hour, but I have to be at work soon and I heard you opened early," the man said, moving toward Greg.

"What seems to be the problem?"

"I'm having a bit of trouble with the ignition. It doesn't seem to catch right away—it sort of stutters." The man demonstrated, and the van coughed as he twisted the ignition a couple of times, then hummed to life.

"Well, why don't you pull it inside and I'll have a look."

"Um," the man said slowly, looking Greg dead in the eye, "how long do you think this will take? I don't have much time."

"Just a minute. If it's anything serious, then you can bring it on back later when you're finished with work."

The man nodded and then pulled the van into the garage when Greg lifted the heavy door open.

There was something about this man Greg didn't like. There was something in his gaze that seemed off balance, that made Greg a bit uneasy. His eyes were bloodshot and his thinning hair looked as if it hadn't been washed in days. Greg couldn't imagine where he was going to work, in heavily muddied jeans and a black sweatshirt that looked like it had been stained with oil or paint.

A quick check under the steering column revealed two loose ignition wires which Greg quickly tightened. He tested the ignition and the engine caught right away. Good. Now the guy could leave.

"Just a second," Greg said to the man, "let me just check one more thing." He couldn't believe what he was doing and he didn't know why, but he slipped under the car. He pulled a pen out of his pocket and wrote the vehicle-identification number on his arm where he could pull his sleeve back down over it.

"Well, sir. It was just a couple of loose wires. I tightened them and you've got nothing to worry about."

"Thanks. How much do I owe you?"

"Forget it; it really was no trouble."

"Sure?"

"Yeah. My father would kill me, says I'm not much of a businessman. But I just can't see charging people for nothing. So maybe you'll bring your car back when there's a real problem or tell your friends about our garage."

"You bet. Thanks a lot. Mind if I use your restroom?"

"Outside and around back," said Greg, following him out.

When the man rounded the corner of the building, Greg wrote down the license-plate number. It was probably a silly thing to do, there were so many green minivans around.

The sky was a crystalline blue and there was a light breeze. Greg looked up and immediately saw two vultures circling low off in the distance. *Today was something's last sunrise,* thought Greg. He didn't notice the driver coming up fast behind him as he turned and headed back into the garage.

chapter twenty

Jeffrey awoke before Lydia the following morning and lay beside her, watching her breathe, watching the delicate rise and fall of her chest. One arm was draped over her rib cage, one thrown above her head, hair spread around her pillow. He brushed a jet-black strand from her cheek and allowed himself to be overwhelmed. She opened her eyes slightly, peered at him through lowered lids, and smiled.

"Feel okay?" she asked.

"Never better. You?"

"I feel good," she said simply. "This feels . . ."

"Natural?"

"Yeah. I just thought it might be weird, after all these years, to wake up beside you like this. But it feels like I'm finally in the right place, you know?"

"I know," he said kissing her lightly on the mouth.

"The temptation is to lie here all day with you, but we really need to get moving," said Lydia as she sighed, sitting up and looking at the clock.

"You're right," he said, the memory of last night's events and the knowledge that Lydia was in danger moving over his thoughts like a stormcloud. "Let's go talk to Benny Savroy."

———

The home of Benjamin Savroy and his mother, Greta, looked like a gingerbread house in all its impossible charm and sweetness. Painted red with white shutters, each windowsill held a colorful flowerbox. The lawn was perfectly manicured and lined with lush green shrubs and a white picket fence. Lydia and Jeffrey approached the house by its cobblestone walkway. To the right of the path was a gorgeous flower garden, as lush and well tended as the church garden. She noted many of the same plants and the same wet black earth that she had seen at the Holy Name. She wondered if Benny tended both gardens.

They were greeted at the door by a woman who looked like everyone's favorite grandmother. Small and plump, with thick gray hair pulled into a braided bun, Greta was wearing a red T-shirt under a denim jumper. Her ruddy complexion seemed to glow and her blue eyes sparkled with warmth and kindness.

"Listen," she said with an unmistakable New York accent, blocking the doorway, "Father Luis called to say you private investigators might be dropping by. I don't want anyone bothering my son. He's a good boy and he never causes trouble."

"Mrs. Savroy—" began Lydia.

"*Ms.,*" she interrupted.

"Ms. Savroy, we don't want to bother your son. We just want to ask him a few questions."

"Why?"

"In connection with the murders of Maria Lopez and Christine and Harold Wallace, and the disappearance of Shawna Fox, all members of the Church of the Holy Name," said Jeffrey. "We are asking the parishioners and volunteers of the church questions to determine if they have seen or heard anything unusual."

"If you think my son had anything to do with that, you're

nuts," said Greta, flushed and nearly shaking with anger. "He has the mental capacity of a twelve-year-old."

Lydia found her reaction defensive and incongruous with the situation, watching as the woman furiously wrung the dishtowel she held in her hand.

"No, ma'am," said Jeffrey, his tone at once soothing and authoritative, "we just want to know if he's seen anything. You can cooperate with us, or we can have the police come and take him in for questioning."

She considered Jeffrey for a minute, eyes narrowed, hands wringing.

"If you upset him, there's going to be hell to pay," she said as she stepped aside, then led them down the hall to a cozy den. Benny sat on the floor, still wearing the beige coveralls Jeffrey had seen him in earlier. He was at least six feet tall and must have weighed in at well over 250 pounds. His sandy-blond hair was neatly combed in a side part and framed his round face, which was the same color and consistency as Play-Doh. His hands looked like bear claws. He was sitting on the floor and watching an episode of *Batman Beyond* on a large-screen television, drinking a glass of milk.

"Benny," Greta said in the sweet tone Lydia had expected to begin with, "some people are here to see you. They want to ask you some questions."

He turned around and looked at them.

"Benny, turn off the television," his mother directed. He did so and then stood to face them. As he pulled himself up to his full height, Lydia and Jeffrey involuntarily took a step back.

"I saw you at the church," he said.

"Yes, you did. Why did you leave in such a hurry, Benny?" asked Jeffrey.

"You talked about bad things. I got scared."

"Why were you scared, Benny?"

He paused, rocking and looking at his mother. She nodded.

"I don't know," he said softly, sitting on the couch and wrapping his arms around himself.

"Do you take care of your mom's garden out front?" Lydia asked him, sitting down on the couch beside him so that she was more at eye level with him.

He nodded.

"And the garden at the church, too."

He nodded again. "I like flowers. They never do bad things. They're just quiet."

"I know what you mean. People do bad things but flowers don't. Right?"

He nodded with enthusiasm, his eyes brightening, happy to be understood. "You just put the seeds in the ground and then make sure they get water and sun. And then a flower comes. Not too soon, but it does come. It's God that makes the flowers grow."

"Do you know Father Luis and Juno?"

"Yes."

"Do you like them?"

"Yes."

"Do you know anyone else at the church?"

"Not really."

"Are you sure?"

Benny gazed at his mother and began to rock again. Then he looked to the floor and Lydia followed his eyes. Benny was wearing a pair of Timberland Toledo boots. Lydia took her cell phone from the inside pocket of her jacket and handed it to Jeffrey, who took it and walked outside.

"I want you to think carefully, Benny. You are not in any trouble and you haven't done anything wrong. Has anybody taken you for a ride in a green minivan? Did someone take you to the park the other day?"

"Benny, what's wrong?" Greta asked, as she saw his eyes grow red and well up with tears.

Benny released a low moan and shuddered. Greta pushed Lydia aside to get near her son and put her big arms around him. "It's all right, honey. Try to relax," she crooned.

"Ms. Savroy, where was your son on the night before last?"

"He was in his bed. Where do you think he was? He's nothing but a child mentally. He doesn't go out by himself at night. What is going on?"

Benny's moaning grew louder. He rolled his head back and his mother tightened her grip on him.

"What about yesterday between the hours of six A.M. and eight P.M.?"

"I don't know. That's when I work. I'm an ER nurse at the hospital and I worked a double shift yesterday. Here probably, or at the church. He can't drive."

"Flowers," Benny said, his breathing becoming shallow, "belong in the ground."

In the next moment he fell to the floor, convulsing. And Greta, pulled with him, began screaming, "I told you! I told you not to upset him. This is what happens. Oh, God, Benny! Someone call 911. He's having a seizure."

Lydia ran to the kitchen phone and dialed 911. As she explained the situation and gave the operator their location, she noticed one of Father Luis's crucifixes hanging on the wall above the phone.

Lydia watched as the paramedics loaded Benny's unconscious body into the ambulance and Greta crawled in after him. She had felt guilty and sad as she instructed a police officer to remove Benny's shoes to compare to the print mold they had taken. She recognized Benny as a pawn in the killer's game—just like she was. She didn't know how Benny had been involved, but she knew that he was, and that she had made him remember things he had probably been able to forget, causing him to seize. Through the back window of the ambulance Greta glared at Lydia with unabashed hatred as they pulled away, headed for the hospital. A squad car followed behind.

"I like flowers. They never do bad things. They're just quiet."

"Well, the shoes are the same size as the print we found at the park and the forensic report stated that the impression was made by someone upwards of two hundred fifty pounds," Morrow said, startling Lydia as he came up behind her. "It looks like we might have our man."

"You're kidding," said Lydia.

"You don't think so?"

"No," she said, incredulous. "He's fucking retarded."

She shook her head and walked away toward Jeffrey. Lydia had been starting to hate Morrow a little less, wondering if she had been too hard on him, even feeling a bit guilty for having held a grudge since St. Louis. Now she remembered why she disliked him so intensely. He hadn't given a shit about the prostitutes that were killed in St. Louis. He'd just written them off. He'd said, "Johns kill whores every day, Miss Strong." And he'd ignored her when she'd told him more would die if he didn't listen to what she had to say. Whether it was because he was lazy or because he didn't want to admit that something like that was going on under his nose, he'd shut the door on her. Three more women had died before the case was solved by the FBI. Now he was just jumping at the first person that came along as a suspect: someone who obviously couldn't have committed these crimes, whatever his involvement turned out to be. Someone who would have a hard time defending himself.

"We are not going to let Benny take the fall for this just because these locals are looking for a victory here. He's not the one," she said to Jeffrey, as she passed him and went back into the house. She took the stairs up to Benny's room.

Jeffrey watched her storm off and turned to see Morrow, who seemed to have had all the air knocked out of him. Morrow wasn't aware that Jeffrey was observing him while he followed Lydia with his eyes. There was something in the way Morrow looked at her that made Jeffrey, unconsciously, put his hand on his gun.

Moving past the police officers who were overturning cushions and looking into drawers, she sat on Benny's bed made up with *Star Wars* sheets. It was a child's bedroom—shelves were filled with toys, posters of Power Rangers hung on the wall, an old computer sat on a blue faux-wood desk. A wastepaper basket was shaped like a football. An oversize polar bear sat on a wicker loveseat by the window. Next to Benny's bed on the nightstand was a photography book filled with color shots of flowers. She flipped through the pages, wondering how long it would be before Benny was able to speak again.

"*Flowers belong in the ground,*" he had said. What did he mean by that? It had raised goose bumps on the back of her neck when he'd said it. "*I like flowers. Flowers don't do bad things. They're just quiet.*"

"Flowers don't do bad things. But people do, right, Benny?"

she whispered. Then she slapped the book shut, standing up suddenly, and ran down the stairs.

"Jeffrey," she said, as she came out the front door . . . and walked over to Benny's flower garden. She touched the earth with the toe of her boot and wondered if her thoughts could be right. *"Flowers belong in the ground." But people don't, right Benny?* Jeffrey had come to stand beside her.

"What's up?" he asked.

"I think we need to dig up this flower garden."

Lydia wanted to be the one to tell Greg. He needed to hear this news from someone who knew what it was like to lose the only person that mattered. But she didn't have to take it on alone. When Jeffrey had offered to come with her to Greg's garage, her first instinct had been to tell him no.

"I can handle it," she said.

"No doubt," he answered, "but I want us to be a team, Lydia. Let's deal with the hard stuff together from now on."

He'd looked a little surprised when she agreed. "Can I drive?" he asked, smiling.

"You're pushing your luck," she answered, but walked to the passenger side of the car.

"Wow, this is just like *The Taming of the Shrew*."

She smacked him hard as they got in the car.

She had watched them load what was left of Shawna's body into the ambulance. The killer hadn't even used a body bag for her, just put her in the ground underneath the red larkspurs in Benny's beautiful, perfectly tended garden. It made Lydia so angry to think that some people never even had a chance at happiness in this world. All those New Age psychobabblers talking about how you make your own happiness and create positive energy in your life didn't know shit about Shawna Fox. One of the faceless shrinks Lydia had gone to see had accused her of wallowing in her grief for her mother, had told her she was destroying her life with negative thinking. "Maybe you're right," Lydia had answered. "When someone cuts your heart out of your chest and expects you to walk around the rest of your life without it, you let me know how it feels. You tell me when you find a way to stop 'wallowing.'" The irony of that statement was hitting her only now as she and Jeffrey drove to Greg Matthews's garage, to tell him they'd found Shawna's body.

"Oh my god," Lydia said.

"What?"

"I was just thinking, when you lose someone you love, if feels like someone has taken your heart."

"Okay . . ." he answered, not sure where she was going.

"Remember how we were talking about what that meant? To lose your heart or to have your heart taken?"

"Yeah. So you're saying maybe the killer lost someone close to him?"

"Right. And maybe that's why he wants vengeance."

"Against whom, though?"

She remembered something Juno had said to her on the first day they spoke. He'd said, *"There are many people who believe that I have the power to heal. But there are many that disbelieve it—vehemently. These types of people have perpetrated acts of violence against me and this church in the past, may God forgive them."*

"What if Juno tried to heal whoever it was . . . but couldn't?"

When Juno awoke that morning, he knew something was wrong. He lay still in his bed and listened to the air. There was a stillness like the pause before speech, as if the church had taken in a long breath and was holding it. He had been loath to move, feeling that once his feet touched the floor, nothing would ever be the same again.

As he went about his morning routine, feelings crept up on him, rose within him like a tide. Emotions he had rarely known seared through him—fear, and an unspeakable sadness. He tried to ignore them and go about the business of the morning. The door to his uncle's room was closed, and Juno almost knocked but he hated to disturb the priest, thinking he might be preparing for mass.

He could feel as he entered the church that the side door to the garden had been left open. He could feel the outside air inside, and smelled the sweet scent of the flowers from the garden. He walked to the doorway but could not bring himself to step outside, remembering when he had fallen in the blood just weeks before. He pulled the door closed and walked to the altar, sat on the stool there to practice his guitar.

So soothed and rapt was he by his own playing that he almost didn't hear the phone ring back in the office. He thought certainly by the time he reached it, the caller would have hung up, but when he answered, Lydia was on the line.

"Juno?"

"Yes, Lydia, hello."

"Juno, I have a question for you. The boy you last attempted to heal, what was his name?"

"It seems like a long time ago," he answered.

"I saw the name when I was searching the Internet before all this started, but I can't remember it now. Do you recall it?"

"Yes, yes, it was . . . Robbie. Robbie Hugo."

"Was he the only person you tried to heal that died?"

"Yes."

"What happened to his parents?"

"Well, his mother, Jennifer, was a parishioner here. Her husband was not a religious man. I don't remember his first name or even ever meeting him. She went to Colorado sometime after the boy died and I assume her husband went, as well."

"Do you know anything else about them?"

"Not really. I'm sorry."

"Juno, do you have a volunteer or parishioner at the church named Vince A. Gemiennes, someone who might not have been on the list your uncle gave us?"

"Well, I'm not sure who's on that list. The name does sound familiar. You'll have to ask my uncle, he'll know better."

"Can you get him?"

"He's preparing for mass," Juno answered, an odd reluctance overtaking him.

"Juno, this is pretty important."

He knocked on his uncle's door and when, after a moment, there was no answer, he pushed it open. "Uncle?" He walked into the room and put his hand on the bed which was made and cold as ice.

He returned to the phone. "Lydia, he's not here. It's very odd."

"Okay, Juno, there should be a squad car in front of the church. Go outside and tell them there's a problem. If there isn't a car out there, go inside, call 911, lock the doors, and don't move until the police get there. Do you understand me?"

"Yes. Lydia, what's happening?"

"Sit tight and I'll be there as fast as I can. I just have one thing I need to do first."

Juno ran, as best he could, twice jamming his foot against he didn't know what. The world so familiar to him seemed suddenly like an obstacle course where malicious, hard objects moved themselves into his path to impede his progress. When he finally reached the door, he called out for the police. But he got no answer.

Simon Morrow was fuming. After the body found in the Savroy's garden had been taken to the ME's office, Morrow had come to the hospital to sit outside Benny's room and wait for him to wake up. Retarded or not, he was involved. There was a body buried in his garden, for Christ's sake. And that bitch had made him seem like the biggest idiot in the world for thinking Benny was a suspect. He *was* a fucking suspect. And Morrow fully intended to be the first person to get the information out of him.

He leaned his head back against the cool plaster and tried to get comfortable in one of the metal-and-vinyl, stiff-cushioned chairs that lined the waiting-room walls. In the background he could hear the quiet rushing back and forth of nurses on soft-soled shoes, the occasional tone that issued from the intercom before a doctor was paged to the ER.

He was tired. He'd barely slept last night.

He had been in the office late, sorting through old records, remembering his last few years on the job. He wanted so desperately to be the one to solve this case. He wasn't a forensic expert or a victimologist or one of those special high-tech detectives that they had on all the TV shows these days. He was just a regular cop who came of age in the department on the street. He walked the grid, assembled the clues, and made the collar. So he'd gone through every arrest that stuck out in his mind since he'd come to New Mexico. He couldn't shake the feeling that he was forgetting something.

He remembered a time when he had been so sure of himself. No problem he couldn't fix, no case he couldn't solve. That was so long ago. A lot had changed.

Even after he had returned to his home and gone to bed, he had stayed awake, thinking, watching the ceiling fan rotate. He had just been drifting off as the sun started to peek in through the blinds, his wife still sleeping soundly beside him. A loud grinding noise woke him suddenly. His retired next-door neighbor was mowing the lawn at the crack of dawn for the second time in a month. *Son of a bitch,* he'd thought, knowing that any hope of sleep was gone.

"Didn't you talk to him about that?" his wife had murmured sleepily. She had turned over to look at him and he noticed that her pale skin was creased from the way she had slept.

"Yeah, but he said he had to do it in the morning. He's too old to mow the lawn in the heat of the day. So I suggested he get someone to do it for him. He misunderstood and thought I meant he couldn't take care of himself. He got all pissed off."

"We should get a caretaker. That lawn is a bear."

"How would you know? You've never mowed it in all the years we've lived here."

"Yeah, and you've never mopped a floor or cooked a meal."

He remembered the conversation with a chuckle, as he shifted in the waiting-room chair. He snorted, "A caretaker . . ."

And then Simon Morrow remembered what he had forgotten.

As Simon Morrow was stepping into his prowler, his cellular phone rang.

"Morrow," he answered.

"Chief, we just got a 911 call from Juno Alonzo. He says his uncle is missing and that the squad car that was supposed to be watching the church isn't there," reported the desk sergeant.

"All right. Get a uniform over there and then call Jeffrey Mark and Lydia Strong and ask them to head over. I'll be there as soon as I can."

"Can do, Chief."

He hung up with a pang of guilt. No one was going to take this collar from him. He couldn't believe he hadn't thought of it before. But it didn't matter now, because he was going to end this thing. And it would be just him.

It was funny how God worked. The ignition in his van had been giving him trouble for weeks. That had been partly why he'd rented the Jeep the night he'd done God's will for Maria Lopez. Also, he had wanted to see how smart Lydia was. She was smart all right, very smart.

He wasn't sure he was going to be able to pull that off. He could have easily been caught that day, but he'd had faith and God had seen him through. He'd used a fake license, not a very good fake, that he'd made on his computer, and then laminated it at a Kinko's. And the credit card . . . he'd actually changed his name to Vince A. Gemiennes with the social security office. He got a new credit card with that name but gave a false address, 124 Black Canyon Road. But he'd never stopped using his old name, never got a new driver's license. He'd remembered how his wife had changed her name when they were first married but how it was ages before she changed things like her driver's license, how her paychecks still came in her maiden name. There was never any problem.

But in the end, he'd been scared. He asked the girl if he could see his file, said he wanted to make sure he had given her the right credit card. She just handed the folder to him because she was busy and he slipped the copies out. She hadn't seemed especially bright, so he wasn't worried that she would notice later. Then, when he was done with the Jeep, he just dropped it off and left in his minivan that he had parked in the airport long-term parking lot.

Then, without his even realizing, God had led him to Greg Matthew's garage. It was the closest to his home, so he'd stopped in there because he couldn't have the ignition being hateful that way. He had a lot to do and a long way to go and he couldn't risk another rental. So he'd brought the minivan to be fixed. It wasn't until Greg had come out and seen him that he realized who Greg was, the boyfriend of Shawna Fox. He didn't know what to do; he had been very scared. He was sure that God had led him there for a purpose, but he couldn't see why. Then God showed him the way again. When he saw Greg writing down his license-plate number, he reached for an old piece of pipe he saw leaning against the garage and neutralized the threat to his plan.

The time was almost here. He fairly quivered with the rapture of doing God's work. Though everything had been taken from him, in the place of all that was lost he had become God's avenger, His warrior, His angel of death.

Standing in his son's room, he said his farewell to the place where his son had dwelled in life. A feeling of power coursed through him. He remembered the feeling from his surgery rotation as a second-year intern. The ability to save a life, the knowledge that one mistake could end a life. To have a human body sliced open, vulnerable before him, was a thrill that heightened all his senses, made him feel infallible, omnipotent. All that had been taken away from him was being returned to him now.

The room really was a masterpiece—a shrine, in a way, to his son. The cool wind blew in through the window, billowing the baby-blue curtains and ruffling his sandy-blond hair. The air was never cool like that in rural South Carolina where he grew up. The heat was like a live thing wrapped around him, raising sweat from his brow and entering his lungs, expanding there like wet gauze. He pushed the hair back from his face. It was ugly to remember his childhood, horrible to remember what he felt like when he was ten, always angry, always afraid. He stared at his hand. It was his father's hand, white, roped with thick blue veins, big hard knuckles like stones buried beneath thin, dry skin. He remembered his father's touch so well, dirty and violent, but something craved nonetheless.

He rose and walked over to the tray of surgical instruments by the metal table and picked up a scalpel. Its sharp edge and what it could do made him think again of Lydia Strong. She was in his thoughts more and more. He needed her to complete his mission. Without her, all that he had done for God would mean nothing. He would let her know her role soon and she would be powerless to deny him. Because that was God's will. He knew just the bait to draw her to him.

He walked from the room and moved slowly down the hall to the living room, where the flickering blue light from the muted television set cast an ugly strobe on the nearly empty room. There was a vague odor of beer and garbage.

He looked at his watch. It was almost eight. He slammed the door behind him as he left the house, but he didn't lock it. After all, he wouldn't be back.

chapter twenty-one

"Okay, we'll be there as soon as we can," Jeffrey said to the cop he was speaking with on Lydia's cell phone.

"What happened?" Lydia asked when he hung up.

"Looks like Juno wound up calling 911 to report his uncle missing like you told him to. The squad car that was supposed to be there was not. Morrow wants us to go to the church."

"Where's Morrow?"

"I didn't ask."

"We'll go as soon as I talk to Greg. I don't want him to find this out from someone else. I need to be the one to tell him," she said, anxious now for Juno, as well.

They were pulling up to Greg and Joe's Auto Repair and as soon as she saw the building, she knew something was wrong. There was an air of desertion to it. When she had come the first time, there was an aura of activity. She'd been able to hear music playing from an old radio, see lights on inside the garage, smell paint and gasoline. Today the door was closed, the lights were off, there was an unnatural quiet.

"Busy place," said Jeffrey. "I hope he has time to see us."

Lydia pulled her Glock from the glove compartment.

"What are you doing?"

"There's something wrong. It's the middle of the morning and the garage isn't open."

"So maybe he took the day off."

"Maybe. But I don't think so."

Jeffrey unsnapped the holster on the .38 special at his waist as they stepped out of the car. Ever since things had started to heat up, he'd regretted leaving his own Glock in New York, wanting to avoid the hassle of getting it on the airplane. They walked to the garage door, which, as they got closer, Lydia could see, was ajar.

"Greg," she called, "it's Lydia Strong."

When there was no answer, she pushed the door open. Stepping inside, Lydia felt the walls for a light switch, which she couldn't find. So they made their way in the dim light coming in from a high, dirty window above the door. They felt their way along the empty shell of a car up on cinderblocks, toward the office where a desk lamp glowed, Lydia in front and Jeffrey at her back.

"Greg," she called again. This time she was answered by a low moan.

They moved faster toward the sound and found Greg on the floor of the office semiconscious, his head lying in a pool of blood. She bent down to him as Jeffrey dialed 911.

Lydia grabbed his wrist to check for a pulse and as she did, saw a number written on his arm. "What is this?"

"What?" asked Jeff, as he hung up with the operator. He bent down and inspected Greg's arm. "It's a VIN number."

"Why would he have written this on his arm?"

"Maybe he didn't have any paper?"

She shot him a look, putting her hand to Greg's forehead. "Call the number in to Jacob Hanley in New York. You'll probably get it faster."

Jeffrey looked at his watch. "Jacob's probably not even in yet. I think I'll call Craig."

Lydia always called Craig Keaton "the Brain" behind his back. He stood a full head taller than Jeffrey but looked as thin as one of Jeffrey's thighs. Clad forever in huge baggy jeans, a white T-shirt under a flannel shirt, and a pair of Doc Martens, his pockets were always full of electronic devices . . . cell phone, pager, Palm Pilot, all manner of thin black beeping, ringing toys. A pair of round wire spectacles, nearly hidden by a shock of bleached-blond hair, framed blue-green eyes. Craig called himself a cybernavigator, though his title at Jeffrey's firm was Information Specialist. He specialized in knowledge of all computer research tools and was, before being recruited for Mark, Hanley and Striker, an infamous hacker wanted by the FBI. He was eighteen when he was arrested and could have faced more than a little time in federal prison, but luckily for him, Jacob Hanley was his uncle. All former FBI agents with more connections between them than a motherboard, Mark, Hanley and Striker were able to get Craig a deal. He worked for them, he kept his act together, and he reported to a probation officer for the next three years.

Now, more or less plugged in to the Internet and the Bureau systems 24/7, more or less legally, Craig could gather almost any piece of information needed at any time of the day or night. Lydia wondered when he slept, and joked that one day Jeffrey would go to Craig's basement office and find that he had become a disembodied voice, sucked into the computers like some character in a William Gibson novel.

"I'll call him," Lydia said.

"Because he has a crush on you and you think that will make him work faster."

"Exactly."

As Lydia dialed, Jeffrey knelt down next to Greg, putting a hand on his shoulder. She heard him say, "You're gonna be all right, buddy, hang in there." She hoped he was right.

"Hi, Lydia. How's it going?" answered Craig, seeing her number on his Caller ID box. "To what do I owe the pleasure?" She found his attempt to be suave incredibly cute.

"Hey, Craig," she said, as sweetly as she could. "I need you to work some magic for me—yesterday."

"You got it. What's up?"

"I need a name and address on the following VIN number: VZN61LG-PSEA."

"That's it?" He sounded a little disappointed. But she heard the soft clatter of his keyboard. "Let's see. DMV systems are always a little slow."

Lydia thought she was going to have a brain aneurysm waiting for him to come back to her with the information. She heard the wail of approaching sirens.

"Okay," he said, after less than a minute, though it seemed to Lydia like an hour. "We've got a 1995 Dodge Caravan registered to Bernard Hugo at 1412 Mission Lane in Angel Fire, New Mexico."

The corners of her mouth turned up in a sad, tight smile of recognition. She had to assume that Bernard Hugo was Robbie's father and that he hadn't gone to Colorado after all. "Craig, you are the best. I am taking you on a drinking binge as soon as I get back to New York."

"Cool. When are you in town?"

Paramedics came in through the garage door, and Jeffrey moved away from Greg as they approached.

"Soon, honey. I have to run, Craig. You're the best."

" 'Bye, Lydia."

"You'll break his heart," said Jeffrey.

"Let's go," she answered.

"Shouldn't we call Morrow?"

"No. Fuck that guy."

"We should call," Jeffrey said as they got in the car, Lydia in the driver's seat. He dialed the number.

"*The cellular customer you are trying to reach is not available,*" said the recorded message.

chapter twenty-two

There was time to turn around and do this the right way. All he had to do was to pick up his cell phone and make a call. Chief Morrow sat in his prowler and looked at the front door of the house. He could tell it was empty. Empty houses gave off an aura of abandonment and most cops could see it. At least they hoped they could.

He should have called Jeffrey Mark by now. He should have at least brought backup. But it was just a hunch. He was just checking up on a hunch. If it was nothing, then it was nothing. If it was something, well then, either he would be dead or he would be the hero cop who saved the day. He was banking on the latter.

Lying in bed this morning, he had finally remembered Bernard Hugo. He remembered Hugo's grief. After Robbie Hugo had died, the church and the community had rallied around them in a way Morrow remembered as remarkable. And at the gathering at the Hugo home after Robbie's funeral, which Morrow had attended in his official capacity, the house had been filled with people. Robbie's mother Jennifer had been strong, hosting her guests with grace and smiling bravely. Bernard Hugo had sat in a corner staring blankly out the window, his face ashen and tight, eyes glazed. Morrow remembered his face as the very embodiment of grief.

There had been whispers, he remembered now as it all came

back, about Bernard's mental illness and whether he could bear up under the strain of grief. Simon Morrow guessed that he hadn't been able to. He wondered what he would find inside. He hefted himself out of the car and walked to the front door. He noted that the lawn was overgrown and the house needed a coat of paint. When he knocked, the door pushed open. Morrow stepped inside. From the door he could see the living room and the kitchen. A hallway leading to the bedrooms was to his left.

"Bernard Hugo," he called. "Police. I'd like to ask you a few questions."

The house answered with silence and he heard his voice echo lightly in the nearly empty room. Most of the furniture he remembered was gone. There was just a television, a recliner, a rickety old card table. He took another step inside and pulled out his gun.

The odor assailed him. Garbage, beer, general filth, and something else. Some other odor lingered, mingling with the others. He pulled a surgical glove from his pocket and deftly slid it on his left hand while still holding his weapon with his right. He wasn't going to fuck this up. The door had pushed open, so he felt it was within his rights to enter. He wouldn't touch anything. Just look around. If he found anything, he'd call it in right away. At least he would be the first on the scene.

Keeping his back to the wall, he walked down the hallway and looked in the master bedroom, where a bed was the only piece of furniture. The bed was bare except for a crumpled-up beige-and-green top sheet. There was little else to see except a closet that stood open where a few items of clothing were sloppily hung on wire hangers and old shoes cluttered the rack that hung on the door.

The door across the hall was closed and Morrow tried to push it open with his foot, keeping his back to the opposite wall, but he couldn't. So he moved to the right of the doorjamb, turned the knob, and pushed the door open fast. It banged against the wall inside the room. He entered gun-first. And when he stood in the doorway, he saw what he had come for. And he wasn't sure whether to whoop with joy or be ill.

As he slid his cell phone from the inside lapel pocket of his suit jacket, he heard cars pull up the gravel driveway. From the window he could see Jeffrey Mark and Lydia Strong walk up to the door. He walked down the hallway to greet them.

"Chief, what are you doing here?" Jeffrey asked.

"I was following up on a hunch that proved to be right," he answered, trying not to seem smug. "What are you doing here?"

"We got a tip on a vehicle and it led us here. Why didn't you call for backup?"

"I wasn't sure there was anything," he answered. "I came here to ask some questions of this guy Bernard Hugo. I just remembered he was working as a caretaker at the church on and off for the last few months."

"Is he here?"

"No."

"But you came in here without a warrant? Jesus."

"Relax. I didn't touch anything."

"That's not the fucking point," shot Jeffrey. "If anybody finds out you were here, you'll lose anything you've found in court and this guy will walk. You wanted to handle this without the FBI, and then you pull a stunt like this that could put your whole case in the toilet. What were you thinking?"

"I was thinking about stopping a guy who has probably killed three, maybe four people, Mr. Mark. Watch your tone. I'm not a rookie. The door was open and there was a notable stench. I had probable cause to enter."

Jeffrey stared at Chief Morrow as the four police officers

around him shifted uncomfortably and looked away. He reined in his anger at Morrow's carelessness. And when he spoke again, his voice was more restrained. "Fine. It's your case, Chief. Let's see what you got."

Simon Morrow was moved to silence by rage as he walked them to evidence he had found.

"Holy shit," said Jeffrey, as he entered the room.

If insanity had a bedroom, this would have been it. The metal gurney where Bernard Hugo had removed the hearts of his victims was scrubbed clean and stood in the middle of a room that looked to have been a baby's nursery. Beside it was a tray of surgical implements—scalpel, bone saw, and other horrible metal tools Jeffrey couldn't name but hoped would never be put to use on his body. Powder-blue curtains hung on the window frame, and a wallpaper border with ducks and balloons could still be seen edging the ceiling. The rest of the wall was covered, however, with newspaper articles and photographs. The maniac collage that papered the walls included images of Lydia from the media, articles written about her and by her, covers from her books, articles about Juno, about the death of Robbie Hugo, baby pictures, some of the very articles that Lydia had clipped from the newspaper at the beginning of her interest in this case. Over it all, the rantings of a demented mind were scrawled in blood. Jeffrey saw immediately the message they had found on Lydia's bedroom mirror among the rest of the deadly graffiti, including: *Sinners must die . . . I am God's warrior and evildoers shall feel my wrath. . . . She will bring the message of God.*

"Holy shit," Lydia said as she walked in the door.

"His name is Bernard Hugo," said Chief Morrow, "and he's been a volunteer caretaker on and off at the church for the last six months. He used to be an orderly at the hospital, but after his son died and his wife left him, he lost it, stopped going to work, got fired."

"I know. His son died after a failed heart transplant," said Lydia; "Juno visited him, supposedly attempted to heal him. And the boy died hours later."

Morrow thought on it a second. "You're right. I had forgotten about that."

Lydia wanted to jump on him. *How could he have not made these connections earlier?* But she knew it wasn't really fair. The whole thing was so insane.

"The guy doesn't even have a speeding ticket, you know?" Morrow said, as if reading her mind. "There had always been rumors about him, according to my wife. Apparently he had been on track to become a surgeon years ago. But he'd had some kind of mental breakdown. He was on so much medication that he couldn't even become a nurse after that. So he settled for being an orderly at St. Vincent's Hospital.

"I remember when the kid died. My wife and I went to pay our respects and he was destroyed, I mean he could barely function. Then I heard a couple of months later from my wife that his wife had left him, went back to her family in Colorado. Then he lost his job. I wondered how he would survive but then I heard that he was doing some volunteer work at the Church of the Holy Name and I figured he'd found God."

"But maybe he was just looking for victims," said Jeffrey.

"Or both," said Lydia. "I think we have some more gardening to do."

Juno sat alone in the back pew of the church. His hands were neatly folded in his lap and his head hung low. The glow around him that Lydia had always perceived, seemed dim and she was not sure how to approach him. He was fragile and fading like a specter. She stood watching him, listening to the police shuffling around her, speaking in low voices as though mass were in session.

There was a horrific amount of blood splattered on the walls that contained the garden, across the flowers, and even on the face of the Virgin. A rosary lay near the door. Lydia didn't hold out much hope for Father Luis. She had asked the police to hold off on digging up the garden for a few minutes, until she talked to Juno. And now she stood wondering how she would begin, his fear radiating off him like a visible aura. She approached him slowly.

Juno heard Lydia's footfalls and sensed her hesitation. He wanted to tell her not to worry, that he already knew. But his voice failed him and he sat silent and waiting. She could not know that he had lost not only his uncle this day, the man who raised him, but his mother and father as well.

Sitting in the last pew, praying, Juno had become invisible to the police. They'd rushed into the church just minutes after his call. He heard them run through the living area behind the church and then move out to the garden, where, he noted, the rushing ended and voices became hushed. He could only imagine what they found there, for no one had told him. So he waited. Whispered phrases floated to him on the wind that blew in from the open door; phrases like "blood splatter," "handprint," "blood-soaked cloth."

Then, as two officers walked passed him, he overheard one of them whisper, "This poor guy has had nothing but tragedy in his life. His uncle was the only parent he ever had. I'll tell you about it later." He recognized the man's voice as someone he knew from childhood, a boy named Jimmy O'Neill who had attended cat-echism classes at the church.

At first he was confused and wondered who Jimmy was talking about. Then he realized that he meant him, Juno. He almost laughed in disbelief as he thought, *Until now I have never known any suffering.* He couldn't imagine what the man meant. His blindness, maybe?

But a cold dawning was moving over him. Then Juno remembered a day long ago on the playground behind the church. In a downward spiral of thought, he remembered Jimmy taunting him one day when they were children, making fun of his parents, saying that they had died in some horrible way. He remembered his conversation with his uncle. And then he remembered nothing else about the incident. It was a blank wall in his mind that he could not pass through. He remembered his uncle's words: *"Jimmy has told you something and I have told you something. You must look into your heart and decide what you believe. If someone told you that God did not exist, would you believe them?"*

He could not remember what he had decided that day. He could not remember thinking about what had happened to his parents ever again. He knew he had sewn his uncle's story of his parents into his soul, like a jewel in the seam of a coat. The knowledge of it, though he never saw it or touched it or thought of it after that day, was a secret treasure that he owned, one that defined him. Now it was as if he'd ripped open the seam and found not a gem, but a lump of clay.

As he sat in the pew, Juno's knowledge of himself and his life turned to quicksand. He was afraid to speak as Lydia approached him. He was afraid he would not recognize the sound of his own voice. She sat beside him and placed her hand on his.

"I know how you are feeling right now. And what I am about to tell you is not going to comfort you," she said softly.

He nodded.

"Outside, the wall is splattered with blood. A lot of blood. It appears as if the garden has been disturbed as well. In a few minutes, we are going to start digging there. And I am not sure what we'll find, but . . ."

He just nodded again and held up his hand. Eventually, he mustered his voice and whispered, "Do you know what happened to my parents?"

"Your parents?" she asked, after a pause, hoping he hadn't lost his mind. "Do you mean your uncle, Juno?"

"No. I mean my parents. Do you know what happened to them?"

"Yes . . ." she said, unsure where he was leading.

"Will you tell me?"

"Are you saying you don't know?"

"Yes."

"What have you thought all these years?" she asked, incredulous.

"If I told you, you wouldn't believe me. Or you'd think I'm insane."

"Try me."

In the lilting voice one would use to tell a fairy tale to a child, Juno told Lydia the story he had believed all his life.

"My mother was a beautiful angel held prisoner by an aging wizard. For sixteen years, he kept her hidden in a dovecote at the top of a tower with a hundred steps. Her hair was as black as the bottom of the ocean and her eyes as blue as ice. And the wizard loved her in his own twisted way. But because she was stolen from God Himself, he hid her among the doves. He fed her only the finest fruit and honey.

"Serena, my mother, was not unhappy. She loved the company of the birds and the wizard was kind to her. And she had been in the tower for so long that she considered it her home. She had no desire for freedom, she could barely conceive of what that would mean. The wizard told her the world was a dark and dangerous place, and he kept her there to protect her from the evil forces that would surely try to harm her. She was grateful.

"In the evenings when the moon was full, Serena would sing for the doves. Beautiful songs in an angel's voice that would carry over the trees and up to the stars. One of these nights, a handsome young shepherd, named Manuel, was walking home from tending his sheep when he heard Serena's song. He followed the sound of her voice and saw her in the window at the top of the tower. Instantly, he fell in love.

"He called to her. But she was frightened and backed away from the window. He walked around the tower, looking for the door, and finally found it but it was locked.

"He stood there awhile calling to her. But she did not reappear. Despairing, he sat against a tree and tried to figure out a way to make her open the door. Soon he fell asleep. Later that evening, he was awakened by the sound of someone walking through the woods. Quickly he hid himself and watched as the old wizard pulled a golden key from a chain around his neck and opened the door. The shepherd heard the wizard lock the door from the inside. He decided this might be his only chance to get into the tower. So he picked up the heaviest, biggest rock he could manage and stood by the door, waiting for the wizard.

"When the wizard emerged, the shepherd hit him on his head with the rock and the wizard fell unconscious.

"Manuel ran as fast as he could to the top of the tower, where he found Serena sleeping on a bed of dove feathers and gold dust. He sat beside her to admire her beauty, his heart aching with love for her. When she woke and saw his kind and handsome face, she, too, fell instantly in love with him.

" 'Come away with me, Serena. I am only a poor shepherd but I will love and care for you all your life,' he said.

"She said she would and he kissed her passionately. It was a kiss so full of love, that a baby was made and appeared beside Serena on her bed. They called him Juno, and that was me. Overjoyed, the young lovers carried me from the tower. But when they stepped outside, the wizard was waiting for them. Enraged, he pulled a sword from its sheath at his side and ran my father through, killing him instantly. My mother was stricken with grief and wailed with all the pain of her broken heart. It was a cry so loud that God Himself heard it and recognized it as the voice of His lost angel.

"He appeared to her and the wizard as a blinding light. He cast the wizard straight to hell. Then He spoke to my mother.

" 'Weep not, my lost little angel, I have come to take you and Manuel home.'

"She saw Manuel's soul rise from his body into the light and soon she was beside him. They were going to God.

" 'But what of our child?' they asked.

" 'He has a life to live before he can join us. He has many things to do on Earth. One day, you will all be together again.'

"And I was blinded by the light of God."

Lydia didn't say anything, trying to understand what kind of person you had to be to believe a fairy tale all your life. How innocent, how trusting, how pure he had to be never to imagine that his uncle had lied. What kind of world did he imagine, where the mystical existed so believably? "And you believed this until when?"

"I think until just now. You must think I am an idiot. Someone like you, always searching for the truth. I have hid from it all my life in this little church. The world is nothing like I have believed it to be. I think on some level, I knew. But I just never examined it. I didn't want to know the truth."

"God, why would you? The world can be a twisted, fucked-up place. What a gift you had all these years, to live like you have. You had something that I'm not sure even exists anymore. Pure faith."

"Blind faith. If everything you believe in is a lie, then you're a fool, not a saint."

She marveled at the change in him. The monklike demeanor he had held was gone, and an ordinary man, angry, confused, and grief-stricken, sat beside her, clutching her hand. He'd lost his glow of inner peace. And she grieved for that loss, almost more than for his other losses.

"Just because your uncle told you a story meant to protect you doesn't mean that everything he taught you was false. Plenty of people who are not fools have faith—faith in God, faith in the basic goodness of human nature. You don't have to give those things up."

"What about you, Lydia? What do you have faith in?"

She searched her mind, wanting to come up with something to satisfy them both. But she didn't know. She didn't want to say what she'd realized in that moment, that she had been searching for faith in *him*. She'd started to convince herself that he could heal the pain she had been carrying inside her since the death of her mother, that he held the truth that could set her free. It was that search that had been drawing her to him.

"Because you see the truth," he said, when she didn't speak, "you don't need faith."

"Because I see the truth, I need it even more; faith that there is something larger, something better than what we see. There are people who believe you healed them. What about that?"

"I never healed anyone. People lied to themselves. And I was starting to believe it, too. They were searching, just like you were. For something larger, something that could fix the injustice of suffering. They let themselves believe a fairy tale. Just like I did."

"But I saw you in my dreams," she said.

"I can't explain that, Lydia."

"And that's the space that faith occupies. In things we can't explain and can't understand."

Now he sat silent, trying to grasp at the fading concept of himself and his world. He wondered who he would be, now that everything he had known was slipping away. "So, do you know what happened to them?"

"Yes. Do you want me to tell you?"

"Yes."

As carefully as she could, she relayed the fate of Serena and Manuel Alonzo, giving him the whole truth as she had learned it from archived articles from the newspaper. She felt he deserved that. "Your parents were poor, living here in the barrio of Santa Fe. Your father worked in construction and your mother was a nurse's aide at Santa Fe General Hospital. They married very young and it was an abusive relationship. Your father beat your mother, Juno.

"When she found out she was pregnant, she became afraid for your life. She was afraid you would not survive the beatings. She was too afraid to divorce him or leave him, fearing that he would find and kill her anyway. So she killed your father, set their house on fire while he was passed out from drinking.

"She went to trial and was found guilty. She gave birth to you in prison and died in labor."

Lydia told the story in all its earthly ugliness. And when she was done, she told him about Bernard Hugo and what they had discovered. And Juno wept, feeling grief and pain for the first time in his life. She sat beside him with her hand on his back and nodded to the officer standing by the door, who had stood waiting for her signal to start digging up the garden. Lydia was certain it was here they would find the victims' hearts. She wasn't sure why Hugo had buried them here, she wasn't sure what his message was, but she had a vague sense now of the way the killer's mind worked, of his essence. And though she didn't know what his ultimate goal was, she knew he intended to have vengeance against Juno for not saving his son. The only thing she really didn't understand was why he chose the victims he did. Was it just a matter of opportunity? Were they just unlucky enough to fly into his radar?

"Juno," Lydia said gently, a thought occurring to her suddenly.

He had lifted his head from his hands and seemed to be staring off at the altar, lost in his grief. He came back to himself when she spoke to him.

"Did any of the victims ever come to you for counsel? Did you heal any of them, Juno?"

He seemed to deflate even further as he considered her question, and realized the implications of the answer he was about to give. In that moment he truly had lost everything he believed to be true.

"I've seen all of them," he said softly. "Christine and Harold came to me a year ago to help them overcome their addictions. Shawna came to me to help her with her anger. And Maria, she came to me when a doctor found a lump in her breast."

"And what happened with each of them?"

"Christine and Harold seemed to have beaten their addictions when they disappeared. Shawna became involved in the church and that seemed to give her some peace. When Maria's tumor was removed, after her visit, it was found to be benign. She claimed that before she had seen me, she was sure she was about to die from breast cancer, and that as I played my guitar, she could feel the cancer leaving her. She was quite vocal about it."

"So you helped all of them. In ways, you healed all of them. That should mean something to you, Juno. Each of their lives was better for your interaction with them, whether it was divine or not."

"Lydia," he said, "if your question implies what I think it does, then all of their lives were ended because of their interaction with me."

"No, Juno, all of their lives ended because of their interaction with Bernard Hugo. Don't confuse that. Do not take that on. You acted in a way that was true to yourself and true to your belief in God."

"So did Bernard Hugo."

chapter twenty-three

Lydia sat in the doorway and watched as the police began to overturn the garden, removing the flowers first and then raking through the dirt carefully, trying not to damage what might be found, if anything. A headache had started to settle behind her eyes, the events of the day bearing down like a weight on her brain. She kept trying to move the images of Juno weeping and of Bernard Hugo's chamber of horrors from her mind so she could focus on what their next move should be. But all she could do was watch, wondering what or who they would find buried in the garden. She thought she knew.

The flowers were piled on the ground like corpses and Lydia found herself mesmerized by the rhythmic sound of the raking in the dirt. The sun was hot and the officers were sweating heavily in their efforts. There was no other sound except the wind and the occasional car driving by. Lydia stared at the statue of Madonna and Child and wondered what those stone eyes had borne witness to, as she heard a rake make contact with a hard surface beneath the dirt. As if answering some kind of macabre cue, Medical Examiner Henry Wizner appeared at the garden gate.

It seemed as if time slowed as the police officers moved out of the way and Wizner knelt by the garden, opening his black bag. He removed surgical gloves, a small paintbrush, and a spade. With the brush he carefully whisked away the dirt to reveal a small glass circle, around which he carefully dug with the spade. Lydia moved over closer to him as he reached with his gloved hand and pulled a glass mason jar from the earth. Inside, floating in a clear liquid Lydia could only assume was formaldehyde, was a human heart.

"It's time to go, Juno," Lydia said, approaching Juno from behind. He sat where she had left him an hour earlier, barely having moved.

"What did you find?"

"Maybe we should talk about this another day."

"My uncle?"

"No."

Juno just nodded.

"Why don't you come back to my house?" she offered. "You can stay there as long as you need to."

"I need time alone. I need to be somewhere familiar." He answered slowly, his voice as slight and far away as he seemed to be. "I need to try to understand everything that has happened here."

"I can't let you stay here, Juno. You are part of his plan and he'll be coming for you."

"And for you."

"Yes, I think so. But don't worry about me. Where do you want to go?"

On the way back to the Hugo house, she brought him to the home of Mrs. Turvey, the woman who had tutored him as a child. She was old but hearty; she took him in her arms and he seemed to find comfort there.

"Lydia," he called to her as she walked away from him, "take care. Don't do anything foolish."

His voice had an odd strength to it and she turned to face him.

"Don't worry about me, Juno. Just take care of yourself."

Now Lydia walked around Bernard Hugo's home and tried to get a sense of him. It was difficult. A few tattered items of clothing hung in the master-bedroom closet; the bed had just one dirty, rumpled top sheet; no photographs sat on the bedside table or hung on the wall. Downstairs there was only a worn recliner and a card table. There was nothing in the refrigerator, except a carry-out bag from the Blue Moon Café and a few cans of Budweiser.

The bag was evidence and she called it to the attention of one of the officers scanning the small, nearly empty house. Lydia wondered if Maria Lopez had handed him that bag, and how many times he'd gone to the café before he'd killed her. He was as alone and disconnected as his victims.

She walked back upstairs to look at the "operating room." It was so eerie to see her image, her articles, her book covers on the wall of a maniac's death chamber.

Chief Morrow was on his cellular phone giving a description of Bernard Hugo to the state police, who would then distribute it to neighboring states. "You guys are going to make sure the area airports, and train and bus stations are covered?" she heard him ask. "Right . . . right. . . . Well, the only place I can think of might be Colorado. His wife is there. No, I don't recall her maiden name but I can get it. I'll get back to you."

Lydia walked over to the table. It looked so cold, so cruel. The table, the implements, as well as the rest of the room, were immaculately clean now. But she imagined the table covered with blood, imagined Shawna lying on it, her chest sliced opened, and she shivered. Lydia wondered if the killer wanted to see her there, too.

Jeffrey walked up behind her and she jumped a little.

"I'm sure he's on the run," he said to her, with too much conviction, as though he were trying to reassure himself as much as her. "He's not going to get far."

"He's not done yet."

"There's no way he can get to you or to Juno. I'm not letting you out of my sight. And there are two detectives parked in front of the Turvey house to protect Juno. It's over, he must see that."

Lydia just nodded. She knew with a cool certainty that Bernard Hugo was somewhere close by, waiting, that he wasn't done with whatever he had set out to do. Jeffrey placed an intimate hand on her hip and she leaned into him. She felt her face flush as the warmth of his presence washed over her. It was such a new feeling, to feel personally happy, even though the sight that faced her was grim.

"How are you feeling?" he asked.

"Horrible and wonderful," she answered. "Horrible about this, wonderful about . . . everything else."

"I know," he said, grabbing her hand and squeezing.

It had been a long day and the sun was going down as Lydia sat on the stoop outside the Hugo home, writing longhand in her notebook the events of the day, narrating them already. In the house behind her, she could still hear the activity of the crime scene. Jeffrey's voice was clear and strong, full of authority. The sound of it comforted her as she wrote. A parade of people rushed back and forth, carrying evidence away, delivering coffee and files.

She looked up from her notebook when she heard a vehicle approach, and saw Wizner emerge with three police officers and walk toward the house. "I think you'll be interested in this, Ms. Strong," Wizner said without stopping or looking at her as he passed. She got up to follow them.

Jeffrey looked up from the conversation he was having with one of the forensics officers when Wizner walked in.

"Well, Mr. Mark, it looks like those organs weren't put to such good use after all."

"That's what I hear, Wizner," said Jeffrey, not in the mood for a flashy presentation.

"They were buried in the church garden . . . four human hearts preserved in jars of formaldehyde."

"How long will it be before you are able to determine whether the hearts belong to the victims?"

"I'm on my way to the office right now. I just thought you'd like to know first what we found."

"No sign of Father Luis?" asked Chief Morrow.

"No bodies in the garden, only the hearts," Wizner answered with a ghoulish smile, as if he'd just said something witty.

After another hour, the room and the house started to clear out as Forensics completed the gathering of evidence. All Hugo's equipment had been removed, and only a few technicians remained, combing for hair and fibers, searching for minuscule blood samples in the carefully scrubbed and sanitized room.

Jeffrey and Lydia stood alone in the room and stared at the walls.

"You certainly figure rather prominently in his imagination," said Jeffrey.

"It must run in the family," she answered, trying to sound light but failing.

She got up and walked over to him, and without hesitation wrapped her arms around his waist, pressing herself against him. She felt his body relax and he folded her in his arms. She didn't care who saw them or what anyone thought. She was just glad she didn't have to face her demons alone anymore.

The chief approached them. "Jeff, can I have a word with you?"

Lydia bristled at her exclusion, but she tried not to eavesdrop as the two walked out into the hallway, and pretended instead to be looking closely at the collages on the walls. At first the chief looked contrite and almost ashamed. Jeffrey's jaw was set the way it generally was when he would reprimand Lydia. And then she saw the chief's face flush in anger as he raised his voice a bit.

"Don't forget who runs the show here, Mr. Mark," he said, and stormed from the house, climbed into his car, and pulled quickly down the drive, his tires spitting up gravel.

"What was that all about?" she asked as Jeffrey returned to her, shaking his head.

"Let's get out of here. This place is starting to give me the creeps."

They walked out the front door of the house and got into Lydia's Kompressor, and started for home.

On the way back, Lydia shared with Jeffrey her conversation with Juno.

"It doesn't seem possible that someone could believe a story like that," Jeffrey said skeptically.

"I agree that it's hard to believe, but trust me when I tell you it's true. He had no idea what actually happened to his parents until I told him."

"How did he take it?"

"Badly. It was sad. He was such an innocent and that's lost now. Bernard Hugo murdered his innocence."

They were both silent for a moment as Lydia drove fast on the dark, winding road toward home, the Mercedes hugging curves, graceful and silent.

"So, if you were Bernard Hugo, what would be your next move?" Lydia asked Jeffrey.

"Well, it depends. If I came back this way and saw my house swarming with cops and I was sane, I'd probably dump the mini-van, steal another vehicle, or hop a bus and get out of Dodge."

"But if you weren't sane, if you needed to stick around for some reason, where would you hide?"

"In all those miles of desert and mountains . . . all I need is a tent and some supplies. But why would I want to stick around?"

"Because the man who killed your son, the man whose heart is the most false of all, is still alive. His heart is still beating and every day it does, it's a greater insult to God."

chapter twenty-four

Simon Morrow hadn't said a word since he returned home. He'd just sat in the old lawn chair that had been in all the backyards of their marriage. His wife knew well enough to leave him be; so she'd left a plate of food on the table for him and gone out with her friends. It was moments like these when he remembered he was an alcoholic. He felt a hurtful need for a beer as the light dimmed around him and evening fell.

He'd left the scene in disgust. After the hopes he'd had this morning, he'd felt crushed by the events of the afternoon. *Is this what it means to be a broken man?* he wondered. That's how he felt. He knew his wife felt differently. She had told him once that he was her hero. It was after the whole incident in St. Louis. She'd said it was because he recognized his faults and worked to make them better. She'd cried a little when she told him how much she admired him. The fact he knew she was sincere made him feel like that much more of a heel. But he'd always hoped one day to feel worthy of her pride, of her love. Tonight he believed that day might never come, and it hurt—almost as much as his need for a double scotch neat.

He wondered if Bernard Hugo was long gone or if he was hovering someplace nearby, unsure of where to go and what to do. Simon Morrow wondered if maybe he understood a little of the desperation Hugo must feel right now. They had both lost something that had caused them to lose themselves a little. Different, certainly. But wasn't there always something recognizable in the most insane human reaction to pain?

How often had Simon Morrow wished he could return to the St. Louis station house? Not to go back there for a visit as the man he was today, but to go back to the man he had been in the days he ran the place, pretty damn well, he thought. How highly he'd thought of himself then. Never a moment of self-doubt, self-recrimination. What he wouldn't give to walk those halls again as a young man. He wondered if Bernard Hugo felt the same way.

Morrow rose and entered his house through the sliding glass doors that led to his comfortable living room. He grabbed his car keys off the countertop in the kitchen, and pulled a light jacket off the back of a table chair. He walked out the front door and went to the police cruiser parked in his driveway. He felt a twinge of self-loathing as he crawled behind the wheel, as if he didn't deserve to be operating department equipment. He thought he'd just take a little ride over to the hospital where Bernard Hugo used to work.

Each of Juno's other senses told him he was in the wrong place. The air smelled of roses and peppermint. The bed was too soft, the sheets too fragrant. He could hear Mrs. Turvey puttering downstairs, cleaning dinner dishes and humming softly. He must have dozed after dinner. He had eaten a great deal in spite of his grief and everything he had learned today. But now he was awake. And he knew with certainty that he was in the wrong place. He must return to the church immediately. It wasn't his mind that told him this. It was not a desire to be surrounded with the things that were familiar to him. And it was not a desire to be alone. It was something larger, something outside himself that told Juno he was in the wrong place.

It wasn't far and he could certainly walk. He had done so a million times as a child. He was sure he remembered the way. He had his cane with him. Mrs. Turvey had told him when she'd leaned it against the doorjamb. He would need to wait until she went to bed. Otherwise he would only worry her, or she would try to stop him somehow. So he would lie and wait until the house was silent. And then he would go home.

chapter twenty-five

As they pulled up to the house, two uniformed police officers greeted their car.

"The repairman for the alarm system was here today, Ms. Strong," said one of the baby-faced officers. "He put a new breaker box inside the garage and says it should be fine now."

"Perfect," said Jeffrey, "but a little late."

"Yes sir," answered the officer.

"Come up for coffee if you get cold, guys," said Lydia, pulling her cream suede jacket around her against the chill.

"Thank you, Ms. Strong."

It felt strange to her, as she turned the brushed-chrome knob and entered through the front door, that Bernard Hugo had been in her house. The hand that had murdered and removed the hearts of innocent people had been on the same doorknob that hers rested on now. She had felt invaded last night but now that she knew who he was and what he had done, it bothered her even more.

"I wonder why he didn't wait for us to come home last night."

"Who?"

"Bernard Hugo."

"Well, we're armed, for one."

"How would he know that we're armed?"

"It's a reasonable assumption."

"Still, if he was really motivated to kill me . . ."

"Maybe he doesn't want to kill you."

"What else could he want?"

"I don't know, Lyd," he said, moving close to her and leaning in to kiss her.

In the melee, Lydia had barely had a chance to acknowledge the way their relationship had changed, what had happened between them last night. But it felt so natural, far more natural than pushing him away for years had felt. It was as if they had slipped into the relationship they were meant to have all along and the only difference was an overwhelming sense of release.

"What's the plan?" asked Lydia.

"I'm going to take a shower. You make some coffee and then we'll head out. It'll be a romantic first date—we'll look for the Dodge minivan, horn in on a few stakeouts, check out some possible serial-killer hiding spots."

"You sure know how to treat a woman, Mr. Mark. And then we'll go park in front of where Juno is staying?"

"Sure."

As he turned to walk away, Lydia slapped him on the ass. He spun around and looked at her, totally floored by the playful gesture.

She smiled. "I've always wanted to do that."

He laughed and walked up the stairs to the shower, feeling light with love for her.

As she stood in the pink glow of the kitchen lights, placing ground coffee beans in the filter, she actually felt a little giddy. Then she immediately felt guilty. *You have no business acting like a schoolgirl with five people dead and a serial killer on the loose.*

The phone rang as she turned the coffeepot on. "Hello?"

"So what are you going to call the book?"

"Excuse me? Who is this?"

"You know who this is."

The room swirled around her as she realized it was Hugo. She internally kicked herself for not having the line tapped. She couldn't believe she hadn't thought of it.

"What do you want, Bernard?" she asked, forcing herself to be calm and rational, hoping that Jeffrey would emerge from the shower so he could pick up the other line.

"I want to know what you are going to call the book you write about me."

"What makes you think I would write a book about you?" she asked, thinking fast.

"Well, that's what you do, isn't it?"

"What's that?"

"Write books about killers. I really should thank you."

"Thank me for what?"

"I have read everything you have ever written and you have taught me everything I needed to know to become God's warrior."

"Is that what you think you are?"

"My son was the sacrificial lamb. He was taken from me and his innocent life lost so that I might do the Lord's work."

"And the Lord's work entailed the killing of five innocent people?"

He laughed and the throaty chuckle made Lydia go cold inside. " 'An oracle is within my heart concerning the sinfulness of the wicked,' " he said.

"More Psalms, Bernard?"

"I'm surprised you recognize it."

"Look, why don't we just end this, Bernard?" she said.

"I fully intend to."

"Where are you? Let's get together. You can tell me your side of the story so I have the complete picture for my book. You'll have a chance to deliver God's message. Otherwise the whole world is going to think you were just a cold-blooded murderer. Tell me where to meet you."

There was a silence on the line and Lydia prayed. *Please let him be delusional enough to fall for this ridiculously obvious setup.*

"You would come alone?"

"Of course."

"Then come at midnight."

"Where?"

"Pray, and God will give you the answer."

The line went dead. She looked at the clock and saw that it was nearly eleven-thirty. She put the phone down in the cradle and before she lifted her hand from the receiver, it rang again.

"Ms. Strong?" It was the quavering voice of an elderly woman.

"Yes?"

"It's Mrs. Turvey. I'm afraid Juno is gone."

"Gone? What do you mean?" asked Lydia.

"He's left, taken his cane and gone. I went in to check on him and didn't find him in bed. I'm so worried."

"What about the police outside?"

"They said they didn't see him go."

"Don't worry. I'm sure he's fine," she lied. "I'll find him. You stay where you are in case he calls or comes back."

"All right."

There was a hurricane in her mind, the possibilities floating like debris. Growing frantic, she pounded on the bathroom door.

"What's wrong?" called Jeffrey from the shower.

"I just talked to Bernard Hugo. He called here. I think he has Juno."

"Are you crazy? What are you talking about?" he asked, throwing a towel around his waist and opening the door.

"Jeffrey, I have to go. There's no time. Follow me to the church with the cops downstairs," she yelled as she ran down the stairs away from him.

"Lydia, don't you even think about facing off with this guy on your own. . . . Lydia—Fuck!"

But she was already gone. Seconds later he heard the Mercedes speed off from the driveway. He was dressed in under five minutes, and after her. If Bernard Hugo didn't kill her, he was going to do it himself.

Simon Morrow wondered how long it had been since the lights had been turned on in the records tomb of the hospital. He stood at the door with an orderly at his side and flicked the light switch but the fluorescent bulbs didn't so much as flicker.

"They turned the lights and the temperature control off down here," the orderly said.

Morrow pulled a flashlight from his pocket and shone it over the edge of the file cabinets. The place was covered with a thick film of dust. Which made it easy to see the recent path someone had made to the end of the room, almost the length of a football field at least.

"How long has it been since anyone was down here?" Morrow asked the orderly.

"No one ever comes down here. All these records have been computerized."

The last happy days Bernard Hugo had known were spent working at this hospital. That had been Morrow's second hunch today. So far, he was two for two. He followed the trail Hugo had left in the dust, his gun drawn, the beam of his flashlight leading him through a maze of file cabinets, and finally to a small area where he found a sleeping bag, some empty, greasy McDonald's bags, and a pile of medical textbooks.

"Where are you, Hugo?" he whispered as he picked up one of the texts.

He exhaled a slight whistle as he flipped the pages, seeing that every white space had been inked over with insane images of death and gore. There were gnarled hands with claws dripping blood and innards; an image of Christ on the cross, His torso open, revealing an empty chest cavity; a decapitated dog. Over every image, Hugo had written Juno's name, inked heavily as if he had raked his pen over the same letters again and again. The image on the inside of the back cover of the book caused Morrow to drop the text to the floor and run, as fast as he could, for the door.

The orderly, who had accompanied the chief to the basement, grudgingly lifted the book to see a sketch of a church. A thunderbolt clapped from the sky and the church was in flames. Inside, a man, woman, and child huddled together happily. On either side of them two figures hung from crosses: a disemboweled woman and a man with his eyes gouged out.

chapter twenty-six

The bark of the trees felt familiar beneath Juno's sensitive finger-
tips. The sound of the wind was a song he had heard before. And
he felt the clearing on the skin of his face and smelled the flowers
from the garden, just as he had as a child. Juno had found his way
home. It had taken a while, but it was if the church was homing
in on him, pulling him into its arms.

But as soon as he climbed the few low steps, pushed open the
heavy wooden doors, and stepped inside, he felt that the energy,
which he knew like the feel of his own skin, had been altered. He
felt the soft chuckle raise the hair on the back of his neck before
he heard it.

Juno did not respond, only lifted a hand to steady himself
against the last row of pews. Maybe he had come for this. After
all, Lydia had warned him that he might be a target of this maniac. Maybe this was Juno's cowardly way of committing suicide,
unable as he felt to face the world that had been revealed to him.

"It's all so perfect," said Bernard Hugo. "We are all truly part
of a divine plan. Don't you think so, Juno? I didn't even have to
come for you, you came to me."

Pain and rage radiated off Bernard Hugo in pulsating waves
that moved through Juno like electricity. But his voice was measured, like a metronome, and as cold as liquid nitrogen. Juno

sensed it was best to stay silent, feeling that the sound of his voice would be like a match to a fuse.

"When a predator stalks its prey, creeps through the woods or the grass, in that second before the chase begins, the prey always has a final moment of realization—an awareness that has crept into its eyes, its sensitive nose lifted suddenly to the wind, an inner silence of delicate ears straining for sound, of lean, taut muscles tensing for flight. Humans assume that a scent caught, in the last minute, on the wind, warns the prey. But I think it's something else. A disturbance in psychic energy, a spiritual knowledge that one has entered the last moments of life on this earth, a mental connection with the creature who will have the final impact on one's existence. Do you think that's true?"

Juno sat, knowing it would be futile and ridiculous for a blind man to run. He wasn't afraid to die, if it came to that. "Who are you and what do you want from me?"

"Who *am* I? Don't you even know me? You, the murderer of my son, don't even know my name?"

"I have never hurt anyone in my life.".

"You claim to be a holy man and a healer. And you are nothing but a liar. You are false to God, like all of them. But you are the worst of all." His voice was rising and he was moving closer to Juno. "At least the others were false only to themselves. But you fooled everyone. In the end, when my son lay dying, your prayers meant nothing. You were no closer to God than anyone else."

"Have you killed all these people because I am not a healer, because I was not able to heal your son? I tried—God knows, I would have done anything to be what people thought I was."

"And all this time," Bernard continued, unhearing, "I have been under your nose, stealing the dirty sheep from your diseased flock and offering their purified hearts back to God. I am

His warrior, His angel of death. All was taken from me so that I could do the Lord's work. And you never even knew me. Your uncle knew me as Vince. Vince A. Gemiennes—the name God gave me."

"So you think that by killing those innocent people, you have given your son's death meaning?"

"They had no right," he yelled, almost shrieking. "They had no right to live when my son, as pure and good as an angel of God, died. There must have been a reason God wanted him to come home, there must have been a reason that I suffered so much pain."

"God forgive you, Bernard, for what you have done, for your misguided acts."

" 'And I will strike down upon thee with furious anger those who attempt to poison and destroy. And you will know My name is the Lord when I lay My vengeance upon thee.' "

Juno heard the scratch and flare of a match being lit.

"I only wish you could see what I have planned for you."

And the heavy sigh of flame to gasoline was the last thing he heard before he felt the radiating pain of a blunt strike to the base of his neck, and then there was nothing.

Lydia parked her car a few hundred yards from the Church of the Holy Name and sprinted the rest of the way, to keep the element of surprise on her side. She didn't know how she was certain that Bernard Hugo and Juno were in the church together, but there was not a doubt in her mind. Then as she got closer, she caught the scent of fire.

She ran up the front steps and pushed with all her strength on the wrought-iron handles of the heavy wooden doors. She ducked down beneath the black clouds of smoke billowing out of the open doors. She pulled up her sweatshirt, covering her mouth and her nose. Shouting for Juno, she saw him lying on the altar, surrounded by flames. Above him loomed Bernard Hugo.

"What are you doing, Hugo?" she yelled, as she removed the Glock from the pouch at her waist.

When he heard her, he spun around.

As she moved in closer, she could see that Juno was spread out on a cross laid across the altar and that Hugo was preparing to nail his wrists and crossed ankles to the wood with a gigantic hammer.

"Stay where you are, Lydia. You were only to bear witness to the end. You came too early," he said, looking at her with disapproval.

"I can't let you do this. Stop right now or I'm going to fire."

He ignored her and lifted the hammer above his head, preparing to strike an iron nail through Juno's left hand, the flames rising around him. She fired a round from her gun and Bernard Hugo fell to the ground in a lump.

She ran up the aisle to Juno and shook him, trying to rouse him.

"Juno, please," she begged. But he was deeply unconscious. She dropped the gun, put her hands under his arms, and had begun to drag him to the door, her throat already constricting from the smoke, when she felt someone grab her by her hair. Bernard Hugo pulled her head back violently until it rested on his shoulder. She could just see his eyes and was overcome by his vile breath. She saw the gleam of his scalpel, and thought of the gun she had carelessly dropped to the floor.

"I've been waiting for you, bitch," he hissed.

"I've been waiting for you, too," she answered. She dropped Juno and thrust her elbow back into Hugo's abdomen with all her strength. As he doubled forward, he brought the scalpel into her thigh and pulled up. She felt the searing pain and screamed but it was somewhere outside of her as she reached, unthinking, and wrested the instrument from her leg. He had missed the artery that he doubtless had been aiming for, but still, blood sprayed from her wound. She edged away from him, struggling to her feet, the scalpel in her hand.

"Come on, you fuck, I'll send you to see Robbie," she said as he moved toward her. In one swift motion, he had her wrist in a hard grip she couldn't escape, and he squeezed until her hand involuntarily opened and the scalpel dropped to the floor. With her free hand she grabbed his shirt and pulled him in and hit the bridge of his nose with the top of her head. He staggered back, stunned, blood pouring from his nostrils. She scampered for the scalpel and brought it around just as he was on top of her again. She jabbed it forcefully into his eye, though she'd been aiming for his jugular. He roared with pain and fell back twitching. She didn't think it was in deep enough to have touched his frontal lobe. She only hoped the pain was enough to keep him unconscious. She grabbed the Glock from the altar where she'd dropped it and waited. He did not move. The flames were all around her now, licking up to the ceiling.

She shoved the gun in the waistband of her pants and reached again for Juno, her leg beginning to throb, a feeling of lightheadedness overtaking her. The only thing she wanted more than to kill Bernard Hugo, was for Juno to live. She fought dizziness and the ardent desire to go back and put a bullet through Hugo's brain, as she dragged Juno toward the door.

She looked behind her to see if the door was blocked by flames and when she turned to look at Hugo again, he was gone.

"Fuck!" she yelled, panic and anger doing battle in her mind.

She struggled to move faster, Juno seeming heavier by the second. The door was ten feet away.

He came at her horribly through the smoke, the scalpel jutting from his eye, bellowing in rage and pain. She deftly moved to one side and he stampeded past her, tripping over Juno and falling, the scalpel driving farther into his head.

And she was on him, gun drawn. She flipped him over and straddled him, one knee on each of his arms. She stuck the barrel of the gun in his mouth. He was not dead. He struggled for breath, his nose broken and his mouth full of steel. She tried not to smile. She didn't think anymore about the fire or the debris beginning to fall around them.

"You miserable, cocksucking psychopath," she said. She had forgotten about the flames, about Juno lying unconscious. It was only her and him. The room seemed to wail with sound and fill with light. Everything warped and slowed around her. The only thing she knew in that moment was rage. It was a rage that had been born the day her mother died, and had dwelled within her, growing like a parasite all these years. Today, she realized, was the fifteenth anniversary of her mother's death. And this thing inside her had devoured every happiness that was ever offered to her, had sucked every possible moment of peace and joy from her heart. And it had led to her being here, straddling a monster in a burning church, holding a gun to his mouth. If she pulled the trigger, she would put an end to him and the havoc he'd visited upon her, and have revenge for his victims. But what would she be, then? Would she destroy the worm that was eating away at her inside or would she become what she most feared and hated?

"That's enough, Lydia."

And she looked up to see her mother standing before her. She looked for Juno and he was gone.

"You came home early because I got caught smoking," Lydia said, sobbing and thrusting the gun harder into Hugo's mouth. "He killed you because I did something wrong."

"He was waiting for her, Lydia. If it hadn't been that afternoon, it would have been another time. It had nothing to do with you or what you did. Jed McIntyre was sick and so is Bernard Hugo."

But then it wasn't her mother at all, it was Jeffrey. Morrow stood behind him, and the flames were almost out. And she could see the flashing lights from police cars and fire engines through the thinning smoke.

"I want this to be over now," she said, coughing from the smoke.

"Just give me the gun, baby. You stopped him. This is finished and we can go home."

She let the gun drop to the floor and Jeffrey came to her and lifted her away from Bernard Hugo. He carried her from the church to the ambulance waiting outside.

epilogue

Six months later—Hanalei Bay, Kauai, Hawaii

When the bright morning sun and roosters wake Lydia from sleep here it takes her a few moments to remember where she is. She looks out the window to see mystical green mountains rising from a crystalline ocean, the mist rolling in as if from heaven. And sometimes it takes her longer to remember *who* she is. It's like that here, where perfect, temperate days run together and the sound of the ocean and Jeffrey's breathing beside her are a lullaby. Lydia Strong made it through fifteen years without knowing peace. Now that she has found it, she can't imagine how she survived.

Recovery has been slow for Lydia. Her physical wounds healed quickly. But the issues she'd been forced to deal with surrounding the death of her mother had left her feeling fragile and hollowed out. Jeffrey strongly urged her, as he had so many times, to seek counseling. But she was not one for head-shrinking. So he had brought her here, to this magical place where rainbows and geckos worked a spell on her. The pain, and the guilt, and the grief, and the loss, and the fear didn't disappear, exactly, but became more like rough textures in the fabric of her life. Part of her but not all of her.

She'd spoken to Juno and he was recovering, moving on in spite of his grief. Father Luis Claro's body had been found in the back of Bernard Hugo's minivan and was buried behind the church. The repairs to the damage from the fire are almost complete. And another priest will come to take over the congregation. Juno will stay on as caretaker, and continue to play his guitar. He's found a way to reconcile all that he now knows with the faith he has always had in God.

"I'm not sure what brought us together, Lydia. But it was something larger than us, wasn't it? We are both better for what happened here. We learned from each other. And things have happened that neither of us can explain. It's as you said. That's the space where faith resides," Juno had said.

Bernard Hugo lies in a coma in a state hospital, breathing on his own. Lydia is trying to find out how much it costs to keep him there. It's a detail she wants for her book. If he ever awakens, he will face charges on five counts of murder, among other things. She doesn't hate him. It's hard to hate someone you understand so well.

Jed McIntyre had dwelled in a place of similar pain—different in its nuances and outcome. But similar in that they both sought a kind of justice. Jed sought vengeance for himself. Bernard wanted justice for his son. His logic was faulty and full of holes, of course, and maybe only an excuse to satisfy an urge to kill.

She imagines him teetering on the edge of psychosis most of his adult life, his dark urges caged by medication and maybe even by the happiness of his life. Then the loss of his son had released the beast inside.

She understands him perfectly. Lydia believes that all human action can be understood, if people are honest about their own hearts. The urge to rage in pain, to lash out and destroy, even to kill—she knows it well.

Benny Savroy remains unable to discuss his involvement

with Bernard Hugo, any mention of the events bringing on a sei-zure. According to Simon Morrow, the DA is reluctant to bring charges, though physical evidence puts Benny at the Lopez dump site and his fingerprints were found in Hugo's minivan. It seems unlikely that someone so developmentally challenged could have been involved on any level that would make him culpable, but stranger things have happened.

Simon Morrow got all the credit for the investigation, in the local press and with the FBI. Lydia and Jeffrey kept their end of the bargain and let him have it. After all, he did eventually solve the puzzle, just one step behind Lydia. He seemed to walk a little taller after the press conference. And she doesn't begrudge him that. Compared to some of the other people she has met in her life, he isn't that bad after all. Besides, Lydia will have the final word when her book comes out. And she does like to have the final word.

Lydia thinks about Greg sometimes. He came to visit her at St. Vincent's as she recovered, and looked some sad combina-tion of relieved and haunted. Recovering himself, from the head wound inflicted upon him by Bernard Hugo, Greg had been pale and thin the last time Lydia sat with him. With Hugo unable to confess or provide details, Greg will always have to guess about Shawna's final hours. Lydia wonders if he will ever find peace. She prays that he will.

Jed McIntyre still sends his letter every month. But Lydia no longer receives them, having asked her publisher to destroy them when they arrive.

And Lydia is in love with Jeffrey. She no longer tries to hide it from anyone, not even from herself. Sitting on the lanai, watching the small, calm waves roll in and out of Hanalei Bay, she is starting to become acquainted with happiness.

A classified envelope arrived in the mail for Jeffrey today, delivered by a hippie on a beat-up red bicycle. He's frowning as he leafs through the pages. And Lydia has been in front of the computer for hours, putting the finishing touches on the book she'll call *Angel Fire*. Bernard Hugo had one prayer answered, at least. He'll have his book.

And as she sits out on the lanai drinking a whiskey sour that evening, Jeffrey comes to join her. The sunset is just finished, the sky still orange and black like a sleeping tiger. He takes the glass from her hand and sips from it, then hands it back to her. He notices that she isn't smoking but says nothing.

"I guess we'll need to head back to New York next week. Something has come up."

"All right. I have to turn in my manuscript anyway. Besides, there's something I want to look into. Your place or mine?"

He smiles. He had been reluctant to bring it up, unwilling to break the spell they'd been under here.

He'd wondered whether they would stay together for a while or if she'd be off on another story when she was feeling more like herself again. Either way, it would have been okay. Because he is home for her now and that is all that ever mattered.

Acknowledgments

There are so many people that have had a part in the writing and publishing of this book. And for each of them I feel a unique and heartfelt gratitude:

To **Heather Mikesell,** in everything I have written since I met you, I have counted on your keen insight, eagle eye, and unwavering support—but have never taken it for granted.

To **Carolyn Nichols,** for taking the time to look at my homeless manuscript and see beneath the flaws to something better, and for bringing it to the attention of literary agents.

To **Elaine Markson,** my agent, for taking me on, and shopping this book with unflagging enthusiasm, finding the best possible home for it, and for enduring my neuroses with endless patience.

To **Kelley Ragland,** my talented and inspiring editor, who made this book better than I ever thought it could be, who, with careful guidance led me to my own voice, taking me beyond being a writer to becoming an author.

To **Marion Chartoff, Tara Popick,** and **Judy Wong,** who always believed that this day would come, even when I strayed far from my dreams.

About the Author

Lisa Unger, writing as Lisa Miscione, is an award-winning *New York Times, USA Today,* and international bestselling author. Her novels have been published in more than twenty-six countries around the world. She was born in New Haven, Connecticut (1970) but grew up in the Netherlands, England, and New Jersey. A graduate of the New School for Social Research, Lisa spent many years living and working in New York City. She then left a career in publicity to pursue her dream of becoming a full-time author. She now lives in Florida with her husband and daughter. She is at work on her next novel.

an excerpt from

the darkness gathers

BY

LISA UNGER,

writing as Lisa Miscione

coming in November 2011

chapter one

The voice on the tape was thin and quavering. Lydia Strong had to rewind the tape and turn up the volume. In the background, she could hear the wet whisper of cars passing on rain-slick roads and, once, the loud, sharp blast of a semi's air horn.

"It's Tatiana," the message began, followed by a nervous little noise that was somewhere between a giggle and a sob. "Are you there . . . please? I can't believe she's doing this to me." The girl inhaled unevenly, holding tears back from her voice. She went on in another language, something throaty and harsh, Eastern European–sounding. Then she switched back to English. "I'm not supposed to call anyone. I don't have much time. I'm somewhere in—" The connection was broken.

The package had been sitting beige and innocuous in the pile of mail that had collected in Lydia's office during the two weeks she had been gone. The small, soft envelope mailed to Lydia care of her publisher and forwarded was just one item in a mound of mail she had received from what Jeffrey Mark called her "fan club." Prisoners, families of murder victims, aspiring serial killers, and miscellaneous psychotics drawn to her because of the books and articles she wrote about heinous crimes and the people who committed them. Winning a Pulitzer Prize and solving a few cases along the way as a consultant with the private investigation firm of Mark, Hanley and Striker, Lydia had become an icon of hope, it seemed, for the world's most desperate and its most sick and twisted.

She was about to toss the envelope into the trash with the rest of the letters, but when she lifted the pile, the Jiffy, heavier than the other items, fell to the floor with a dull thud and the slightest rattle. She looked at the package for a second, then reached down to pick it up. There was no return address, though it had been postmarked from Miami more than three weeks earlier. Written in capital letters in the lower-right-hand corner was an urgent plea: "PLEASE READ ME!"

She observed the moment where she could choose to open the package or choose to throw it away, never the wiser to its contents and the impact it might have on her life. But something about the smallness of it, the innocence of its soft beige form and the slight rattle that indicated to her a tape cassette piqued her curiosity, lit a tiny jolt of electricity inside her.

Lydia extracted a pair of surgical gloves, a letter opener, and a pair of tweezers from her desk drawer. She opened the package with the letter opener, careful not to disturb the seal, then removed a tape cassette and a handwritten note with the tweezers. The note was written with big loopy letters in a faltering cursive hand.

Dear Miss Strong,
You are a good woman of strength and honor. And you must help Tatiana Quinn and all the other girls who are in need of rescue. There are too many who are already past helping. But if you begin with Tatiana, you may be able to save so many more. I cannot tell you who I am or how I know this, or we will die. But I beg you to come to Miami and see for yourself. Nothing is as it seems here, but I know that you will see the truth and make it right. I pray that you will.

It was like a thousand other letters she had received over the years, and she felt the familiar wash of anxiety, resentment, and curiosity that generally overwhelmed her when someone asked for her help. But there was something different about this letter. Maybe it was the child's desperate voice, or the earnest tone of the letter, or maybe it was the implication that Lydia was responsible for the lives of the young girls supposedly in danger . . . and the fact that part of her believed that. Or maybe it was the haunting memory of Shawna Fox. But whatever it was, she didn't crumple the letter or destroy the tape. She just sat staring at the youthful handwriting, with its loopy letters full of hope.

Lydia leaned her head back against the black leather chair, closed her eyes, and released a long, slow breath. She felt two weeks of fatigue pulling at her muscles and her eyelids, even as the excitement of "the buzz" made her heart race a little. Images danced through her head: a girl alone on a street corner, huddled in a phone booth, staring nervously around her; the crowds that had gathered at Lydia's book signings during the media tour she had just conducted to promote *Blind Faith;* a murderer's face as she straddled him in a burning church, her gun inside his mouth; Jeffrey's smiling eyes. The tape player by her computer gave off a blank hiss for a few moments before she noticed and reached over to click it off. As she picked up the phone, she heard the elevator door that opened into their apartment. She realized that she was still wearing her jacket, still had her bag slung over her shoulder.

"Lydia?"

She jumped eagerly from her chair, moved quickly from her office, and walked across the bleached hardwood floor of the foyer and into the tight embrace of Jeffrey's arms.

"Hey, you," she said, leaning back to look at his face. His

brown hair was damp from the light rain outside, and she caught the slightest scent of his cologne.

"God, I missed you," he said, kissing her, tasting her.

"Umm, me, too," she answered. She was amazed by the exuberance she felt, the sheer excitement of seeing his face and feeling his body.

"How did it go?" he asked, taking her bag and helping her off with her coat.

"You know, the usual. Inane interviews, packed book signings, bad hotel rooms. I'm never doing another book tour. It's torture."

"I've heard that before," he said, rolling his eyes. "You love it."

She smiled at his knowledge of her. "I didn't love being away from you," she replied.

They walked from the foyer to the kitchen, where they embraced again, Lydia looking over his shoulder at the view out their window. She missed the view of the Sangre de Cristo Mountains from her Santa Fe home, but nothing excited her like the New York City skyline at night. The possibilities were endless. She had to wonder what was happening behind each lighted window. She knew it was all happening—love, death, sex, drug abuse, loneliness, happiness, despair, even murder. But these days, it was what was happening in her own kitchen that excited her most of all. The buzz she had felt before Jeffrey came home, listening to the tape, had almost disappeared from her mind. Almost.

Jeffrey had coined the term *the buzz,* inventing a word for Lydia's unique ability to perceive what others did not—her ability to know when something was wrong, or not what it seemed, or needed investigating. Sometimes the truth left only a footprint in the sand, a scent on the wind. And Lydia had an uncanny ability to detect the most fleeting clues. Listening to the girl's voice on the tape, she'd felt it. She got a lot of crazy mail, a lot of false leads, a lot of desperate pleas. But listening to that tape, she'd heard the unmistakable pitch of fear, of need. A year ago, she would already have been researching. She'd have been on the Internet, looking for articles on a missing girl named Tatiana Quinn in Miami. But instead, she was now immersing herself in the happiness of being home with Jeffrey.

In their friendship, they'd been apart more than they'd been together. They met when she was just fifteen years old. At that time, he was an FBI agent working a serial-murder case; her mother was the thirteenth victim of the killer he hunted, Jed McIntyre. There had been a bond between Lydia and Jeffrey since the first night they met, a bond that had grown stronger over the years. Her mentor, her colleague, her friend—he had been all these things to her. And then last year, as together they worked a serial-murder case in Santa Fe, they had finally surrendered to the feelings that had always been just beneath the surface.

When they'd captured the killer, and Lydia had healed from her injuries, they'd returned to New York City. Lydia had turned in her manuscript and then, instead of jumping right into a new case, she had, maybe for the first time, relaxed as she waited for her book to be published. She took up yoga at a trendy East Village studio where Willem Dafoe studied. She went to Washington Square Park and watched the chess bums play their speed rounds, and wrote poetry. She searched for gourmet recipes on epicurious.com and cooked elaborate meals for herself and Jeffrey. She did not scan national newspapers and the Internet for new story ideas, waiting for something to seize her. She went for walks, talked on the phone, and visited with her grandparents in Sleepy Hollow, realizing she'd seriously neglected them over the last few years. She did not discuss with Jeffrey the cases he was working on with his private investigation firm, Mark, Hanley and Striker, Inc., for which she worked as part-time consultant. She was surprised to find one day, as she strolled down Fifth Avenue, looking in shop windows, that she had never been happier.

The thoughts that had obsessed her since the death of her mother were echoes of another life. It wasn't as though they had disappeared entirely, but she found she wasn't as driven to know what motivated killers, how their minds worked. She didn't feel any longer that she was somehow responsible for caging all the evil in the world like some hopeless superhero. She remembered her life before Santa Fe as feeling like she was running on a treadmill, full speed, but never getting further from what haunted her and never getting any closer to what she imagined might be the cure. She had finally given herself permission to turn it off and stand on solid ground. She now experienced moments of true inner peace.

On the other hand, old habits die hard. And, truth be told, in spite of her happiness, she *had* been getting a *bit* restless and was excited when the book tour began. But after a few days on the road, the hectic schedule, the sleeping away from Jeffrey, the forced remembrance of the events in Santa Fe started to wear on her . . . and she just couldn't wait for it to be over. She had to laugh. She had always despised dependence in herself. Now she welcomed it, as she did all the new things she was discovering, all the emotions she had suppressed for so long. Happiness, sorrow, fear, longing, joy, and, most of all, of course, love were powerful forces within her, reminding her for the first time since her mother had died that she was alive. As if she had killed herself emotionally because she blamed herself for her mother's death and then resurrected herself, as well.

Now she sat with her elbows leaning on the glass kitchen table, legs folded beneath her, watching Jeffrey make her a cup of tea. She had always loved to watch him in the kitchen, all broad shoulders, chiseled jaw, and big hands—occupied not with guns and fistfights but pot holders and teakettles.

"We haven't been apart like this since we've been together," he said, sitting next to her. He placed a steaming cup of chamomile and Grand Marnier in front of her, and the smell was heaven.

"I know. It was torture. I've never had a *home* before that I missed when I was away. Every place, even the house in Santa Fe, which I loved, was just somewhere I kept my things," she said, looking into the cup, tracing the rim with her finger. "But this place . . . our home. I hated being away from it. I hated sleeping without you."

"Let's not make a habit of it." He placed a warm hand on the back of her neck and began working the tension he found there.

"Deal."

She looked around the kitchen, lighted by the orange glow of three pendant lamps hanging over the black granite island, the terra-cotta tile floor, the bleached wood cabinets with their stainless-steel fixtures. It was a warm and cozy room, ground zero for all conversation. Like everything in the apartment, they had designed it together, paying attention to every detail of the home they would share. They'd gotten rid of most of their old furniture and belongings, keeping only what meant most to them.

"New beginnings demand new objects," Lydia had declared. And Jeffrey had agreed. He'd never developed attachments to things anyway. He'd never had much of a home life, so he'd never spent much time on the East Village apartment he'd owned since he left the FBI. He'd started his private investigation firm from there, sleeping on a pullout couch in the back bedroom. Now the firm of Mark, Hanley and Striker employed over a hundred people and filled a suite of offices on the top floor of a high-rise on West Fifty-seventh Street. But his apartment had remained almost empty of furniture. He found the only possessions that meant anything to him were his mother's engagement ring, his father's old service revolver, and a closet full of designer clothes.

Lydia's apartment on Central Park West had looked like it belonged on the cover of *House Beautiful*: sleek, modern, impeccably decorated, but, Jeffrey thought, totally cold and impersonal. "You live in someone's *idea* of the most gorgeous New York apartment," he'd commented once. She'd sold it as is, furniture and all, to some software designer just months before the dot bomb. Jeffrey had sold his apartment, too, throwing in the pullout couch and rickety kitchen table and chairs. They'd both made a killing and then bought a three-bedroom duplex on Great Jones Street, downtown.

A metal door with three locks opened from the street into a plain white elevator bank. A real Old New York industrial elevator with heavy metal doors and hinged grating lifted directly into the two-thousand-square-foot space. By New York standards, it was palatial. The cost was exorbitant, of course, as it was New York City ultrachic, shabby-cool. But Lydia had declared it home the minute they'd stepped off the elevator and onto the bleached wood floors. The private roof garden, which was at least a story higher than most of the other downtown buildings, sealed the deal. From the garden, they could see the whole city. At night, it was laid out around them like a blanket of stars, which was a good thing, since you rarely can see any actual stars in New York City.

Now it was home, the place in the world they shared. But it had seemed empty, a shell of itself when she was gone. Lydia was his home, Jeffrey had realized while she was traveling. He'd had her all to himself since Santa Fe and he'd grown used to that. But he had sensed her restlessness even before she left on the book tour, and he knew she would be getting back to work soon. In fact, he knew the second he had walked into the apartment and saw her come out of her office with her coat still on that something had caught her interest. It made him sad and tender for her, but he knew her well enough to know that he had to let her go in that way if he was to share her life at all.

"So, what were you doing when I came in?"

"Oh," she said, standing, "come with me. I want you to hear something."

"That's what I was afraid of," he said with a small laugh.

"It might be nothing."

"But first . . ." he said, pulling her into his lap and pressing his mouth to hers.

"Yes . . ." she answered, "first things first." She led him upstairs to their bedroom.

Also coming in
2011

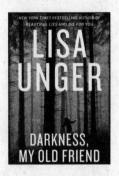

Darkness, My Old Friend

A Novel by Lisa Unger

$24.00 (Canada: $27.00)

978-0-307-46499-6

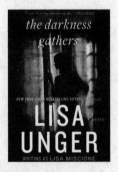

The Darkness Gathers

A Novel by Lisa Unger, writing as Lisa Miscione

$15.00 (Canada: $17.00)

978-0-307-95311-7

AVAILABLE WHEREVER BOOKS ARE SOLD

Want More Lisa Unger?

Use your smartphone to take a photo of the
barcode below for exclusive **short stories,
sneak peeks,** and **behind-the-scenes** access.

If you do not have a 2D barcode reader on your smartphone,
download the software free at LisaUnger.mobi.

Don't have a smartphone? Text ANGEL to 333888.